CITY OF LIKES

CITY OF LIKES

A NOVEL

Jenny Mollen

Nacelle Books

Praise for CITY OF LIKES

"*City of Likes* has Jenny Mollen's trademark lacerating humor and her ear for the outrageous, but this novel brings a new level of pathos to her writing. It's a dark and engrossing satire of motherhood, wealth and friendship, laced with insight into the danger of remaking ourselves in the social media age. To be gulped down in one sitting."
— STEPHANIE DANLER, *New York Times* bestselling author of *Stray and Sweetbitter*

"Jenny Mollen tackles the novel with all the signature hilarity, insight and page-turning candor that she brings to her memoirs. A rollicking, joyful read that will make you want to put down the phone - and pick up a book."
— REBECCA SERLE, *New York Times* bestselling author of *One Italian Summer*

"Jenny Mollen's *City of Likes* is a propulsive story of motherhood, social media, and obsession - and the ways we can lose ourselves in each. A delightful blend of social commentary, dark humor, and good old-fashioned suspense that I devoured in two days."
— EMILY HENRY, #1 *New York Times* bestselling author of *People We Meet on Vacation*

"*City of Likes* is a hilarious take-down of what happens to people when they overdose on social media. It is an escape from social media while still reading about social media; a fantastic awakening to help clear your head and your addiction. And it's hilarious. The greed, the lies, and the interminable desire to get more likes turns

innocent people into horrifying versions of themselves. I couldn't put it down."
— CHELSEA HANDLER, #1 *New York Times* bestselling author of *Life Will Be the Death of Me*

"First things first: I would pay good money to sit at a bar with Jenny Mollen and listen to her hilarious observations about the people around us. And I promise, once you read *City of Likes*, you would, too. Part comedy of manners, part social satire, Mollen's debut novel is a pitch-perfect rendering of our current Instagrammable age. It's viciously funny, and packed full of heart."
— GRANT GINDER, author of *Let's Not Do That Again* and *The People We Hate at the Wedding*

"Loved this fun ride of a book, with sharp humor and a surprising depth of emotions. Filled with delightful takes on how social media affects all of us, *City of Likes* is a must-read."
—JESSE Q SUTANTO, author of *The Obsession and Dial A for Aunties*

For Sid and Lazlo

CHAPTER ONE

I shot up in bed, convinced that I'd just felt a cockroach tiptoe across my forehead. Repulsed, I raked my fingers over my scalp and ran my tongue along the inside of my mouth. "Oh my god!" I screamed. "I think I might have eaten one!"

"You didn't eat one!" My husband called out from behind the bathroom door.

I switched on the light and scanned my bedside table, expecting to see a chorus line of roaches staring back at me. There was a flicker of movement behind the pile of childhood development books I'd spent the last six months forcing myself to read. It was as if the pests were taking a short break to change costumes before remounting their attack. "Iliya, this is insane! We can't stay here."

"It's here or my mother's place," he calmly reminded me.

"How are those our only two options?"

According to the alarm clock, it was almost seven in the morning, but from where I sat, in our windowless tomb of a bedroom, it could just as easily have been the middle of the night. I raised my water bottle and slammed it hard onto my nightstand, determined to draw blood.

"You're not gonna get them," Iliya said. "They're too fast."

"I don't want to get them! I want to call an exterminator!"

"You can't call anyone. We're not on the lease. We're not even supposed to be here."

"How are you so mellow about this? We are living in a roach-infested apartment with two children! This isn't something we can just wait on." I got up and stomped toward the bathroom door and flung it open.

Iliya was leaning into the mirror, flossing his teeth in his neurotic way, until his gums bled. "Cockroaches don't hurt children," he slurred, then spat into the sink before turning toward me. With his angular cheekbones and piercing blue eyes, he looked like one of those male models from a high-end cologne commercial. The kind of guy who says nothing until the last moment, when he locks eyes with the camera and whispers something nonsensical like, "Set your heart on fire with ice."

I folded my arms and glared. "I'm calling Ken."

"You've already called him five times," he said. "You look psycho."

"I *am* psycho!" I exclaimed.

"Besides, Ken's on location."

"In Toronto! That's like five minutes from here." I turned around and headed back into the bedroom, closing the bathroom door on his annoyingly Photoshopped body.

"By what, rocket ship?" Iliya laughed as he caught up with me. "He's busy shooting. You know actors. Give the guy a minute."

"So now he's all Daniel Day-Lewis and too deep in his craft to deal with a roach infestation at his apartment? Is that *really* going to be your defense?"

"Ken is a great guy and he's letting us stay here for free," Iliya said for the millionth time. "You don't even want to know what the roaches look like in Coney Island."

Iliya was right. I didn't want to know what the roaches looked like in Coney Island, nor did I want to know what his mother looked like without clothing. I watched him help himself to two identical black T-shirts in a basketful of clean laundry on the floor.

When Chelsea House offered Iliya the promotion, they expected him to jump without thinking twice. And he did. We all did. Head of global membership was a coveted position, one that he'd been gunning for since his early days with the club. It was, according to Iliya, "an opportunity too good to refuse," even if the bump in pay wasn't that substantial. The company provided us with a small relocation fee, enough to cover the money we lost breaking our lease in LA and throwing our furniture into storage. But there were still hundreds of things to figure out. Iliya was tasked with finding us a temporary place to stay while I focused my attention on getting our tuition back from our son's preschool and enrolling him in another one, selling our car on Facebook, and setting up goodbye playdates and drinks with every friend, co-worker and dog groomer we'd known for the past decade.

I sunk back onto the edge of the bed. "I should have known this was too good to be true. Wait a minute," I said, redirecting my anger. "*You* should have known this was too good to be true." I watched Iliya study the two T-shirts and pretend not to hear me. "A spacious loft in Tribeca for just as long as we needed it? Of course, that's not a real thing! If Los Angeles taught us anything it's to never believe the empty promises of actors." I flopped backwards on the bed, then remembered the roaches. I sprung back up and gave myself a thorough TSA patdown. "Why would Ken do this to us?" I wailed.

"Hey. Ken is a good friend who's worked his ass off for the current success he's having, so I'm not going shit-talk him. His show is doing better than any other show on the History Channel." Iliya was proud of his former AA sponsor. Ken was the only person I'd ever seen Iliya have a phone call with that lasted longer than five minutes.

"Not to be a total buzzkill, but it's about the Oregon Trail." I couldn't resist. "Eventually everybody loses an axel or dies of dysentery." Iliya didn't respond, most likely because he had no idea what I was talking about. His education was cut short at age fifteen, when he escaped the antisemitism of Ukraine and moved to Brooklyn with his mother and little sister. He never ended up re-enrolling in school. In order to help support the family, he went to work right away, promoting clubs and restaurants around Manhattan. And now, all these years later, he was back where he'd started.

Iliya's plan was always to save up enough money so that he could open his own restaurant. It was going to be high-end and Russian, a spruced-up version of Veselka, his favorite East Village joint. He'd been nurturing this dream ever since we met at Geiko, a Japanese steakhouse in Hollywood where all of the waitresses were forced to dress like horny geishas and where we both worked.

I let off a sigh. "Tell me why I agreed to do this again?"

"You didn't like Los Angeles either," Iliya reminded me. "You hated the traffic." He was speaking as if we were two octogenarians reflecting on a life we'd lived centuries ago instead of one we'd abandoned just three weeks prior.

"Everyone hates the traffic, Iliya!"

He winced. "And the endless sun."

"That's just you. I have nothing against the sun. In fact, I like sunshine, and palm trees, and nice people who say 'excuse me' when they bump into you on the street."

"There's a difference between nice and fake. And how many of those 'nice' California people ever offered you a job? The kind of job you deserve?" He tilted his head. "You have to believe me. This city is going to change your life."

It was true, my life in LA hadn't been perfect. I felt trapped in my air-conditioned apartment in the valley. My friends were either singles who suggested we meet for dinner at 9:30 p.m. or new moms who lived all the way out in Brentwood and refused to cross the 405 for playdates which meant I was alone ninety percent of the time and while I wanted to get back to work, I couldn't get hired to save my life. I'd only recently started trying to find a job, after Roman had turned four, but it felt as though the entire industry had changed in the few years I'd been sitting on the bench. New platforms were popping up quicker than I could download them, let alone figure out how to optimize them.

New York was the biggest marketing hub in the world. The city was bursting with energy and opportunity. And not just professional ones. Whenever we visited, it felt like a giant cruise ship where I could be a parent upstairs but also disappear downstairs to a life that was entirely my own. In theory, it was everything I'd been looking for. But the reality was already proving to be different from the postcards.

"Which of these shirts do you like better?" Iliya asked, switching gears.

I stared at him blankly. "Is this a trick question?"

"No. Why?" Iliya looked at me with that foreign-guy cluelessness that he'd perfected.

I shook my head. "They're the exact same shirt."

"No they aren't."

"Umm. Yeah." I showed him the matching Gap tags.

"One is more washed. It's a different vibe."

"Feels like the same vibe to me," I muttered. "I guess go with whichever makes you feel richer and skinnier?"

"I'm already skinny." Sometimes my humor was wasted on him.

While Iliya pulled one of the shirts over his head, I marveled at the body of the man I happened to marry. Towering over me at six feet three inches, Iliya was more masculine than any guy I'd ever been into. Which wasn't saying a lot, as the guys I dated before him turned out to be gay. Iliya gave me a warm smile. "It's going to be okay, Meg. This isn't our new home. It's just until we can afford our own place." He kneeled down to kiss me. "I gotta hurry," he said. "Saro is flying in from London." Saro was the CEO and founder of Chelsea House, someone Iliya emulated and feared in equal parts. "I'm still taking Roman today, right?" Iliya was waiting to see if I would offer to take our son to school.

"It's your turn," I said, trying to stand my ground. I'd taken the kid to the last ten drop-offs. "Speaking of Saro, I saw that Chelsea House is hiring someone to run their website. Did you know about that?"

"I didn't," he said, averting his eyes. "Have you seen my wallet?" I grabbed a pair of jeans sitting on top of the dresser and fished out a dilapidated Velcro billfold. Iliya had used the same wallet since he'd turned twenty-one and refused to replace it. He claimed it kept him humble. It also served as a reminder that he hadn't yet reached his financial goal. Over the years, people would give him new ones, which he would graciously accept then cast off into one of his junk drawers.

"Well, they are," I said, my voice slightly quavering. "And I'd kill that position."

Iliya held up his hand and shook his head. "You don't want to run somebody's website. And you know how I feel about us working together."

"But we met working together."

"And you hated me."

It wasn't until after Iliya fired me that we ended up getting together. And it wasn't until after our first child that I forgave him for firing me. "But we're stronger now, and we need the money, and I am good. Really good."

"You're better than good," he said. "Running a website isn't what you were born to do. You're a writer."

"A copywriter," I corrected him. "There's a difference."

"And Chelsea House is cheap. You need to find a job that pays real money. Otherwise, what is the point of you going back to work?"

I balled my hands into fists. "The point is that we can't afford to live in New York if both of us aren't working. And if I keep hearing the *Paw Patrol* theme song all day every day, I'm going to have a psychotic breakdown."

"Summer is over," he said. "Roman is back in school."

"Well Felix isn't," I reminded him. "And you're missing the point!"

"Look, I want you to be happy too," he said. "I just don't like the optics. I barely know this New York team. Imagine me going in today telling them that they needed to hire my wife, who hasn't had a job in nearly five years."

"Wow." My voice cracked. "That was really low."

"I'm sorry, that's not what I meant. It's not that I don't think you're qualified. I just think it comes off as nepotism."

"Said the guy who works for a glorified fraternity," I shot back. I found it absurd that Iliya, a dude who could not have been less moved by popularity, was the gatekeeper to one of most sought-after membership clubs in the country. He didn't disagree, not deep down anyway.

But he was a hard worker. And if he didn't want to lose his job, it was best not to think too hard about Chelsea House and all that it stood for. I hated the late nights, the drunken douchebags, the posers who spent all day scrolling their own websites on their laptops, the married women who were always slipping Iliya their room keys. I even hated the maddeningly hot waitstaff who waited twenty minutes before asking if you wanted a glass of water.

But running the club's membership gave Iliya a cachet that no previous job ever had. People kowtowed to him. The club's younger members invited him to their weddings and the older ones to their children's bar mitzvahs. It was silly, but it felt good. And hopefully it would prove beneficial when he finally decided to do something on his own.

"You're going to get a job you love," Iliya said. "You had an interview yesterday, you have more today. You're doing everything right. You don't need me to hook you up with nonsense."

"Thanks," I said, wishing he could see how lost and obsolete I felt.

"You are going to be more than fine." Iliya kissed me on my forehead like I was a child. I hated when he did that.

CHAPTER TWO

I stopped working when I had Roman because we couldn't afford help. I didn't have an extended family that I could lean on, and my mom was only capable of intimacy with cats. My goal was to be the mother that I'd always wished someone had been for me.

Turned out my happiness wasn't to be found at the bottom of a heap of burp cloths and breast pumps. I found myself falling deeper and deeper into a depression. In high school, I worked as a stock girl at Blockbuster video. It was a two-year stint during which I'd watched and internalized the message of every rom-com I was supposed to be rewinding. According to Hollywood, I could have it all! I could have a baby, then take off for the woods of Vermont to make homemade applesauce, only to reemerge as the CEO of my own company with a sensitive-yet-stable veterinarian husband, a cherubic and potty-trained toddler, and a closetful of matching flannel pajamas.

Instead, I found myself isolated and unfulfilled. The highlight of my week was taking Roman to the grocery store and letting him feast on all the free samples so I could get out of making dinner. Being a mom wasn't enough for me. And New York was my chance to finally get it right. I was going to go back to what I knew before kids. I was going to find a job —something fulfilling that would make me not just a more joyful person but a better parent. I was going to beat my depression, finally get my head screwed on straight. I was going to be me again. My reverie in the shower was broken by the sound of my four-year-old son shrieking.

"He better not have seen a fucking roach," I shot to Iliya as I rushed out of the room.

Roman stood naked at the front door shaking like a nervous Chihuahua. "RiRi is here," he said excitedly.

I heard the raspy mutterings of what sounded like an angry Russian prostitute on the other side of the door.

"Is that you, Marina?" I asked, double-checking that it was indeed my sister-in-law and not some belligerent neighbor.

"Of course, it's me! Who else would it be?" Marina exclaimed, bursting through the door the moment I unlocked it. In her platform suede boots, skintight jeans and bright orange Hermes belt, she looked like one of those high-priced call girls who sit in the lobby at the Beverly Hills Hotel staring at their phones and eating Chex mix.

I tried not to judge her babysitting attire as I made my way to the other side of the room, toweling off my hair and scanning the area for roaches with each step. Normal rent for a one-bedroom in Tribeca was ten to twelve grand, at the minimum. But Ken's apartment, along with two others that had better views of the bumper-to-bumper traffic on Canal Street, wasn't technically in Tribeca. Instead, it was situated in a sort of no-man's-land once referred to as West Soho and most recently deemed Hudson Square. Developers had tried to buy the building just after Hurricane Sandy, thinking that with all the water damage, they could score it for a deal. But as Ken had explained to us, the owner was unmoved by the offer. The shady cash-only bodega downstairs generated more than enough money that selling low wasn't worth it. Unfortunately for us, keeping the bodega running was all that mattered to him. Any issue upstairs — whether it was plumbing, electric, or even pest-related — went ignored.

Marina sidestepped around her nephew, making a beeline to the kitchen sink with a half-spilled latte in her hands. "What happened to your clothes, Roman?"

"They were too tight."

Marina threw me a look.

"What was too tight?" Iliya walked out of the bedroom busily answering morning emails on his phone.

"My pants. They were a little tight but also very loose," Roman supplied.

"Roman, they're cotton and tagless," I told him. "You picked these sweat suits out and you promised that you would wear them. We have seven of them now and I'm not giving them away." Roman's pre-K in LA had thrown around the term "sensory" when it came to his strange predilections and more than occasional tantrums. I was still hoping that this phase would be something he'd outgrow. The older he got, the easier he was to negotiate with. Read: Bribe. Unfortunately, the whole thing was like a game of whack-a-mole. The minute I helped him move on from one issue, a new one would pop up. Currently, it was all — and only — about clothes.

"I'm pretty sure Marina brought something for you," I said. "And if you can get dressed, I bet she'll give it to you."

Roman lit up and began to bounce up and down for Marina like a fan girl sitting front row at a Taylor Swift concert. I envied the power she had over him. She was the fun aunt. She was also the only aunt. Which only made her more fun. I was jealous not just that my son adored her but that she only got the best of him. They'd laugh, they'd play, and then she'd get her things and go. She didn't have to deal with the chaos of getting him dressed, the irrational scenes over the food he didn't want to eat or the three-hour adventure that was bedtime. As far as Marina was concerned, kids were easy. It was moms that were hard.

"Okay, look everybody," I said, glancing at my watch. "We've got to get a move on things. Roman's school starts at nine. It's Iliya's morning to take him and —"

"NOOOOO!" Roman cried, digging his heels into the hardwood floor. "I want Mommy to take me!"

I glanced at Iliya, who was in the room physically but may as well have been at his office. He was terrifically engrossed in his emails. "Mommy has an interview today," I reminded the entire room.

"I thought you did that yesterday." Roman blinked at me, confused.

"This is a different job. It's a new day. New day, new job." I tried to sound positive. I wanted Roman to see me as a winner even if I couldn't see myself as one. "And it's *two* interviews. I'm meeting with two different companies, so that's even more of a chance for success, right?"

Roman stared at me blankly, then farted. Defeated, I made my way over to Ken's mini kitchen. While I measured out three cups of formula for Felix, I gave Marina the rundown. "We don't have a microwave, so you need to heat the bottle in a pot. Felix can sleep for another half hour but then you need to wake him, or he'll be off his schedule for the rest of the day. Oh, and we already fed Red, but he still needs to go out and pee," I instructed, lining the cups of formula along Ken's hotplate.

"Aren't you wondering why I spilled my latte?" Marina looked at me, clearly offended that I hadn't yet given her my undivided attention. Before I could come up with an excuse, she launched into her rant, half talking to me, half checking out her manicure.

"So, this dickhead started screaming at me when I pulled up because I wouldn't unlock my car doors and let him in."

"Language!" Iliya hissed to his sister. He drained his coffee and deposited the empty cup by the sink.

"Quiet, both of you," I said gently. "The baby is still asleep. We want him to go for another half hour."

Marina ignored me, focusing on scowling at her brother and then continuing her rant. "It's like, not every Mercedes SUV is an Uber, dude." Marina scoffed as she rummaged through the cabinets for a morning snack.

"But I thought you *were* an Uber driver," I said, taking my time washing Iliya's cup to be sure he saw me doing it.

"A Wing Woman, Meg. That means female passengers only. My car, my choice. Eww! You guys have roaches!" she shrieked, dropping a box of cheddar bunnies to the floor and watching them fly everywhere.

"*Zatknis!*" Iliya cried, shaming his sister in Russian. "The baby!" It was my job to drop to my knees and scoop up the bunnies.

"I'm not gonna lie, guys," Marina said. "This already feels like a hostile work environment."

"Nobody is being hostile," Iliya and I said in unison, terrified that she might pick up her knock-off Chanel purse and its fifteen-pound makeup bag and storm out of our apartment. Marina looked at me, about to say something, when Roman interjected. "Can I have my present now?"

"When your clothes are on," Marina instructed firmly, pointing to the sweatshirt portion of the tracksuit on the floor. And like a miracle, Roman promptly complied.

Looking as proud of herself as if she'd just taught our dog to speak, Marina sauntered over to her bag and pulled out a Super Mario figurine. "It's from when your daddy and I were children. I got him off eBay. Originally he was a prize in a cereal box." Marina could make anything sound exciting, even dry old cereal.

"They used to put toys in cereal?" Roman looked like his mind was about to explode.

"Believe it or not, they still do. If your mommy buys the fun kind." Marina shot me a vengeful smile.

"Roman, we gotta go!" Iliya said, sounding jumpy.

"But I want Mommy to take me!" Roman flung himself between my legs as I made my way toward him with his backpack.

Iliya looked at me, then again at his phone. God, he was so pathetic. "Fine," I said. "Just go. You can do tomorrow's drop-off." Before Iliya and I could kiss goodbye, Felix started screaming from behind a sheet of drywall that Ken had put in place to give the illusion of a second bedroom. His high-pitched cries reminded me of those techno sirens that go off whenever somebody orders a Sex on the Beach shot in Tijuana. I threw up my hands, defeated. "*Annnd* the baby's up!"

"Don't look at me!" Marina said.

"*Pizdets!*" Iliya cursed in his native tongue and turned to me, sheepish as he grabbed his keys. "Please don't hate me."

I watched my gorgeous husband slip out the door, wishing I could hate him.

"How long do you need me today?" Marina asked when her brother was out of earshot. "I made it to the focus group round of my Lastrelle study."

"Your what?" I asked, hurrying to rescue Felix before he combusted. Unbothered, Marina slicked down her vixenish high ponytail and walked to the full-length mirror to admire her outfit and then start to pick apart a face full of makeup. She was beautiful like her brother but hid it under half a dozen layers of foundation that she insisted was "just a little powder and bronzer."

"Lastrelle," she called out. "It's a new technology that takes off four or seven layers of skin and makes you glow. But first you look like a lizard person for a week."

I reappeared holding Felix. At just five months old, he was a clone of his big brother, with Iliya's dark hair and my curled upper lip. "Did you already have this procedure?" I inquired, concerned she was about to peel her entire face off in front of me.

"Not yet," she said. "Later today."

"Mommy! I'm waiting!" Roman was keenly attuned to any and all gravitational shifts in my attention. The desperation on his face said that he'd just been abandoned in a hot car.

"Okay. Yes. We're going." I hunched down on the floor, balancing Felix in one arm as I attempted to wedge Roman's little feet into his tiny shoes. "You wanna grab Felix?" I asked Marina. But she was in a trance, squeezing a nonexistent zit on her chin.

If I were interviewing nannies to help me out with the kids, Marina would have been my last choice. She was messy, unreliable, and always looked like she was dressed in a slutty Halloween costume. But she wasn't a child molester, didn't wear my shoe size, and my kids adored her. Also, she was cheap.

"So what time do you need to leave?" I asked, trying not to let my frustration show. This was so typical of Marina. She would always pretend to want to help but when the time came, she'd find a way to weasel out.

"Like three-fifteen. Latest." She shrugged, finally taking Felix into her arms and beaming like she was Mother Teresa.

"Ok. That's the soonest I can get here," I said. "Roman's school isn't out until three." I looked at Roman, who was starting to pull on his shirt. If I didn't get him out of the house, he was going to be naked and sobbing within the next two minutes. "Right," I said. "Okay. Fine."

"Oh, did I tell you about the dentist?" Marina asked just as I was about to grab my bag.

I tried to be polite while still gathering up my things, laser-focused on Roman like he was a Jenga tower that might fall at any moment. "I have a date with a dentist who offered to make me a free night guard," Marina continued. "God, this place really is a shithole…" She touched the wall. A sliver of old paint broke off and fell to the floor. "Are you sure it's safe to live here?"

Roman perked up. "What's a shithole?"

"Nothing, honey." I shook my head. "Take your backpack. Don't forget to take Red out!" I reminded Marina as I kissed Felix one last time.

"Da, Da, Da!" she nodded. "Oh, and don't forget to text me your Wi-Fi password, your Netflix info, and your Seamless account!"

"You got it," I called back, slowly realizing that I'd just gone from having two children to three.

CHAPTER THREE

The city was ridiculously hot for September. Way hotter than Woody Allen movies had led me to believe, with their depictions of autumn in New York as a season that called for oversized blazers and tweed slacks. I didn't have access to any oversized blazers that weren't Iliya's, and I didn't have any slacks that weren't maternity wear. The last time I shopped for myself was before I had Roman. Once he was on the scene, he was the priority and every bit of extra cash I'd squirreled away went toward buying onesies and then the next size up in whatever leisure suit he was currently obsessed with. My go-to outfit was black jeans with some kind of band tee that made me look like I was a prepubescent boy permanently stuck in the bleachers at a Death Cab for Cutie concert.

But I had an interview today, so I tried to class things up with a ruffled button-down blouse and mules that I could half-walk in. "Let's take a picture to remember this moment!" I said, pulling out my phone and snapping a shot in a mirrored wall of what I hoped would be my last day of unemployment. I uploaded the picture to Instagram. My account was set to private and not even my husband followed it. It was half diary, half vision board, a way to catalog my life. I used it to look back and see what my body had looked like six months ago or to approximate how happy I'd been the year prior. I also posted pictures of experiences I longed to have, the Italian grottos and Tibetan temples I hoped to visit. I never had the money to do one of those study-abroad programs in Europe, and the only place I'd ever traveled for work was Nashville, to supervise a biscuit mix commercial.

Sweat dripped down the back of my neck as I stuffed my phone back into my purse and rushed across Canal Street, heading south.

Reaching into a sandwich baggie filled with what had now been coined by Marina "boring" cereal, Roman pulled out a handful of whole grain oats and sprinkled them on to the sidewalk, leaving himself a trail back to Marina in the event that we got lost.

Sunlight seeped through the cracks of the few prewar spice warehouses still waiting to be converted into ten-million-dollar lofts. Men pulling breakfast carts lined with donuts and everything bagels ambled across the vacant cobblestone streets, expertly avoiding potholes and sidewalk scaffolding. Iliya had explained to me that Tribeca was always under construction, always reinventing itself. The neighborhood was like a cat who'd lived nine lives, or Madonna before she started adopting all those Malawi children. What had started out as farmland had morphed into a hub of wealthy white people crammed into brightly lit buildings, as if afraid of the dark.

I'd never been wealthy by any stretch of the word. I grew up poor with an English teacher mom who had three kids by three different men. My dad owned his own plumbing company and did okay but got remarried and moved to Palm Springs with his new family when I was still in middle school. He always sent me a card on my birthday but sometimes got my age wrong in his inscription.

With Iliya's new bump in income, we were better off than we had been in a while. We'd saved a tiny bit and probably could have afforded a down payment on something modest in my hometown of Salem, Oregon. But New York was a whole different stratosphere. It would have taken a lucky lottery ticket or some elderly gentleman making Iliya an indecent proposal for us to even dream of living like the people who seemed to levitate around us. When I took Red out for his late-night walk, I liked to stand on the street corner while I waited for him to pee, looking up at my neighbors and trying to guess what they had ordered for dinner or what they were watching on TV. It was fun to admire them though, pacing back and forth in their all-glass habitats in the sky like wild animals on display.

From Beach Street to Barclay, blondes pushing sticky-fingered children in geared-out strollers barreled down the sidewalks like drag racers, brushing past each other without so much as a glance or nod of acknowledgment. Everybody was frantic and frazzled, even when there was no reason to be. People didn't meander in New York. Even when you tried to stand still, you almost had to fight against some unseen current constantly propelling you forward.

Roman had been in his new preschool for just over two weeks, and I had yet to remember to pack his lunch. There was just so much going on. By the time I got both kids to bed, I could barely remember to brush my teeth and charge my cell phone before burrowing under the sheets and passing out. Lunch was always one step beyond me.

Roman didn't seem to mind my forgetfulness, as it gave us a few extra minutes of time together before drop-off. We popped into a sweltering deli to pick up a sandwich and an apple, and then completed the walk to his modestly air-conditioned school.

"I love you, Mommy," Roman said when we reached the top of the school steps. He held my face, kissing me more intensely than any man ever had. No goodbye with Roman was ever easy. It was always hard to tell who was feeding off of whose anxiety.

He still clung to me as he ran through his ritualized list of questions. "Where are you going to be?" "Will you pick me up?" "If I want to call you, will the teacher let me?" I nodded over and over, offering whatever reassurance I could.

"I don't want to go," he whimpered softly into my sleeve. Kids and parents were streaming past, and I didn't dare look up. I didn't want to see their pity and judgment.

"Roman, you can do this," I said, prying myself free and steering him toward his classroom. Before Roman could lunge for me, I raced back downstairs, where a mother gave me a rueful smile. She was wearing a fashionable peasant dress and carrying a bucket bag with fabric samples spilling out of the top. A bright yellow bike helmet jauntily dangled from her elbow.

"It's hard, but trust me, by next year they will turn into different kids," she said.

"You promise?" I followed behind her and watched her unlock her bike.

"That's what everybody says, anyway." She shrugged. "Where are you guys thinking of for kindergarten?" Her tone was a mixture of curious and competitive.

"Still figuring it out," I said noncommittally. Ken's place was only temporary, and I couldn't enroll Roman anywhere until we had a permanent address.

The mom gave a flat smile. "If you're thinking of going private, you'd better get it figured out soon."

I held back a groan. My friend Bethany had warned me that New Yorkers were obsessed with private school. Getting your kid into the right school was a ferociously competitive sport that made the Hunger Games look like ping-pong. At the time, I'd tuned her out. We could never afford the hefty price tag of private school. But the more people talked about it, the harder it became to ignore.

New Yorkers had this weird way of both lauding and shaming you. If you opted for public, you were gritty and cool. But if you didn't try for private, you were a greedy monster who clearly cared more about yourself than setting your kid up for success.

"Well, before you make any decisions, you may want to do a neuropsych eval on him," the mom suggested.

"A what?" I looked at her in confusion.

"Just an assessment of what you're dealing with. It's like a blueprint for your child's brain. He seems wonderful, but he clearly has... needs." She gave me a slapped-on smile.

"What needs?" I felt queasy. "*Special* needs?"

"I'm not an expert," she said airily. "But everyone has needs. My daughter has her own cornucopia of shit going on. It's just the world we live in now. Imagine if our parents had actually taken the time to figure us out."

Roman had never been easy. I was the first to admit that. But he was smart and always seemed to be on the right track developmentally. I had struggled with dyslexia as a kid, but I was fairly certain that that wasn't his problem. There were other things that concerned me though, and other people were starting to see them too.

The mom watched me as her words sank in. "You just want to be sure that he's going to a school that can support him not just academically but emotionally," she added gently. "I'm Sari, by the way."

With her curly strawberry blond hair and the tiniest smattering of freckles across her nose, she looked like the middle-aged version of my childhood Cabbage Patch doll — only richer.

"I'm Meg," I said with a smile that I hoped would conceal the intimidation inspired by her supersized diamond engagement ring. "Is he your first?" Sari asked as she walked her bike toward the street corner.

"Yeah. He has a baby brother at home," I said, following along. "Eldest kids are always the most difficult." Sari sighed knowingly. "He's probably a genius. My daughter is either going to be a CEO or a serial killer. She's smart as hell but when it comes to empathy or normal social cues, she doesn't have them. That's why we're doing private. I can't let her get lost in the system."

I could feel the corners of my mouth quivering. Was that what I was doing to Roman, setting him up to get lost?

"It's expensive," she went on, "but I just want her to have all the tools she needs. You only get one shot, you know?" I could feel my armpits dampening. "Yeah," I trailed off.

"I hate to sound like a snob because I'm really not a snob." Sari was talking faster now. "I'm super down to earth. I live in *Brooklyn*, for god's sake, but public schools in the city are a shit show. And if you have any issues at all, you slip through the cracks. It's sad. So sad."

"What cracks exactly?" I asked.

"In public school, the ratio of students to teachers is like 30 to one. Also, lice," she added in an ominous tone.

"So which school is your daughter going to go to?" I was hoping to gain some insights for myself.

"It depends on who accepts her." Sari hit the walk button at the corner, but didn't bother waiting for the light to turn before stepping into the road and making her way across, oncoming traffic be damned. I picked up my pace and followed in lockstep, eager not to miss a word.

"Abington would be my first choice," she went on. "Nobody is better than them when it comes to child development. They are on another level with all the additional support, the OT, the cog behavioral specialists, the tai chi and meditation classes, and that nut-free kitchen. It's like if Maria Montessori had a three-way with Julia Child and the Dalai Lama." She turned to me, as if expecting a laugh to come tumbling out. But I was too overwhelmed.

"Wow. I want that," I said wistfully.

"Who doesn't?" she practically snorted. "But you need a golden ticket to get into Abington! Every parent in the city is gunning for a spot."

Deflated, I looked down at the sidewalk.

"My husband went to Ellsworth, which is also respectable, but I already know that Waverly would be miserable there."

"Waverly," I repeated. "That's so different!"

"My husband and I met at the Waverly Inn. Good thing we didn't meet at the Spotted Pig." She laughed, then got back to business. "I have a whole list of places I'm going to tour, but we'll see." Sari stopped short, as if nervous that she'd given away too much information. "Which way are you going?" she asked, hopping on her bike.

"Umm, that way." I pointed in a random direction. "If you ever have time for a coffee, that would be great," I threw out. "I'd love to pick your brain and see your list of schools."

Sari nodded, feigning interest as she tucked a curl behind her ear and checked the time on her phone. "I'm late right now for an install, but let me get your number from the class list and I'll shoot you a text with some times."

"I'd love that." I smiled, wanting to believe that I'd hear from her.

The further away I got from Roman's school, the easier it became to breathe again. A weight was lifting. An unbearable blanket of guilt, love, and responsibility. I'd loved my parents, boyfriends, and of course my dog, Red, but motherhood was different. This was a vomit-inducing kind of love. An infinite joy mixed with infinite terror that never seemed to go away. My postpartum depression lasted, well, postpartum. It wasn't just a phase; it was a new way of seeing the world after children. While I wouldn't have traded motherhood for the world, I felt like my life was bifurcated in two disparate halves: the Meg I'd been before my kids and the one I was after. As I hurtled toward my first job interview of the day, my worries about resuscitating my dead-end career were compounded by this new belief that maybe Roman had bigger issues that I was neglecting to see. He was my first, so I really didn't know what to compare him to. When I looked at other children walking with their parents, though, I felt envious. Nobody was bolting out into the street, tearing off their shoes because they detected a grain of sand, asking ten thousand times if they were going to be late to wherever they were headed.

When Roman wasn't spilling over with anxiety, he was spinning or daydreaming or bouncing up and down. It was terrifying. He was my kite and I was his string. Maybe I should have just let him soar, but tethering him to my wrist often felt like the only true way to protect him. My friends liked to tell me that I was overreacting, that he would outgrow whatever problems were revealing themselves at the time. I desperately wanted this to be true. But I couldn't be sure that it was. I took a deep breath and tried to focus on the only thing I could control at present. I'd promised my son that it was going to be a good-luck day.

The second interview was the one that mattered. It was for Lippe Taylor, a big-time marketing and consulting agency. The first was more of a random opportunity that came up through a publicist I'd worked with on a cauliflower rice campaign several years back. It was for a start-up company that made matcha tea. She'd told me upfront that the brand didn't have much capital, which was publicist code for "They're going to pay you peanuts." I almost declined the opportunity to meet for a job that couldn't cover the cost of a babysitter. But I was rusty when it came to pitching myself and figured that I could use a practice run before the big interview.

As I waited for the light to change, I pulled out my compact and checked my teeth for mystery flecks. All clear. I reapplied my lip gloss and grinned at myself. I'd get through the interviews and google the fuck out of private schools later that evening.

CHAPTER FOUR

After crossing Broadway and a few more streets I'd never heard of, I realized I'd overshot the mark. Matcha Pitchu had a brick-and-mortar coffee shop on the corner of Lafayette and East Fourth. I was now on Second Avenue, and on track to be late if I didn't hightail it.

Berating myself for not taking a cab from school and opting to wear herbal deodorant on this sultry day, I finally swooshed into Matcha Pitchu. I was out of breath and even more out of sorts.

A man who appeared to be a fifty-year-old, caffeine-addled former punk rocker greeted me at the door and introduced himself as Seth. After offering me an iced tea and a beanie with his company logo, he led me up a flight of stairs. I trailed behind him, admiring his artificial sandy blond hair and neck full of sterling silver jewelry.

The corporate office was in an open space decorated in psychedelic colors and alien-themed tchotchkes that you'd buy at a roadside kiosk in Roswell, New Mexico. It reminded me of the dorm room of a guy I used to hang out with for free weed in college. A glass wall separated several rows of desks from the brightly lit conference room that also doubled as a test kitchen.

"We are still a tea brand, but I'd say forty percent of our current business is CBD, and I expect it to just keep growing," Seth said. As he talked, his overly dyed unibrow moved up and down his forehead. "We carry brownie bites, lotions, and all the kitsch shit like cock oils and mints, but what we've found is that there's still a hole in the market." He gave a lopsided smile that could have been the result of bad Botox or a mild stroke. "Nobody is targeting moms! And moms control eighty-three percent of household purchases. That is just moronic!" he exclaimed, handing over a chalky sphere. The label told me that it was infused with 20mg of sustainably sourced CBD. "Do you know much about CBD?" he asked.

"A bit," I lied, still trying to figure out why anybody would purchase what I was holding.

"It's a bath bomb," Seth announced in the proud tone of somebody introducing me to the lightbulb.

"So did you always want to be a copywriter?" he asked, momentarily interested in somebody other than himself.

"Yes," I said. "I mean, it wasn't my childhood dream, but it's the thing I do well. And I like doing things well." I smiled. He seemed to like what he was hearing.

I could come up with snappy copy. But my real gift was an ability to read people. One look at a person and I knew exactly what they wanted. Just as I'd get a sense of a person, I could understand a brand and instantly be able to communicate on its behalf.

It began in college when my roommates started making me write their MySpace bios and Facebook status updates. After college, I moved to Los Angeles with the hopes of landing a staff job on a sitcom. I was a part-time hostess at Saddle Ranch on Sunset, with two shitty pilot scripts and three creative-writing credits from Santa Monica community college to my name, when I finally found my voice. I'd get jacked up on lattes from the adjacent Starbucks all morning then go back to my studio apartment on Martel, boot up my computer, and fire off jokes that nobody could hold against me.

I didn't know what copywriting was aside from the depiction of 1960s ad agencies I'd seen on *Mad Men*. But that was before a neighbor who worked at Brigman Stern, one of the most prestigious West Coast firms, came to me one night in a panic over a vegan bagel account she'd been assigned. The product Fagels (fake bagels) needed a catchphrase, and I offered up: "Once you go Fagel, you'll never go bagel." It was stupid and never in a million years did I expect it to leave the confines of our building courtyard. But the client did cartwheels, and my neighbor was promoted to senior copywriter shortly thereafter. She was so grateful that she rewarded me with freelance gigs whenever she could. I mostly worked in packaged goods, writing text for "alternative food brand" campaigns. I learned more than I ever wanted to about monk fruit sweeteners and sorghum flour, but with time, I found myself bored and wishing I were half as good at writing screenplays. A senior creative director at the company who worked on the Coca-Cola account picked up on my pessimism. "You might just be selling water with bubbles," he told me, "but if you don't believe in your product and think that you are changing the world, you're never going to be able to convince others to buy it." So I learned to believe — or pretend I did anyway.

Seth had me sit on a red velvet loveseat shaped like lips as he kept rambling on about how his products were going to "disrupt the space," though I was unclear what "space" he was referring to. He'd been tight-lipped over email, but now he was making up for lost time. While I was fairly certain the CBD market was already saturated and catered to everyone from moms to miniature schnauzers, I told Seth that his business sounded "very disruptive."

Seth's business partner, Vigo, a shorter, younger finance guy with spiky hair that had an electrocuted air, materialized and helped himself to the spot next to Seth. He offered no words, nor eye contact, but listened intently as Seth continued his rant. The pair sort of reminded me of a real-life Bert and Ernie. Part of me wanted to believe that they were lovers.

"Like instead of downing a bottle of white wine at night, pop one of our Mommy Bombs in the tub and take the edge off," Seth said with a clownish grin. Vigo sat there, straight-faced. It was getting harder to look at them seated next to each other and not picture them in shower caps singing "Rubber Duckie."

My personal opinion, not that it mattered, was that CBD was like lavender. Great in concept, but in no way capable of making a real dent on a person's stress level. At least not the kind of stress I had.

"Mommy Bombs?" I asked, hoping that the name was just a working title.

"You know I invented the matcha latte, right?" Seth said.

"I didn't," I said, looking at Vigo to see if he was going to dispute the claim.

"Before me, it was all chai all the time. Look it up, it's on my Wiki page."

I nodded politely, pretending not to know that anyone could edit his own Wikipedia page.

"CBD is a crowded market at the moment," I said, trying to influence them into feeling a bit less confident. I'd seen other copywriters do this in the past, in order to make a client feel extra services were needed. Once I saw an entire dried fruit campaign go to this moderately talented writer who convinced his clients that after the South Beach Diet, all women feared bananas and that the only way out was an entire rebrand on the fruit itself.

"There are plenty of similar wellness products already on the market, aren't there?" I asked. "So I guess my first question would be: What makes this different? How are you better than the competition?"

Seth started revving up, excited to make a believer out of me. "Look, could these women use Epsom salts and add a couple drops of CBD oil to their tub for a similar result? Sure! But they aren't, because there is nothing exciting about that! People want a sexy miracle drug, not some depressing health food store remedy. The success of this project hinges on the way we market it. You know that better than anyone."

"Go on," I said.

"Take a basic necessity, throw some sans serif font on it, shoot it on a muted pink backdrop, and sell the idea of luxury at a price that is accessible to all. Now *that's* the name of the game, right Vig?" The straight man nodded, and Seth went on, "We are just taking things a step further because our bath bombs aren't shitty. They are actually pretty magical. They are handcrafted in small batches with high-end essential oils and top-grade CBD. Not to mention packaging that makes you want to nut."

'I'm sorry?" I asked, certain I must have misheard him.

"But I don't just want this to be a fake status symbol sitting on your bathroom sink next to your high-end soaps, I want this to be a movement! An inflection point in the industry!" Seth continued, like a charismatic funky-haired preacher at a rock and roll church. "Dirty Lemon dude figured out a way to make lemon water sexy. Do you know how cheap and easy it is to make lemon water?" He walked over to the sink and turned on the faucet. I watched as Seth grabbed a lemon out of a fruit basket and sliced it in half.

"There," he said, dramatically dropping the half lemon into a glass of tap water and slamming it down in front of me. "I just made it."

I granted him a smile and brought the drink to my lips. "It's delicious," I said.

He nodded and watched me take another sip. "We thought about hiring Black Reindeer for this… but they botched our nitro-infused chocolate milk launch by convincing us to put the ingredients from the back on the front. Do you know how much motherfucking sugar is in chocolate milk?! Nobody should see that info EVER!"

I looked over at Vigo, who'd picked up a laptop and started typing on it, madly. My spidey sense was that he was the true brains behind the operation but knew better than to interject when Seth was on a roll.

"Do you have a creative director?" I asked. "Art director? People I'd be collaborating with?"

"Nope. It's just us. We're doing this almost entirely in-house. Vigo is the strategy guy and I'm more of the creative force. I also have a bunch of interns and a web guy I like to use. But I need a killer copywriter and I've been told that you are stellar. Or at least the best in our price range."

"That's really nice to hear," I said, my voice ringing with disbelief. How was this guy at the helm of any company?

"We are very collaborative here. You got ideas, throw 'em out there and let's see what sticks. Bottom line is, we want this to be fresh but not young. We need someone your age to make it authentic."

"My age?" I laughed.

"Advertising is a bit like modeling. After thirty, you are past your prime. But so is our demo! And we want to come across as real but also aspirational."

Vigo nodded in agreement, then went back to taking notes as if he were a courtroom stenographer on amphetamines.

"Well, I think you're right about the authentic part," I said. "You need to reflect your consumer, not talk down to them."

"Right. Of course." Seth nodded, trying to understand.

"Instead of the 'This is how good your life would be if you had us' approach, consumers, especially moms, want to feel understood. They are too savvy. Especially millennials. They see through the other shit. You need to become the consumer. You need to talk like them, dress like them, and even joke like them. That's how you establish a bond."

Seth looked at Vigo. "I have goosebumps. Do you have goosebumps?"

Vigo shook his head. No goosebumps.

"So is this an offer?" I asked. Boldness wasn't my specialty, but I was feeling more self-confident than usual. This guy was a joke and I just wanted to go to the Lippe Taylor interview with a bird — or bath bomb — in hand.

Seth pressed his lips together. "Can you give us a minute?"

I watched Seth and Vigo huddle together on the other side of the glass wall like they were discussing a football play. I figured that when they came back in and begged me to come aboard, I would play it cool and tell them that I would give them an answer by the end of the week. People loved to get answers by the end of the week. When you asked for any more time, it was an obvious brush-off. But an "end of the week" answer always felt like a tentative yes not desperate "yes." It was the best way to close out a meeting and an even better way to enter another one.

I pulled out my phone, trying to look nonchalant, when I saw something that made my heart sink. Sitting in my inbox was an email from my contact at Lippe Taylor informing me that the interview had been canceled. "We're going with an internal candidate. We were so looking forward to meeting you and we will keep you abreast of any upcoming opportunities." Before I could respond,

Seth burst back in, beads of sweat dripping down his cheeks. He looked like a peroxide blond beer that had been left out of the cooler.

"Okay. So… I wasn't sure over email, but now that we've met you, Vigo and I believe that you are the *only* person for this job. You can speak to this crowd in a way that we can't. And I think we share the same worldview."

"We do?" I looked at him, nonplussed.

"This bath bomb is every mom. You want to escape your kids, but you also don't want to be out at the nightclub. You want to have your cake, but you don't want the calories after nine p.m. You are part of that 'self-care isn't selfish' crowd. You're privileged, but still put upon; blessed, but batshit; fun, but functional —"

"Sorry," I stopped him. "Are we talking about me or the figurative 'me'?"

"You… But also the *figurative* you!" His eyes were bulging with excitement. "We don't have a ton of money so the retainer would be modest." He coughed and glanced down. "Twenty grand for six months. We're also open to offering points."

"How many points?" I asked with my best poker face. I'd never been offered a point in anything.

"We'd need to look at the math —" Vigo interjected. It was the first time I'd heard him speak. His voice was low and creaky.

"Look," Seth said. "You get this company up on its feet and we can talk about it."

I was blinking, my head swimming in confusion. I wanted a job. But did I want to hitch my wagon to these two? For what amounted to an annual salary of forty grand?

"Two skews are ready to go!" Seth jumped back in. "'C-section blues,' 'TGI-Monday,' you know, because Monday is when the nanny is back. That one was Vigo's idea!" Seth looked back at Vigo, who groaned. "We want to launch with a total of five," Seth told me. "But cute so far, right?"

"Yeah," I told them. "I totally see it."

I was nodding my head, unsure if I saw anything or I just really needed a job.

CHAPTER FIVE

No matter how many times I entered Chelsea House, I always felt like one of those imposter colognes they sell at big box stores. Not quite Georgio, not quite Calvin, but something that came in an aerosol can and potentially caused some sort of contact dermatitis. Maybe it was by design — the straight-faced hipsters holding open the front door, the Rasta-chic gatekeepers positioned behind the front desk, the waitstaff with their Pilates-toned bodies encased in perfectly asymmetrical Belgian-designer uniforms. Even though I knew most of the people working there by name, I could never shake the feeling that I was about to be thrown out for simply lacking whatever ephemeral quality everyone else possessed.

Chelsea House encouraged members to think of themselves as part of an elite cabal of artists and dreamers sent down to earth to exchange ideas and energies in a super chic setting that offered movie screenings, free Wi-Fi, swimming pool access, and endless plates of painstakingly massaged kale salad.

Originating in London, the club thrived on its reputation for excluding anyone whose job involved wearing a tie to work. Bankers from the Upper East Side all the way down to Battery Park City begged and pleaded their cases, but rarely made it past the membership committee, of which Iliya was now the head. He'd been an interesting choice considering that Iliya, who'd come of age under the Coney Island boardwalk, didn't have an elitist bone in his body. Off the record, he thought the whole concept of Chelsea House was bullshit. But the concept liked Iliya. He had a strong work ethic, and his looks didn't hurt either. Normally, the club liked to give all their membership director positions to people already living within the community from which they'd be picking and choosing, but with the opening of new clubs like the Wing, the Soho House, the Norwood, the Well, the Wonder, and the The (a nonbinary concern that insisted on being called a "collective" and not a "club"), Chelsea House was losing not only its edge, but its supremacy. And Saro Stark, the master of the Chelsea universe, believed that Iliya was the only person fit for the job. He wasn't entirely wrong.

When I walked into the sixth-floor clubroom, I found Iliya in a back booth. He appeared to be comforting a distraught waitress. Though he was merely listening to her as she sobbed, I felt the hairs on my neck go up as I called his name across the room. No matter how pure the waitress's intentions, she would eventually try to fuck him. They all did. Even the ones who liked women.

"Iliya," I said in as bright and calm a tone as I could muster. Iliya glanced up, totally unfazed. He wasn't worried. Maybe it was a sober thing, but giving in to temptation, whether it was a glass of whiskey or an eager hostess, was something he deemed the province of the weak. It was beneath him.

"Hey, Meg," Iliya said. He appeared surprised, but not unhappy to see me. The waitress adjusted her blouse as Iliya stood to hug me. "Logan, this is my wife, Meg," Iliya said, somewhat stiff.

Whenever he introduced me to new people, especially women, I always felt their eyes linger on my face a few moments too long. I could read their thoughts. They wanted to know how *he* was with *me*.

At thirty-five, I was neither young nor old. I was still able to rock jean shorts, but past the age where guys tried to communicate with me through music. I was a plain Jane with a black bob and boobs that didn't require a workout bra. In a place like France, where women could look like boys and still be sexy, my stock might have been higher. But where I grew up, most people wrote me off as a suicidal goth or militant lesbian because I owned Doc Martens, listened to Ani DiFranco, and had hair that didn't reach my shoulders. Which was fine with me. I'd seen enough horror movies to know that girls like me had the best odds for survival. The cheerleaders and prom queens were always the ones who ended up slaughtered or electrocuted with their own blow dryers.

The buxom twenty-something smiled, extending her hand. All I could focus on was the large ink merwoman on her forearm.

"I like your mermaid," I said in a sugar-sweet tone, overcompensating for my insecurity.

"It's a siren," she corrected me.

"Even better." I laughed awkwardly and Iliya shot me a look. I was overdoing it. "What?" I gave him a playful hit on the shoulder. "I'm a big fan of using my feminine wiles to lure men to their deaths. You know that."

He sighed. "I do."

When I first met Iliya, I was twenty-five years old and bartending at Geiko, the Japanese steakhouse whose employee dress code had been put in place well before the #MeToo movement. I'd heard all about the brooding night manager from the other waitstaff before actually speaking to him and had already determined that I wanted nothing to do with him. Which of course meant that I wanted everything to do with him.

He made me nervous to look at, and I knew he wasn't the type of guy you could expect to call you back, let alone commit to something exclusive. He was dark and mysterious, with his Russian accent and all-black wardrobe. I was hired to work day shifts and he only worked nights, as I could only assume his daylight hours were spent sleeping in a sarcophagus.

For my first two months on the job, our paths never crossed. But when I switched to evenings, there he was, the vampire from every Anne Rice masturbation fantasy I'd ever had. He drove a motorcycle, smoked cigarillos, and wore a leather bomber with a mandarin collar. I fucking hated mandarin collars. But his fashion sense was one of the few things about him that allowed me to feel mildly superior. He might have been hot with his chiseled cheekbones, but he was still a dork in a fucking mandarin collar that nobody had the balls to inform him was hideous.

As a manager, Iliya wasn't allowed to involve himself with staff, even though I had full knowledge that before I'd worked there, he'd hooked up with more than his share of cocktail waitresses in the coat closet. This was before he stopped drinking and before he got promoted, but the rumors never died.

Aside from when he was using the same three Spanish phrases on whatever busboy he'd come across, pretending to be a laid-back man of the people, sober Iliya was intense. He was detail-oriented, not a little neurotic, and harder on me than the lunch-shift manager, whom I could control with flirting. Iliya tried to be delicate when he eventually fired me, calling me out on the fact that I spent half my time behind the bar gossiping with the busboys about his outfit choices and the other half eating maraschino cherries. In closing, he explained that it was obvious I didn't see myself in the restaurant business for the long term.

"Do you really think anybody working at this place sees themselves here long term?" I replied, wondering if now was a good time to give him my thoughts on mandarin collars.

"I do," he said plainly. The look he gave me told me I should be ashamed.

What I'd failed to realize then was that Iliya had worked his ass off to become a manager at Geiko. And my mocking the restaurant industry as a whole only seemed to make him more annoyed.

I left that afternoon burning with shame and hoping I'd never see him again, but also sort of hoping that I would do something with my life that would land me on the giant billboard outside his office window.

Two weeks later, while aimlessly drifting around Cost Plus World Market at the Grove, I bumped into him. Literally.

It was a gloomy Sunday afternoon and instead of channeling my depression into another screenplay about my parents' divorce that I'd waste 200 dollars to print at Kinko's, I decided to max out my last working credit card on redecorating my apartment. I was holding a basketful of tea lights, paper star lanterns, and a handful of summer sausages when I heard someone *pssst* in my direction. I half thought I was being accused of shoplifting and spun around nervously. Iliya looked less greasy under the fluorescent lights. His leather jacket was nowhere to be seen and he was wearing actual colors: blue jeans and a thin maroon V-neck that looked like it might belong to an ex-girlfriend. I jumped back and one of my sausages went flying down the aisle. Iliya promptly went after it. I tried to act cool, disinterested, and like I'd never tried to find his Facebook page when he walked back over. "What?" I said, as if he'd been nagging me for weeks.

"Why are you always so angry?" He grimaced and put his hands up in the air.

"Well, you did fire me," I said, snatching back my sausage and stuffing it into my basket.

"I'm sorry," he said softly. "If it makes you feel any better, upper management wanted me to do it three months ago."

I shrugged and pretended to organize the contents of my basket, trying my hardest not to let this new information wound me.

"You changed your hair," he said.

"No, I just brushed it," I corrected him, shocked that he noticed my hair now or ever. "How's your restaurant career going?" Condescension tinged my voice.

"Good." He nodded. "How are things going with you, work-wise?" I swallowed and pretended I didn't care what he thought. "I'm writing jingles and helping my friend from college cut demo reels. You have one? You should play a Dracula in something," I said dryly.

Iliya smirked. He started to say something, but then stopped. "Are the sausages really great here or something?" He scratched his head, staring at the multiple links of beef in my basket. "You sure have a lot of them."

I huffed, pulling my basket closer to my chest. "What are you here to buy? Were you looking for something?" I shot back.

"Just you," he said without flinching.

I felt my stomach drop the way it did on roller coasters.

"I saw you through the window and wanted to make sure there were no hard feelings between us," he said.

"There is nothing between us," I gulped, very much wishing that there was something between us.

"Okay." He nodded and moved to go, then hesitated. "Now that I'm here… maybe I need a new French press, a disposable table-cloth? Obviously, it seems like summer sausages are a must!"

I didn't want to laugh, but I couldn't help it. He was funnier than I'd realized. And perceptive, the way that only women usually were. I rolled my eyes, trying to stay strong. But I knew that I was screwed. Even if he walked away, never to be seen or heard from again, I was going to think about him, obsess over him, and probably spend the next three months reading his horoscope and replaying this exchange in my head.

"You always roll your eyes at me!" he mused as we walked toward the end of the aisle. "Is that all men or am I special?"

"I do it to all men," I said, turning into another aisle and praying that he followed me. He did.

I could only play it cool for so long. I watched him speak Russian to the elderly checkout woman and help her bag my groceries. Next thing I knew, I'd agreed to have dinner with him. We went to some stroganoff place in Glendale. I rode on the back of his sleazy motorcycle, drank two shots of vodka, and gave him permission to enter my apartment afterwards (something I knew better than to do with a potential vampire).

I started the evening proudly telling him that nothing was going to happen between us because he wasn't my type and ended the night begging him to fuck my brains out in his mandarin collar. We were married a year later.

"Aren't you supposed to be at your interview?" Iliya asked, discreetly kissing me on the cheek.

I pouted. "Lippe Taylor canceled."

"I'm sorry." Iliya grabbed my hand. "You okay?"

"Yeah, actually. I got the first one." I smiled, trying to seem excited.

"You got the first job." He perked up. "That's great."

I nodded. "They're making weed bath bombs for moms. Oh, excuse me, CBD."

"I thought it was a tea company." Iliya's eyes narrowed. "That seems like a weird fit for you, no?"

"You mean a weird fit for you," I corrected him. "I have no issues with CBD. And it's supposed to be for moms."

"Moms doing drugs? You really want to get involved with that?" Iliya probed, his judgment loud and clear.

"They aren't ingesting it. They're soaking in it. Who knows if it even does anything." CBD isn't even a drug.

"Well, I don't want any," Iliya said. "Are they going to pay you decently?"

"Yeah," I lied. "I might even get a point in their company."

He scowled. "That means they *aren't* paying you."

"They *are* paying me! I just got a job offer! Can we be happy for a minute before picking the whole thing apart?"

"I'm sorry." Iliya gave me a slow smile. He was backing down. "That's great that you got something. I told you that you would."

"I know, you're always right." I was still annoyed.

"You want to eat lunch?" he asked, trying to defuse the tension.

"With you?" I cocked my head. I knew what he meant.

"I can't right now. It's crazy here." Iliya barely pressed the button for the elevator before he was back on his phone, shooting off more emails. "That mer-waitress was cute," I couldn't resist saying as we waited. Iliya rolled his eyes.

"Are you going to be home later or…"

"I doubt it." Iliya looked back down at his phone and shook his head, frustrated with whatever he was reading. He was still screwing up his face at the screen when the elevator doors opened.

"I got to take care of this," he said with a sigh that was meant to evoke pity. "Bubby is on the roof. She'll handle you."

"So glad I'll be handled," I said dryly, walking into the elevator before he could hug me goodbye.

The doors shut and I took a deep breath. *Don't cry, Meg,* I told myself. "UGGH! Don't you just wish everybody would just fuck off sometimes?" a voice behind me roared. Startled, I looked over my shoulder. I'd been so caught up in the waves of resentment that I hadn't noticed the blonde in oversized sunglasses standing behind me. My fellow passenger had a faint accent that I couldn't quite pinpoint.

I wiped my eyes, mortified. "Yeah," I said, forcing a laugh. "I guess I do."

"Emotions are powerful. No need to hide them," she said, taking a tissue out of her clutch and handing it to me. "He would have been lucky to handle you." She took off her sunglasses and gently squeezed my hand. With one blue eye and one green eye she was unquestionably striking. But it was her intensity that stopped me in my tracks. Her focus was practically invasive. I had to look away. "You are far too powerful to be fucked with," she told me as the doors opened. "Don't take any more shit, okay?"

"Thanks," I said watching her walk off in tall dark combat boots and a voluminous pink babydoll dress that made her seem at once a woman and a child.

Iliya's understudy, Bubby, spotted me and rushed over in her Gucci slides and a cashmere sweater embroidered with the sentiment *Think outside of my box.*

Her real name was Jami, but Iliya nicknamed her "Bubby" because she ate her bagels with the dough scooped out, drank only hot water with lemon in the morning, and was always complaining about her sciatica like she was a seventy-three-year-old widow from Boca, not a twenty-seven-year-old dictator of New York society. I looked across the rooftop for my elevator companion but was disappointed to see she had vanished.

"Meg," Bubby said brightly, taking me by the elbow. "Let me get you set up."

CHAPTER SIX

Bubby installed me in a corner spot. The rooftop pool was already packed with beefcakes in banana hammocks and lifestyle bloggers surreptitiously trying to snap pictures of their pedicures as they waded into the water.

Unauthorized photography was strictly forbidden at Chelsea House. If you were caught so much as taking a selfie, you were promptly asked to leave. The house was as rigid as a state legislature. Their latest policy, mandating that children have their own memberships in order to gain roof access, had members fuming. As Iliya had explained it, it was a measure against the place turning into a giant summer camp in the warmer months. While they were happy to accommodate hotel guests and certain families with pull, the club wasn't looking to turn into a day care facility. Only problem was, that's what it had been the previous summer, and members were up in arms.

"How are you?" Bubby inquired.

"Good. Better. I think I found a job. You know that tea shop, Matcha Pitchu?"

"Yeah, but no," Bubby said, displaying only slightly more interest than Seth had shown in my career trajectory. "Do those two dudes look like they're about to fuck?" I looked over to see two trainer types grinding in the hot tub passionately enough to rub off each other's spray tans. "Because there is absolutely no fucking allowed on the rooftop," Bubby reminded me, like I was the one considering it.

"I think they're just..." I started before she cut me off.

"I'm sure you're freaking out about schools."

"How did you know?" I asked.

"It's September. That's when all moms start freaking out about schools. Isn't Roman a kindergartener?"

"He will be soon." I nodded, impressed that she remembered.

"So you really are in the thick of it!" she laughed. "Don't worry, everybody is in the same boat. Going through this gauntlet is a New York rite of passage. The bar bill this month is going to be off the charts." She grinned.

"Don't look too pleased," I said.

· "How could I not? I love it! The desperate frenzy. The cutthroat nature. The eventual reckoning with one's real status in the world. As a person without kids, it's deliciously satisfying to watch the unraveling."

"Well, I don't know if I can unravel any more than I already have."

"Oh, you *can*, believe me," Bubby said, encouragingly. "You're doing private, yeah?"

"To be honest, I really don't think we can afford it. Tuition at these places is outrageous."

"You find a way. I used to commute two hours roundtrip every day to go to Spence, and it changed my life."

"It's *that* different from public school?" I asked.

"The education is great, sure, but it's all about the connections and relationships. In New York, when people ask where you went to school, they're talking about high school. Not to scare you."

"It's fine. I've been scared my whole life."

I started to say something else then stopped. The blonde from the elevator was back on the scene. Now shoeless, she was dangling her feet into the pool.

"Do you know her?" The words almost slipped out of me.

"Do you *not*?" Bubby tried to swallow her laugh.

I looked at the woman again, "No…Who is she?"

"Aren't you supposed to be in advertising?" Bubby shook her head in disbelief. "You really *are* new to town. That's Daphne Cole — or as she's better known on Instagram, Sweaterweather365."

"I don't really deal with fashion," I said. "That's more of a New York thing."

"Fashion is a New York thing?" Bubby snickered. "I'm pretty sure there's fashion in LA too." Daphne's and my eyes met. I felt a prick of embarrassment, then glanced away.

"She was a fashion influencer, but then she had kids and now she's more of a mom-fluencer but with killer fashion," Bubby explained. "She's mega."

I'd worked with a good amount of wellness gurus, DIY crafters and smoothie artists, but this was new ground. "What exactly *is* a mom-fluencer?"

"It's its own subgenre. Like, she is still a super high-end fashion chick but now she also does deals for diapers and those little whistles you stick up baby's asses to make them fart… you know, the Windy?" Bubby looked over at Daphne, cocking her head and furrowing her brow. Daphne's hair was falling out of its topknot in waves and her boots were cast aside as she delicately traced shapes in the water with her toes. She wasn't overly skinny; she had hips and curves, cracks and crevices. What was most striking was a quality I couldn't put a finger on. She was gorgeous, magnetically so. It was almost blinding.

"Her style is siiick, right? Those Bottega boots are sold out everywhere. And the Cecilie Bahnsen dress? I can't! So many *Killing Eve* vibes. Apparently, her closet looks like Hirshfield's." Bubby added, sotto voce, "When you are that rich you can take fashion risks. You don't need to mess around with basic black."

"Where did she come from?" It was all I could think to say.

"I think she's like first-generation Albanian or Bosnian or one of those Balkan countries. Her accent sort of ebbs and flows. Her mom was a housekeeper, or groundskeeper, or what are those people who have, like, a skeleton key to every room?"

"A female butler?" I asked.

Bubby shook her head. "Story is she worked for a few high-profile old-money families uptown. Daphne used to help organize closets before she was old enough to work retail. You know how Paris Hilton treated Kim Kardashian like her closet bitch? That was basically Daphne. Came from nothing, worked her way up, and now she's crushing it. Can build an Eiffel Tower out of French toast, gets gifted Chanel bags, never seems to have a bad fucking hair day, and just announced that she's designing a capsule collection for Revolve. With her kids."

I laughed nervously, baffled by how somebody with kids could possibly be that productive. "How many kids does she have?"

"Two. Twins. Vivienne and Hudson," Bubby said. "I'm embarrassed that I know that, but I do. The kids are part of her whole schtick. The husband gets dragged into it sometimes too. Kip? He's like a finance dude. Of course. Sort of a frat boy type… Cute, but in, like, a dorm room non-consensual hook-up kind of way."

I squinted, trying to picture what she meant.

"Anyway, yeah… I hate when people are so perfect, don't you?" Bubby was staring at Daphne's back. It wasn't tan, but it glowed.

"Jesus, yes." I smiled, trying to mask my growing feelings of inadequacy.

When Bubby bopped off to do her job, I pulled out my phone and wrote to Seth and Vigo to accept their offer. I had planned on waiting until the end of the week, but I was bad at waiting and too nervous that they might change their minds by then. I needed to know that I had a job even if it was a dodgy one that wasn't going to cover the cost of a New York City education. I needed my family and the people around me to know that I had a purpose. Maybe I wasn't some self-made fashionista crushing the motherhood game, but I was still somebody. I was the person who needed to know that most of all.

When I finished my lunch, I took the long way toward the elevators, passing the spot where Daphne had been sitting. The ice cubes in her otherwise empty glass were precariously balanced on top of each other like discarded toys wedged into Roman's closet. I felt a strange stirring, regret mixed with happiness. Even if Daphne was long gone, she'd still seen me in the way I hadn't felt seen in a years. We'd shared a moment, and that was never going to become untrue. Biting down the smile forming on my lips. I headed home.

CHAPTER SEVEN

Marina left our apartment at three-fifteen, not a second later. I made dinner, cleaned the kitchen, fed and walked Red, washed two kids, killed three roaches, and sent four bitter texts to Iliya. Taking matters into my own hands, I researched home extermination remedies online and applied a mixture of sugar and borax along our baseboards, under the cabinets, and around the sinks.

"I just can't get comfortable!" Roman tossed and turned, restless well past eight p.m. I'd been in his room for almost an hour. Sweet Felix was catatonic in the crib beside us.

I placed Roman's weighted blanket back over his body and once more tried to extricate myself from the room. "Okay, I'm gonna go for real now—"

"Mommy?" Roman grabbed me, his grip tightening around my waist.

"Yes?" I whispered.

"I'm scared."

"Of what?" I asked, looking at his glowing purple night-light that made me feel like I was on mushrooms.

"Are you gonna die before me?" He blinked, ever so seriously.

My heart dropped. "No. Nobody is dying," I lied, finding myself moving closer toward him when I was supposed to be creeping away. "No, but I mean, like, someday you are going to die, and Daddy is going to die, and Felix is going to die —"

"That isn't happening ever!" I stopped him. "I love you, and you are healthy, and Mommy is healthy, and Daddy is—"

"Dying first because he is older than Mommy," Roman informed me, wrapping his fingers around my wrist. "I love you so much. I'm going to be sad when you go to Kevin's."

"Kevin's?" I looked at him, confused.

"That's where you go when you die, up to Kevin's," he informed me stoically. It hit me that in the game of telephone that is being four years old, he'd understood "heaven" to be "Kevin's."

"Who is telling you all this? Marina? Your school?"

"Oh Mommy...." He didn't answer. "Don't get old...." He was starting to drift off.

"You are completely safe, and Mommy is going to be with you forever," I assured him in a whisper.

"Can you just brush me?" Roman flopped over and pulled up his pajama shirt, presenting me with his back like an overindulged house cat. I used a skin brush on him twice a day to help keep him focused, but the brush was stimulating, and I didn't like using it before bed.

"How about a little massage?" I offered.

"A big one," he said, and I couldn't bring myself to refuse him. "Down. More back. More. Stop. Front. Sides. Face."

"Face?" I laughed.

"Daddy does face and ears," he groggily informed me.

I missed the daddy that shared bedtime massage duty with me, the co-parent that lightened the emotional load. I tried my hardest to remind myself that Iliya was working for all of our benefits, and that overseeing an army of attitudinal servers wasn't how he wished to be spending his night.

Once Roman was basically asleep, I scooped Red up in my arms and placed him on top of Roman's comforter. I wanted him to sleep there, at the foot of the bed, like those movie dogs that forge a special bond with a troubled teen and change their lives forever. Red wasn't going for it, though. He came right over to my feet.

I'd always believed that having a dog and then having a child was like falling in love with somebody new while still living with your ex. And I had a feeling Red shared this view. Sure, he'd seen enough of Roman's acrobatics on the couch to know that closing his eyes anywhere near Roman was enough to land him in one of those canine wheelchairs. But it was more than that. He saw himself as my dog, and my dog only. The kids were simply interlopers.

The second I started my Seal Team 6 crawl out of the boys' bedroom, Red followed me. At last, I got in my own bed with Red in one arm and my laptop in the other.

I had work to do. Both Bubby and my new mom acquaintance, Sari, had made it sound like child protective services would come for me if I didn't at least look into Abington.

According to the school's website, tours were already underway. Financial aid was awarded to a select number of kids, and the school itself was barely a mile from Ken's roach motel. If for no other reason than to be able to tell myself that I had tried, I submitted a request for a tour. Then I reached for my phone in a sort of mindless haze and found myself staring at the explore page on my Instagram.

I typed the letters slowly. "S-W-E..." Before I finished the word, Daphne's face appeared, right under the Sweetgreen account.

I felt a prick of excitement as her feed sprung to life: private beaches, presidential suites, and room-service trays spilling over with exotic fruits. There were charcuterie boards and paper mâché castles as tall as the ceiling and children's bento boxes filled with gourmet desserts. There were carousels and costume balls, cold Champagne, tricked-out cars, and oh, the clothing — capes and dresses and shoes and handbags. It was retail porn, lifestyle porn, vacation porn, and food porn with the occasional bathroom bikini selfie that teetered into the realm of porn-porn.

Daphne's body looked smaller in the photos than it had on the roof. The pores on her face were nonexistent, as if she'd been attacked by a giant eraser. I tried not to think too much about her captions, most of which sounded like they'd been lifted straight out of a "Quote of the Day" desk calendar.

But just when I wanted to cringe, I'd stumble upon a post where she would pour her heart out with a rawness that was rare to find among influencers of her caliber. She talked about things that women didn't often talk about — her struggles with depression, her dissatisfaction with her body, her thyroid autoimmune disease, her screwups with her kids, and her guilt about preferring Netflix over fucking her husband.

I wasn't unfamiliar with the world of influencers by any means. I'd ghostwritten captions for quite a few of them, when they were working with brands that had hired me. But perhaps because I understood the machinations behind the posts, I'd never found any of it all that interesting. There was something different about Daphne. Something that was impossible to ignore. It didn't matter if you cared about her Balenciaga bag or botched Botox or brown-bag lunch challenge. She sucked you in. The commentators seemed to agree. "Where are the other honest portrayals of motherhood?" one follower wrote. "Sending love and light your way, my queen," somebody else chimed in. "You are saving my life," added another.

Mixed in with the autobiographical content and sponsored brand posts with everyone from Prada to Pampers were pictures of her fraternal twins, a boy and a girl who appeared to be slightly older than Roman. Wide eyed and moon faced, they were photographed from all angles in high resolution and with such frequency that after only five minutes of looking, I was certain I'd be able to pick them out of a crowd. While I never could have felt comfortable sharing my kids the way that she did, from a brand perspective they were what grounded the whole thing in reality. For as fancy as some of her content tended to be (she wasn't afraid to post a Birkin riding in a chopper), she was still a mom with all the same struggles. It was an authenticity that spoke to me in a way that made me incapable of turning away, that made me feel less alone.

Scrolling back through her feed, it seemed as if she was the originator of nearly every offbeat trend. She wore oversized eighties-looking suits with giant shoulder pads, nylon body suits that had built-in feet, patent leather trench coats with see-through mesh T-shirts, top hats, bowler hats, boater hats, and sombreros — and that was all years ago.

Having met Daphne in real life, it was hard to look at her page objectively. I kept trying to find the woman I'd encountered in person, but aside from the over-the-top-fashion, she wasn't quite there. This was someone different.

In person she'd been sarcastic and mischievous, almost aggressive. Online she was softer and more feminine. Something about her posts told me she was in on the joke, which made me like her even more. She was playing to the crowd, without apology. She'd determined who they were and fed it back to them with a glamorous twist. She was doing the same thing I did. Only she wasn't working for a brand. She *was* the brand.

After scrolling through roughly four thousand posts, I still wanted more. And so I opened my email and started to type. "You guys need a face for your product," I wrote to Vigo and Seth. "And I think I found her."

CHAPTER EIGHT

"Sweaterweather365? I don't get it. That's her *name*?" Seth asked the following week. He presented me with the elaborate tea that he'd been crafting for the past twenty minutes. "But what about when it's hot outside?"

"I hope it didn't seem like an overstep, but I really think this woman would be —" I stopped talking and gasped when I caught sight of the calico cat made solely out of foam and chocolate powder looking up at me from the mug.

"That's Hot Tea," Seth said with a smile.

"Yeah, but the cat. It's practically a photograph!" I shook my head in disbelief.

"No, that's his name. Hot Tea," Vigo explained, breaking his silence to clarify.

"I'm a cat daddy," Seth confessed. "I have Ankimo, Bowie, and Rachel Meowdow. But Hot Tea is the prettiest. Bowie only has one eye and the other two are Cornish Rexes, so they basically just look like raw chicken breasts with whiskers."

"Right," I said, looking over at Vigo and wondering how in the hell these two had ever got together.

It was a little after nine a.m., still early at Matcha Pitchu headquarters. Aside from the two baristas downstairs preparing to open, the place was empty. Seth had been there all night working on new formulas and had demanded that we meet as soon as possible to discuss "next steps." Dressed in flannel pajama bottoms and red Elmo house slippers and with hair that looked as if it had been used as a youth league soccer field, Seth seemed to look more on the verge of a breakdown every time I saw him.

Vigo pulled up Daphne's Instagram on his laptop and showed it to Seth. I'd been working on them for over a week, and this was the first time I'd managed to hold their attention. He'd stopped on a photo of Daphne kneeling on the bow of a yacht in the South of France with a caption that read, "Feeling a bit Nauti and not giving a ship."

"I love these captions!" Seth exclaimed.

"The captions are terrible," Vigo baritoned.

"I thought the same thing.... at first." I pressed my lips together. "But it's a bit. She's making fun of herself. And what's more, she's the most influential mom in the city. There's a self-awareness under there. That's her secret sauce."

Seth hummed and continued to peruse Daphne's page while Vigo typed some things into his phone. "I'm running her through StarShoot," he grumbled. "It's a platform that does the math for marketers. There's an influencer engagement calculator. It's basically 'likes,' plus comments, plus reposts, divided by the total number of followers and then divided by the total number of posts," Vigo explained slowly, as if he were speaking to a couple of foreign exchange students. His face brightened. "Not bad. She has an average ER of 1.97, which is high considering she isn't a celebrity and I had never heard of her before."

"You aren't her demo," I said. "Moms are!"

"One problem." Vigo set his heavy-lidded eyes on me. "We don't have the kind of money that a chick like this would require. Her rates are probably something like thirty grand for a post. Maybe two to three hundred thousand for a full-blown campaign."

Seth's mouth dropped open. "For real? Should I be an influencer?"

"I'd follow you," I said.

It always seemed crazy to me that the act of posing in front of bubblegum pink walls and boomeranging into marshmallow-filled bathtubs was a legitimate twenty-first century career. But I had watched regular people build small empires, frame by frame, avocado toast by avocado toast. I had been in the room when big companies committed to compensating online personalities who'd agreed to a single post more than they paid me for a year's worth of work.

"Those twins hers?" Vigo checked.

I laughed. "I don't think they're child actors."

"Twins scare me," Seth said.

"Okay. I get it." Vigo capitulated. "But some of these captions. Oy vey," he groaned.

"I can fix the captions for our purposes if we can get her," I vote.

Vigo looked to Seth, then back to me, still processing. Finally, a slow smile played across his mouth. "Let's bag her."

It took a week of going around and around with Daphne's agents before we learned that she might be interested. As luck would have it, she didn't have any conflicts or exclusivity in the bath bomb or CBD space. But for a half-day photo shoot, two press interviews, one static post in her feed and a single three-frame story, the agency was requesting 150k. After consulting with Matcha Pitchu's investors and throwing in another 10k he'd squeezed out of his parents, Vigo countered at 50k with five percent of total back-end revenue. It was the best he could do.

Daphne respectfully passed on the offer.

CHAPTER NINE

Corralling Roman across the threshold of Abington School, my adrenaline kicked in. I'd killed myself to get a time to bring him in, but now confronted with the perfect moms streaming through the doors of the Harry Potteresque building, I knew I was in over my head.

My heart rate started to settle as we made our way inside. Beyond the austere exterior, Abington was colorful and warm, with hallways that smelled of buttered toast and freshly purchased books. Large picture windows looked into each classroom. I couldn't help fantasizing about what kind of life I'd have had if my parents had actually invested in my education.

"Greetings and salutations!" The words came from a small woman wearing Iris Apfel reading glasses. She stood in front of a large banner that bore the words: "Don't Dream It, Be It."

"*Rocky Horror Picture Show*?" I exclaimed, giddy.

"Pretty sure it was Eleanor Roosevelt," she countered.

I was pretty sure that it was Tim Curry but chose not to argue.

"This is Roman Chernoff," I said. "He's here for a playdate and I'm here for the parent tour."

"Well, as we tell prospective parents, it's not exactly a *playdate*." She delivered her scolding in a cheery tone. "We like to think of it as a *child visit*."

"Oh, of course." I blushed, remembering the jargon the Abington admissions worker had used on our phone call.

"What time was your appointment for?" she asked, eye level with my waist. Discreet as she tried to be, I could tell she was sizing me up to see if I wore a Rolex or any other status symbol that might indicate that I was capable of contributing generously to the school's annual fund.

"I'm Marilyn, the dean of the lower school." She smiled, twisting the simple strand of pearls she wore under her checkered button-down shirt and cashmere cardigan.

"If you wouldn't mind, leave your contact info with Norma." She motioned to a gray-haired woman seated and looking forlorn in the corner. "And then head on over to the Mandela room." She pointed down the hallway with her tiny doll-like fingers. She reminded me of that little woman from *NCIS: Los Angeles* who was always telling the team what to do.

"I don't want to go on a playdate!" Roman shrieked as we entered the wood-paneled conference room filled with stoic-faced parents in folding chairs. "It's a *child's visit*." I corrected him calmly, looking to the other parents for approval.

"Who am I visiting?" he rebutted.

"You know… I really don't know." I laughed, hoping someone would come to my rescue.

The crowd remained quiet, avoiding eye contact like a bunch of fifteen-year-old girls in a Planned Parenthood waiting room. Coordinated in gray sweaters, navy suits, and Marilynesque pearl necklaces, each parent looked more uptight and stressed out than the next.

With fewer than twelve spots available for incoming kindergarteners and a sibling policy that gave preference to kids who already had an older brother or sister at the school, they were ready for war. And so was I, just to a laser degree.

"Meg?" a familiar voice called out. I turned around to see Sari sitting in the corner. Her tote had been traded in for a sophisticated black Chanel bag. And her curly hair was now styled into a Heather

Locklear bouffant. She looked as though she'd woken up early to get a Cosmo from Dry Bar. She motioned for me to join her.

"I woke up early to get a Cosmo from Dry Bar. Is it over the top?" she asked under her breath, touching her head.

"You look great," I reassured her.

She smiled. "I wanted Waverly to get one too, but her hair is just too thin to hold anything," she confessed, glancing at her daughter. "Say hi, honey," Sari instructed the kid. Waverly looked at me stone cold, then pretended to shoot me with a finger gun. As the imaginary bullet grazed my ear, I instantly felt better about Roman's chances.

"Are you nervous?" Sari asked. "I'm crawling out of my skin." Before I could respond, she leaned in closer and whispered to me.

"You know the price doubles when they go to the upper school, right? And they also want a donation each year." She scanned the room, sizing up the competition. "Did you know that they hire outside investigators to advise on what your value is? It's crazy. Where else are you guys looking?"

I managed a flat smile. "This is it so far," I said, and immediately understood that I'd provided the wrong answer.

"GIRL! What did I tell you last time we spoke? You need to cast a wide net. You won't get in everywhere. Nobody does, unless you are a crazy billionaire or something. You aren't a crazy billionaire, are you?" She stopped short, more interested in me than she'd ever been.

I laughed. "Just crazy."

"Oh, thank god. We need more normal people around here." She paused. "And by normal I obviously mean, like, normal rich. I'm not saying you're *poor*. Look, I live in *Brooklyn*," she reminded me, pronouncing the borough as if it were a venereal disease.

Just then Marilyn poked her head in the doorway. She was flanked by two younger women holding clipboards.

"Okay parents, time to bid your little scholars farewell while we take our tour and they have their visits. We're going to split the kids up into groups of three and…" I watched her lose track of her thought as she clocked Roman, who was now wearing his nametag across his eyes like he'd been censored in a photo. My heart quickened and she resumed her spiel. "And we will meet back up in about thirty minutes."

Marilyn had her sales pitch memorized and perfected as she led the gaggle of slobbering parents through each of the building's five floors, strategically stopping in front of all the portraits, plaques and trophies. "So, this is where we have the kindergarteners through fifth graders, and then at our uptown campus, we have sixth through twelfth," she said, escorting us up a grandiose staircase. "This building is obviously more modest than our uptown location, but we still have two gyms, one pool, and our own nut-free cafeteria that provides all meals. We don't allow outside food because of allergies, but we do make everything on premises from scratch using as much produce from our organic rooftop garden as possible. We'll be visiting the garden momentarily."

Sari whispered in my ear as we continued to ascend the marble stairs. "This is such a tease," she went on. "I have friends — two gay dads, biracial, Ivy League educations, the grandma has a wing named after her at Lenox Hill — and they didn't even get an interview because their flight back from Nairobi was delayed and they applied on October first. In the end, they were waitlisted at every school." Before she could give the appropriately mournful shake of the head, she let off a horrified gasp. I followed her gaze, expecting to see blood. It was Daphne Cole, talking to a group of friends.

Daphne was dressed in knee-high snakeskin boots with jeans and some sort of bondage-type spine harness over a plain white tee that most definitely didn't come from the Gap. Her hair was longer than I remembered with a darkened root that blended into a caramel blond. I could feel the sudden quickening of my breath.

"I can't. I literally cannot," Sari said. "That's Daphne Cole." Our tour group was moving ahead but the two of us stood frozen in place like two unfortunate citizens of Pompeii.

Daphne was talking to a shorter woman with dark hair and skin that was probably allergic to the sun. She looked familiar in that vague way people do when maybe you'd gone to high school together. Or perhaps she was in one of those United Airlines seat belt videos. She wasn't memorable enough to be the lead, but maybe she could have been the second or third flight attendant who got to wear an oxygen mask and sit next to a real-life kangaroo.

"That's her cousin Lauren," Sari whispered. I could tell by her tone she wasn't a big fan.

"I think maybe I've seen her before," I said, trying to make sense of my *deja-vu*.

"Probably. MommybearTribeca? She pays to get her pics promoted on the gram." Sari rolled her eyes.

Paid-promo Lauren looked rigid, and like she was desperately trying to exude a youthfulness that was just out of reach. I could picture her straining to learn TikTok dances and wearing Minnie Mouse ears to Disneyland.

"Come on," Sari said, and we hustled to catch up with Marilyn and company. They were winding their way down a hallway toward the woodworking studio. Kids wearing matching Kevlar aprons sanded and sawed pieces of plywood that were to eventually become part of the end-of-semester project, a sculpturally innovative, freestanding residence for the school's potbelly pig, Tofu. Roman was going to flip out when he learned that the school had its very own pig.

"So they're related?" I asked Sari. It had been minutes since Lauren and Daphne were within our view, but she knew who I was talking about.

"By marriage. They were roommates who married cousins. Lauren moved to New York when she was, like, twenty-two. She met Daphne when they were both interns at *Teen Vogue*. And when Lauren met her husband, Sheldon, she introduced Daphne to his cousin Kip."

"Sounds incestuous," I whispered.

"They didn't get together right away. Daphne was too busy dating some married banker with a burner apartment in Gramercy."

Our group rounded another corner. This hallway was filled with science projects and abstract seascapes made out of kidney beans glued to construction paper. It was all the tactile stimulation that my son's busy brain needed. God, this place would be so perfect for him.

"So how did the whole Instagram thing start? How did she get so huge?" I asked, finding my mind wandering back to Daphne as I followed after Marilyn, who was moving at a surprisingly fast clip for somebody with such small legs.

"Lauren was actually doing it before any of those girls," Sari supplied. "Posting pictures of herself running on the beach in ball gowns. It just never became anything because she has nothing to say. She also has a horrendous sense of style. I was brought in on a remodel she was doing to her Amagansett house, and I swear to god, the whole place was so Miami it made my head spin." Our group had come to a stop. Marilyn had us line up and wait for our turn to peek into the Science Lab. "I'm not talking mid-century Miami — I mean marble bathtubs and Serge Roche palm frond mirrors on every wall," Sari said.

I nodded, as if I could picture exactly what she was talking about.

Our line inched forward, and Sari resumed her lecture in a whisper. "If you did an anthropological study on Manhattan moms, Lauren would rank at the top for most out of touch," she said. "A friend of mine has one of her old nannies working for her; Lauren has a fleet. Not only did she pay shit and never make direct eye contact, she also insisted that all the children's clothing be air-dried and ironed. Can you imagine asking your nanny to do that?" Sari looked at me.

"Definitely not." I shook my head, pretending to have access to both a nanny and an iron.

The tour ended unceremoniously with Marilyn walking us back to the Mandela room to reunite with our kids.

"So that's it," she smiled, bidding us farewell. "I wish every one of you the best of luck," she said. It sounded as if she'd already made up her mind that nobody in our group was worthy of moving forward in the application process.

Roman ran toward me, all smiles. "I got gummy bears!" he announced. I'd never seen him look so jazzed after having been separated from me for over thirty minutes.

"We're done?" I muttered to Sari. I'd missed my opportunity to take Marilyn aside and inquire more about financial aid.

Sari gave a dejected shrug. "It's not like any of us had a chance."

Jacked on high-fructose corn syrup, Roman bounded off ahead of me. "Roman, wait!" I called after him, worried he would do something that might further seal his fate.

"Wait for your mom, little guy," a voice warned.

I gulped when I looked up. Daphne was standing by the front of the school, blocking Roman from barreling headfirst through the exit.

"You again," she said. "How's your life going?" A slight smile crept across her face.

"Better!" I chirped. "Just… you know, doing the school thing!"

"Do you guys know each other?" Sari looked confused, then mad at me for not having said anything earlier.

"Not really. I mean, sort of. I…" I wasn't sure how to explain.

Daphne held up her hand and proceeded to set the record straight. "I tried to pick her up on an elevator."

CHAPTER TEN

Daphne was with Lauren and a delicately featured woman with artfully spiraled hair and arms who looked like she slept in plank position. Lauren squinted and reached out her hand. "We haven't met," she said, clearly trying to decide if I was anyone worth knowing. "I'm Lauren."

"Tanya." The other woman gave a wave.

"And this is… I never got your name." Daphne aimed a smile at me.

"Meg Chernoff," I told her.

"Daphne Cole," she said, extending her hand.

"I know," I blurted out.

Lauren's eyes widened. She let off a cough that escalated into a choking sound.

"Lauren! Are you okay?" Tanya started walloping Lauren's back aggressively, as if she'd been waiting for an excuse to hit her for the entire duration of their friendship.

I turned back to Daphne, whose multicolored eyes were still focused on me. "I know who you are because I work for a company that was trying to get you for a campaign," I said, trying to recover. "A bath bomb thing."

"Oh yeah. That sounded cool." Daphne tucked a piece of hair behind her ear, revealing a constellation of diamonds crawling up her lobe.

"Hey Lauren, I'm Sari," my companion jumped in. "I helped on your Amagansett reno. The place turned out stunning. I really hope AD takes it!"

Lauren made a look of confusion.

"*Architectural Digest!*" Sari said.

"I know what AD is." Lauren's smile said she was disinterested in Sari on every level. "My kids have already destroyed the place. We'll see."

"You're new to town?" Daphne looked at me, one eyebrow raised.

"Is it that obvious?" I asked.

Tanya laughed and Daphne shut her up with one withering look. There was no question that Daphne was the Heather With The Red Scrunchie of their group.

"My husband runs membership for Chelsea House, so we moved out from LA about a month ago," I said. "He's from here. Or well, he grew up near... ROMAN!"

My son was submerging both of his arms into a small aquarium by the window as Waverly looked on in disgust. "I'm freeing him!" Roman said ardently, scooping the water like an animal rights renegade air-evaccing an orca from SeaWorld.

I redirected my gaze to the group of women, embarrassed.

"Speaking of fish," Lauren jumped in. "Can you get our kids hooked up with Chelsea House pool memberships?" She glanced at her gang. "Did you guys know that starting next month kids are going to need their own memberships to be allowed at the pool?"

"I heard about that," I responded. "Crazy, right? I can inquire..."

"Daphne doesn't think kids should be allowed up there," Lauren shared.

"I said that one time, about one kid!" Daphne scoffed.

"Yeah, mine!" Tanya clarified.

Daphne spared a quick glance for me, then looked around at the group. "Tramp Stamp starts in ten minutes. What are we still doing here?"

"How is it? I've been dying to try it," Sari interjected. I'd forgotten she was still by my side. "I've heard that it totally changes your body," she continued. Nobody responded.

Daphne's eyes were set on me. "Is your company on Instagram?"

"Yeah. The parent company is called Matcha Pitchu," I told her. "This new thing hasn't launched yet."

"How about you?"

I gulped. "Me?"

Daphne pulled out her phone. "Meg Chernoff, right?" I watched as she typed my name slowly. "You're private." She looked up at me, perplexed.

A ticklish sensation spread up through my knees. "I have kids. It can be scary. Child of the eighties, too many afterschool specials." My laughter sounded demented.

"I hear you," Daphne said. "Well, let us know if we can help you with anything."

I smiled, unsure if she meant help with the school or New York in general.

"It takes a village," she said.

"Or a vineyard!" I blurted out.

This time everyone erupted in laughter. Even Lauren was amused.

"You're funny." Daphne cocked her head to the side and looked at me again. "See you soon, I hope."

Sari turned to me, slack-jawed, once they'd left. "That was *huge*. You know that, right?"

Still unsure of what to make of the exchange, and a little embarrassed, I called out to Roman.

"Lauren is on the board here," Sari told me. "I'm sure she's the only reason Tanya's kid got in. He got kicked out of Avenues for breaking his math teacher's nose with an abacus. Tanya's husband is also one of the best plastic surgeons in the city," Sari said. "It was sort of a win for the teacher. Her old nose? It wasn't great." She grimaced. "Anyway, forget about how today's tour went! If those women want you in, you are getting in!" I could tell she was on the verge of tears. "I'm so happy for you!"

CHAPTER ELEVEN

Later that night, Roman picked at a plate of chicken tenders that had taken me two hours to heat in Ken's janky electric oven. Felix was over on the floor, fussing in his bouncer.

Iliya had texted that he wouldn't be home until eleven, which I knew meant midnight. The new normal. I wanted to be annoyed that he was always coming home later than he promised, but I was simply too tired to care.

Instead of fixating on Iliya, I thought again about Daphne and what she had said. Was she really offering to help me get my son into the perfect private school, the one with a fleet of therapists and a vegan potbelly pig? I would have been a fool to assume so. And yet, I couldn't help but daydream about my new fairy godmother and all the walnut-paneled doors she might open.

"So, what did they ask you in the interview?" I looked over at Roman, who was now scribbling on a piece of construction paper next to his plate.

"I don't remember." He gave a preoccupied grunt.

"Well, was it good or bad? How did you feel overall?" I pushed my notepad covered in potential bath bomb names to the side and gave him my full attention. "Could you see yourself happy at a school like that?"

Roman blinked up at me. "How do you spell the word *kill*?"

"What? Why?" I craned my neck trying to get a glimpse at what he was drawing.

"When is RiRi coming back? It's no fair Felix gets to play with her all the time." His little brother wedged his entire hand into his mouth and let off a whelp. "Why is he SO LOUD?" Roman covered his ears.

"He's getting teeth. Which means he's in pain. And you were this loud too," I informed him, grabbing a frozen toothbrush from the freezer. Red followed close behind, hoping that whatever I was holding was made of ham.

Felix was teething and, according to Marina, he'd been "super annoying" all day. He had a low-grade fever but nothing severe enough to warrant a trip to the doctor. I was afraid of those chemical teething gels, and sadly all the chamomile drops just didn't work.

"I can schedule a playdate for you and RiRi. I said to Roman I'm sure she'd love some alone time with you," I sat, down beside Felix to massage his gums with one hand. I picked up my phone with the other hand and banged out the words "teething baby."

"Can you get me a cookie?" Roman called out, batting his enormous eyelashes.

"A cookie? You still haven't eaten your dinner." I motioned to his plate.

"I will eat. For a cookie," he negotiated.

Before I could decide whether to laugh or just give in, my phone started ringing.

"Teething baby. Genius!" Seth exclaimed. "Hashtag I love it, hashtag no-pants dance!"

God, "mom brain" really was a thing. In this case, though, it was working in my favor.

"Mom! Cookie!" Roman proudly waved his empty plate in the air.

"What he's trying to say is that he's excited." Now Vigo was commandeering the phone. "Also, he's not wearing pants." This was more than I wanted to know.

"So, what's the last one?" Seth asked eagerly.

"COOOOOKIE!" Roman's demand grew louder.

I gave Roman a signal with my hand, then put on my head-
phones and continued the conversation as I rummaged through
the fridge. "The last bomb? I'm not sure yet," I said, glancing at
Felix, who was drooling in his docking station.

I unwrapped a tube of premade cookie dough and absently
threw a few discs onto a half-greased pan. "But I have been thinking about the brand as a whole and I still hate *Mommy Bombs*," I
said. "It's not sexy enough." I was starting to feel more comfortable
in my role, however undefined it was. "So here's my pitch: I think
you should call it NBD."

"Is that like an NDA?" Seth wasn't following.

"It means No Big Deal."

"Oh, I like." This was Vigo.

"Right?" I was excited. Or I was excited that they were excited.
"And for the final bath bomb…" I racked my brain, frustrated that I
was still racking my brain.

"Magic," Seth said. "I think having the word 'magic' in the title is
good." He started to spitball. "Magic woman, magic juice… magic
woman juice…"

My phone was glowing with a notification. "Sweatherweather365
has sent you a follow request." I felt a spike of adrenaline. And then
it hit me. "Guys— It's Trophy Mom." The minute I said the words, I
knew that they were the right ones.

Seth howled. "That's fucking brilliant!"

"That works," Vigo agreed.

I hung up the phone feeling high on something far more intox-
icating than CBD. Throwing the cookie sheet into the mini oven,
I sashayed back into the living room. Once I'd transported my
slumbering baby to his crib, I sat down next to Roman, careful to

shield my phone with a throw pillow as I opened Instagram and pressed on my profile picture. Before I accepted Daphne's request, I wanted to take a quick inventory. I deleted a handful of sunset pics and a couple of close-ups where my chin looked a tad too Jay Leno.

"What are you doing, Mommy?" Roman asked.

"Nothing," I assured him, massaging the back of his neck. Just then, a DM appeared in my inbox. "Are you going to accept my friend request or what?"

Both taken aback and excited by her forthright method of communication, I put on an episode of *Paw Patrol* for Roman, then slipped off to the bathroom.

"The thing is. I don't have any followers. As you might have noticed," I wrote back.

"I did. That's why I want in. I like the idea of being part of a club that won't have me." I could picture her lips curling into a smile. Her next message was much longer. "Speaking of… I wanted to invite you to this ridiculous, and pretentious supper club my friend Lauren does. It's totally awful but I keep coming back. It's like a car accident or super obvious facelift that I can't look away from."

"You're really selling me." I laughed as I wrote back.

"We're doing it at my place this month." Daphne attached a picture of the invite along with her cell. "If you don't come, I'll never forgive you." She added a winky face emoji. After sending back my number along with a "thumbs up" emoji, I took a deep breath. There was no going back.

"So, what are you doing right now?" She wanted to continue our conversation.

"Watching *Paw Patrol* with a four-year-old. You?" I settled onto the raggedy Turkish bathmat on the tile floor.

"Hiding from my kids in my closet and drinking." I couldn't tell if she was joking.

"I wish I could hide in my closet but it's not big enough," I lamented.

She shot back a laughing emoji. "Welcome to New York…it's been waiting for you."

"I'd try the fire escape but my eldest is sort of like Kathy Bates from *Misery*. If I try to hide, he'll break my legs and never let me out of his sight again."

"You are really funny!" she replied, then started writing something else. My anxiety mounted as I watched the three little dots dance across my screen. "Remind me, what do you do for the CBD company?"

"I am writing their copy and helping with the brand development." I tried to sound somewhat important.

"So you're a writer."

I had to stop myself from replying no. I had imposter syndrome as a writer and felt no right to actually identify as one. Even seeing the word spelled out made me uncomfortable. I had a highly specific skill set. But I was no Nora Ephron, and to suggest otherwise would be far too brazen.

"Copywriter." I included the uncomfortable emoji that looked like Felix when he was passing gas. "Just accepted you," I added, eager to steer us away from the topic of my not-quite career.

The conversation moved from DM to text almost without my realizing it. I stood up to splash some water in my face and turned to go check on Roman. Another vibration. "Going through your pictures. You are an absolute knockout." I almost dropped the phone into the sink. "I don't care if that is creep status," Daphne added, "I just had to say it."

"Are you sure you're looking at the right account?" I replied. "The one with all the stock photography of Croatia?"

"Pixies reunion concert looked fun," she shot back.

Oh my god. She'd seen the picture of me kissing one of my girl-friends outside the Greek Theatre in Hollywood in '07. I cracked the bathroom door open, checking that Roman was still in the same place I'd left him. "I miss my old life," I wrote.

"How was it better?" she probed.

"It was just different," I replied. "Now there are no concerts. Just a kid I have to convince to sleep and a closet that is body-shaming me."

"LOL your body looks great to me," she wrote. "Okay so you miss concerts. What else?" I could tell Daphne was having fun, and truth be told, so was I. While I realized I should have inquired more about Abington and the possibility of her writing me a letter of recom-mendation, I just wanted to keep her entertained and engaged.

"What else do I miss? Hmm…. Concerts, cocaine, cult sta-tus movies, the usual pre-kid life unencumbered by fear or consequences."

"You had me at cult."

I bit down a smile. I hadn't bantered back and forth with some-one in years. It was fun, and it felt good to know that I was still capable of it. Red wedged his way through the door to see what I was up to. After giving me a once over, he shot me a judgmental stare and walked out.

"You are the first person I've met in a long time who truly doesn't give a fuck," Daphne continued.

"That's not true. I give so many fucks," I confessed, closing the door so that Red couldn't come back and guilt me with his all-knowing eyes.

"Seeing you at Abington was a breath of fresh air. You aren't like those other women."

"Neither are YOU." I smiled as I typed. "But I admire how you play to them."

"Oh? Go on."

"Not just the moms at school. All the moms. You give them what they want. They think that you're them when you're just serving up what they asked for, with a side of sarcasm and a whole lot of oversharing. It's very smart."

Daphne didn't write anything for a good minute. A minute that felt like an eternity. I hoped that I hadn't been too presumptuous. "So what do you think?" she said at last. "Should we run away together?"

"I don't have a car," I typed, trying to play it cool. "Would you settle for a Citi Bike?"

"Baby." She stopped typing, allowing the word to sit on the screen all by itself. She was flirting with me. And I liked it. "So are you gonna follow me back?"

"I really only use the app for work. I don't follow anyone."

"And to catalog vacations, and ex-girlfriends," she teased.

"I wish those were my vacations! I've never even been to Europe." I said, dodging the comment about the ex-girlfriends.

"Make you a deal: If you follow me, I'll unfollow everyone else. That's four hundred people I'm willing to leave out in the cold just because I want your attention."

I was smiling so hard it made my cheeks hurt. I could have stayed there grinning all night if it weren't for the sudden blaring of our smoke detector, snapping me out of my trance.

I raced out of my hiding hole. "Jesus Christ!" I cried. The cookies were in ruins. The whole apartment was engulfed in bitter smoke.

"Mommy! We're going to die! We're all going to die!" Roman cupped his ears and closed his eyes, preparing for certain death.

I opened the oven to retrieve the charred pieces of dough. "It's fine, honey! We're fine!" I assured him, opening the windows and jumping up and down, trying to knock the batteries out of the bleating contraption. If this caused permanent damage to Roman's eardrums, I'd never forgive myself.

When the room finally went quiet, I turned to Roman, out of breath and not a little embarrassed. "Honey," I said loudly, just in case I had actually damaged his ears. "I think it's time we all go to bed."

CHAPTER TWELVE

"Mommy? What's Jesus Cries?" Roman asked as I tucked him under his weighted blanket.

"What?" I was still frazzled and shaken by the night's events.

"You said it when you came out of the bathroom. When the house was on fire," he reminded me.

"The house was never on fire," I quickly clarified, making a mental U-turn back into mom mode. "I said... jeans... and... fries." I prayed he was too tired to continue the conversation.

"I love you, Mommy," he said in a drowsy whisper.

"I love you so much, Roman. More than anything in the entire world." I stopped for a moment, marveling at his beauty.

"More than Felix?" he probed.

"Not more; different," I explained.

Having a second child had proven to me that I could simultaneously love two people without one relationship taking something from the other. My heart had expanded when I had Felix the way I'd promised Red it would when I had Roman. The only one who lost in this magical equation was Red. My having an actual child had turned him into an actual dog.

"I love you because you are you and I love Felix because he's Felix," I said. "But I love you both more than anything else there ever was and ever will be." I finished the thought more for myself. My tiny captor had already fallen asleep.

The second I got out of the room, I shot Red a how-could-you look. The apartment had nearly burned down, and he hadn't so much as lifted a paw. Then I went to find my phone and text Daphne. I apologized for going dark on her. "Sorry, my kitchen was on fire." She didn't reply. I started rereading what I wrote over and over as if to be sure it sounded okay and not too insane. *Maybe she went to bed. Maybe she is judging me.* Thoughts spun in my head as I brushed my teeth. *Maybe she is calling Marilyn from Abington. Maybe she is calling the police.* I worried, gargling my mouthwash. *Maybe we weren't supposed to be friends. Maybe I crossed a line by endangering my children that I can never come back from.* I paced into the living room, checking my phone. She still hadn't written. *I guess I should forget about that invite she sent me. Maybe the people who dislike her will hear about her disliking me and take me in. Maybe someday years from now somebody will bring up her name and I will finally be secure enough to admit that we had this weird texting flirtation that lasted roughly fifteen minutes and ended in me almost burning down the carpenter from* The Oregon Trail's *apartment.* Half an hour later, I heard the jostling of keys in the hallway. Iliya walked in, looking dazed and spent.

"What's burning?" He sniffed around.

"The apartment is trying to kill us," I announced dramatically. "It took two hours to heat up the mini oven for the chicken tenders and then two minutes for it to burn the fuck out of the chocolate chip cookies. It makes no sense." I might have been chatting with Daphne slightly longer than two minutes, but I chose to omit that minor detail.

Ilya frowned. "You should have put a timer on."

"A timer wouldn't have helped," I defended myself.

"You could have set off the sprinklers." Iliya shook his head as he clambered onto the kitchen counter to reinstall the batteries in the smoke detector. "Has Red been out?"

"No, not yet. I couldn't with both kids." I surreptitiously glanced back down. No notifications on my phone. That was it. She hated me.

"Can you hand me that plastic piece?" Iliya pointed to the top of the smoke detector, now sitting on the sink. I reached for it and passed it to him just as my phone pinged with a notification. It was Daphne. All she sent was a single kissy face emoji, but it was enough. I could breathe again.

"I can't believe you're still awake," Iliya said as he climbed back down from the counter. He was giving me his look. I knew where this was going.

"I thought you were going to walk Red," I said, watching him move closer.

"I am," he said quietly. He took my phone from my hands and tossed it onto the couch. "Hey." He gave me a glassy-eyed smile. "I'm proud of you."

"For what?" I asked, wishing that I could catch a glimpse of the screen from where we were standing to make sure he hadn't accidentally called her.

"You're working again. It's what you wanted." Iliya started kissing my neck.

"I..." I began, but he stopped me with his mouth. His hands slowly worked their way down my body. He backed me into the mini fridge and dropped to his knees, burying his head between my thighs. I unclenched my jaw and let my eyes flutter closed.

His hands dug into my ass as he picked me up and sat me on the kitchen island. Mumbling under his breath in Russian, he took his time entering me. Pictures and sounds rushed through my mind as I let myself go. I was thinking about him, but I was also thinking about her.

CHAPTER THIRTEEN

We woke up later than usual. Red had spitefully peed on the rug and my phone was still on the couch, at four percent charge.

I rushed to get Roman out the door. As we raced toward school, I apologized about burning the cookies and promised to make it up to him. Roman was in a forgiving mood. He squeezed my hand and gave me extra hugs at the school door.

I was standing at the crosswalk in a pair of vintage boots I'd dug out of a still packed suitcase and a white T-shirt that sadly didn't include one of Daphne's crazy looking bondage belts when Seth called, frantic.

"You're never going to fucking believe this," he started.

"You're bankrupt," I guessed, already surfing around on LinkedIn in my head.

"No, dummy. Daphne Cole is gonna do our campaign."

According to her agents, Daphne had a change of heart and decided that NBD sounded "like a lot of fun." She "believed in the product" (that she'd never tried) and "took a shine to the overall brand aesthetic" (that she'd never seen). It was obvious that this had nothing to do with NBD and everything to do with me. I felt like I was flying.

Her schedule was tight as she had Fashion Week obligations, a capsule collection she was designing, and a trip to Paris for a Zoe campaign in mid-December. But she was excited to "collab," and willing to reduce her rate as long as we covered glam and her agent's ten percent commission. Though she didn't want to do any interviews or appearances, she agreed to a three-hour photo shoot. Two pictures would be approved for promotional usage on the company's website and on her personal Instagram. After that she'd syndicate to her Facebook account in order to amplify reach. The latter was my suggestion. I had enough experience in this world to know that without the paid amplification, sponsored posts ended up as good as dead. I normally didn't concern myself with back-end minutiae, but I didn't trust Seth and Vigo to handle it alone.

It took a week to cobble together the funds, the crew, and the equipment before Seth and Vigo invited Daphne and her team over to Matcha Pitchu HQ for the shoot. If we'd had actual money, I would have forced them to rent a real space. But between the cost of paying employees, the cost of manufacturing the product, and Daphne's fee, they were already strapped. They were so strapped, in fact, that I agreed to let them pay me at the end of the quarter, whenever that was.

"We didn't expect the Daphne thing to actually work out," Seth said. He was wandering around the conference room barefoot, wearing a kimono that easily could have doubled as a hospital gown. "I know it isn't much for her, but that is a big check for us to have to write. If I paid you today, I'd have to shut down the whole operation, you dig?"

I wasn't shocked. I knew the company's financials, and how much the shoot was costing. But I didn't care. Daphne was worth it.

Seth's face lit up. "How is this for a jingle: A soak a day keeps your children at bay." He delivered this in a singsong voice, mean-while sprinkling the contents of a Splenda package in a line across the conference table. I watched him remove a small straw from his pocket and snort the long line of sweetener in one inhale. I didn't know whether I was impressed or horrified. "I'm getting kind of nervous," he said.

I couldn't think straight. It had been over a week since I'd ban-tered with Daphne from my bathroom. And I had no clue what it was going to be like to see her in person. Maybe I'd read too much into her flirtations, and it was going to be a cordial working relationship just like any other. Or maybe she'd act like she had no idea who I was. I'd resisted the urge to text when her deal closed for fear that she might not reply. I had no good reason to think that she would ignore me. I just wasn't comfortable giving my power away and risking potential rejection. I'll admit it. I had a girl crush. Or a crush-crush. It didn't matter that Daphne was a woman, or that I was happily married with two kids. I wanted this feeling to last forever.

Daphne was due to arrive in less than an hour and things were far from ready. A phalanx of interns practiced filling a large porcelain tub with bubbles and foam while two grips argued over where to hang an enormous piece of paper that we planned to use as our backdrop. I helped set up a tripod for light, securing it with sandbags made out of bulk beans that Vigo picked up at Costco and rice plundered from Seth's doomsday stash in the basement.

The photographer, Zed, looked like Terry Richardson if he'd eaten Terry Richardson. He'd showed up with a twenty-year-old assistant wearing a cropped babydoll T-shirt that said, "Fuck the Pain Away." Vigo had sourced the guy off Craigslist and offered him two hundred bucks in cash and a hundred-dollar Matcha gift card for the half-day's shoot. I hadn't seen his body of work, but had a strong feeling it featured plenty of shots of his assistant.

"So what's the plan?" Seth looked at me blankly, as if we hadn't gone over it countless times.

I stared at him. "We are going to get Daphne in that tub and get as many shots of her as we can before noon. She has a hard out." I looked at Zed and Vigo, both of whom had drifted over to us. "Is that not the plan?"

Seth raised his arms in the air. "I'm totally open to just vibing off whatever..."

Zed started nodding slowly. "Let's get her in the tub. I like that... Or is in the tub too on the nose?" Zed backtracked. "Draped on the tub? Under the tub?"

"Guys," I said, trying to keep my cool. "We have a tub so let's use the tub. Let's not overthink this." I was only supposed to be their copywriter but for some reason I now found myself wearing every hat there was.

I sat down in a club chair and checked Daphne's page to see if she'd posted anything new. I couldn't help myself. I just couldn't stop. Even though I knew she was being paid to say half the things she was saying, I still found myself wanting more. I wanted to know about the new "sponge concealer" she was buying, what she packed her kids for lunch and how much of it they ended up eating. I wanted to know what style pants she thought were the most flattering and what children's books she felt promoted self-esteem and helped young readers locate their North Star. I wanted the scripted answers and I wanted the real ones. I stopped on a picture of her leaning against a graffitied wall, wearing a studded skirt and designer fanny pack. I began to ponder if maybe I needed a designer fanny pack of my own when I heard Vigo call out my name.

He gestured at a small entourage of people coming toward me. There she was. Daphne had on a Metallica T-shirt with beat-up jeans and was holding a tan lapdog with a smashed-in face. Her eyes were set on me. "Hi, stranger," she said, her indeterminate accent stronger than ever. She moved toward me, kissing my cheek. "This is Cha Cha, my favorite child," she continued.

The dog looked at me with palpable disinterest and then burrowed her head into her own butt.

"She's adorable." It was all I could think to say. "What is she?"

"Pekingese, according to the breeder. But who knows? He was arrested and his mill got shut down, so I never got her papers," Daphne said.

"I can't tell if you serious."

"Meg. I'm messing with you. I thought you knew me better than that." She smiled coyly.

Lauren humored Daphne with an obligatory laugh then turned to me. "I sent my kids' applications into Chelsea House," she informed me.

"Great. I'll tell my husband to keep an eye out," I said. Daphne introduced me to the rest of her team. Michael, her hairdresser, was a feisty blond with balayage locks just like Daphne's. From behind, he could have played her stunt double. There was Nicky, Daphne's malnourished makeup artist, and her agent, Susan, who was in the corner screaming into her phone. The introductions hadn't been necessary on my end. These people were all staples on Daphne's Insta feed.

Michael and Nicky stared at me. "Where should we set up?" Michael asked, still not removing his sunglasses.

Vigo corralled everyone toward a foggy full-length mirror and wardrobe rack he'd set up in the back of the room.

I gave them a good hour before I started stressing. Eventually, I had no choice but to approach and check on her ETA.

"France will be fun!" I heard Nicky gush. "Especially around Christmas! I've always wanted to go to a Paris show."

"The fall shows are better," Daphne said. "But after New York Fashion Week, I'm too spent to fly seven hours and run around Europe with ten thousand suitcases. It's always so crowded and none of the good restaurants have space. December will be far more chill."

I peered around the rack. Daphne's head hung down and she was staring at her phone while Nicky swabbed at her eye. "How are we doing?" I asked nervously.

"THINGS ARE GOING," Michael hissed into his blow-dryer like it was a microphone.

"Okay, great." I smiled.

"She just needs lashes," Nicky said.

"Sorry." Daphne reached out to squeeze my hand. "I was hoping you'd come find us."

I smiled back, embarrassed by the attention but also in disbelief that we were touching. Michael pretended not to notice but clearly had an opinion, which he expressed by "accidentally" aiming the blow-dryer at my face. Susan reappeared holding Cha Cha and looking flustered.

She had a compact gymnast's build and an arched back, making her look like she'd just dismounted the uneven bars. I knew she had to be at least twenty-five but if she told me that she was only fifteen, I would have believed her.

Daphne stood up and wiped her hands together. "So how long do we have here?"

"Two hours," Susan replied crisply.

"So… yeah, if you are good to go," I said. "We want this to be an easy day. I promise to get you guys out of here as quickly as possible." I tried to sound professional as I inhaled Daphne's perfume. There were notes of amber, vanilla, and other things you'd be inclined to set on fire. I felt my skin getting warmer and my neck starting to itch. But it wasn't just the scent I was responding to.

To simply call Daphne gorgeous would be an understatement. Like standing too close to a mural that stretched a city block and only seeing the square foot that was immediately in front of you, you wouldn't get the full picture; you'd be missing out on the masterpiece. Daphne was so much more than gorgeous. Her beauty was raw and complex and just the slightest bit tortured. She was like nobody I'd ever known before, and yet she felt like someone I'd known forever.

"I have too much curl on this side," she said, playing with her hair in the mirror. "We need to bring it down a bit. I look like a fucking homecoming queen." Daphne turned to me. "Meg, you weren't a homecoming queen, were you?"

I shook my head. "Musical theater geek."

A sly smile appeared on Daphne's face. "I almost believe you."

She was right. I'd been exaggerating. I was a latchkey loner who listened to Portishead and Tori Amos and cut out clippings of models from fashion magazines to glue to my bedroom ceiling. I barely had the courage to sing in the shower let alone in my high school's production of *Mame*.

I used to fantasize about what it would feel like to be one of those popular girls, to have two parents who were married and could afford to buy me a car. I wanted to have family dinners and game nights with brownies made from scratch. To own a wardrobe that came from Banana Republic and a Princess Diana commemorative Beanie Baby that watched over me while I slept. It would have been fun. But even with those luxuries, I don't know if I would have truly fit the part. Because in order to be popular you have to be a bit naïve, like a toddler still unaware of its own mortality. If you've experienced disappointment, if you understand how ephemeral everything is, you'll never feel popular. You'll just feel lonely.

"Let's get this show on the road! I want to make our lunch rezzie," Susan demanded.

At the mention of food, Lauren looked up from her phone. She claimed she was tracking one of her son's Lyft trips but from where I was standing, I could see her scrolling through a BuzzFeed article titled "23 Dogs Who Totally Nailed Wearing Socks."

"Does anybody know the Wi-Fi password here?" she asked.

"Yeah, Hide your kids hide yo Wi-Fi," I said, mortified.

Lauren made a face of disgust. "With a y-o ?"

"Do you have dogs?" I asked, motioning to her device.

"No," she said curtly, stuffing her phone back into her pocket.

Daphne disappeared behind a folding screen, then reappeared in a tie-dyed silk robe. "What do you guys think?"

"LOVE it." Susan swooned.

"It's cute." Lauren shrugged, barely looking up.

"Can I be honest?" I said. Daphne's entourage went silent. I looked down at my shoes for no other reason than I needed to look somewhere. "I really don't think we need all that..." I trailed off.

"All what? It's just a robe." Daphne shook her head confused.

"I mean the tie-dye," I explained. "I think it might be a bit too Cherry Garcia when paired with the CBD." Michael bit his lip. Susan's eyes widened, nervous. Daphne swallowed, clearly not used to hearing that her fashion sense was off.

"It's still a great piece!" Susan assured her.

"I love it," Michael agreed. "Maybe not for this, but it's great."

"Did she just compare you to a Ben & Jerry's ice cream flavor?" Lauren snickered. "Who is the designer?"

"Nobody," Daphne said curtly. "Just some art student off Etsy. I thought the big pearl buttons were sort of fun." She tugged at the neckline, slightly wounded.

Her entourage kept supplying compliments. Daphne responded by stripping off the robe. It fell to the floor. All she had on underneath was a white lace bra and underwear set. "Well, it's Meg's campaign and she hates it, so I hate it. So what do you want me in?" she asked. "I didn't bring a lot of options."

I took a gulp and tried not to stare at her cleavage. "Are you comfortable in just that?" I asked. Before I realized what I was saying.

"This?" she asked, letting out a small laugh.

"Minus the bra." I doubled down, serious. "Who takes a bath in a bra?"

Daphne looked at me and cocked her head to the side. I could tell she was impressed by my boldness. Frankly, so was I. "Not me." Daphne shrugged as she approached the bathtub in her underwear, covering her breasts with her arms. Vigo and Seth stared, slack jawed, as she submerged into the bubbles.

Seth looked at me. "Are we not doing a top?"

"She's in the tub," I said. "What kind of top did you want?"

Zed turned to Vigo and shrugged. "I'm digging it," he said, and started shooting. The moment the camera snapped, Daphne's confidence seemed to disappear. Suddenly, she seemed skittish, awkward even. Her movements were jerky, her expression slightly panicked. I didn't want to say anything, but I could tell she was growing more and more uncomfortable.

"She seems a little jumpy," Vigo worried, looking at Seth. "Should we pull her out of the water?"

"That's the thing with influencers," Vigo said in an undertone. "They aren't real models."

"It doesn't help that your photographer looks like a convicted sex offender," Susan shot back. "He's probably freaking her out."

While Zed was easily an eight on the most likely to kidnap you at a truck stop bathroom scale, he wasn't the issue. Daphne was freezing up for other reasons, I was certain. I thought about all the pictures I'd seen of her in the past and realized that they were mostly selfies. "Would it help if you could see the monitor?" I called out to her.

"YES! PLEASE!" she said through a clenched smile.

I pulled the monitor closer to the tub and sat down next to her.

"Do they think I look chubby?" She sounded so vulnerable. "You can tell me. I can take it."

"What?" I said. "Not at all. It's all good. Breathe." She wasn't relaxing.

"Let's take a ten-minute break everyone," I called out. "Would you feel better in the robe?" I asked her as the crew dispersed.

"You hate the robe." She laughed nervously. "I was a fat kid. My sister and I weighed in twice a day, naked, on two different scales. One digital and one old fashioned. And if we weighed more during our evening weigh-in, Mom made us ride the exercise bike in the basement before dinner. Instead of saying grace before a meal, we would hold hands as she said, 'Over the lips and onto the hips.' She used to refer to my body as 'bodacious'...The word still haunts me."

"Okay. Stop. Get all that out of your head. I am promising you on my life that you are a total smokeshow. These are gonna be some of the hottest photos you've ever taken. And I've seen almost every photo you've ever taken," I confessed.

Daphne smiled and brushed a piece of hair from my face. I could feel the peach fuzz on my cheeks stand up straight. "You have such great hair," she said. "I love how shiny and dark it is."

I smiled, flattered, then mentally smacked myself across the face. Time was running out and we needed these shots. "What kind of music do you like? Do you have a playlist?"

"On my phone," Daphne said, looking over to Susan.

Susan handed Daphne's phone to Zed's assistant, who scrambled to hook up the Bluetooth. Beyoncé's voice filled the room.

"Formation," I said, nodding in approval.

"The only album of hers I ever liked."

"The best Beyoncé was the scorned, vegan Beyoncé," I agreed.

"She's only relatable when she's starving and hates her husband," Daphne said, laughing.

Zed started shooting before I even had a chance to leave the frame.

"The giggly girl stuff is working!" Vigo called out from behind the monitor.

"Meg, stay put," Seth demanded.

"I don't normally do professional shoots," Daphne confided.

"Don't worry," I said. "These guys are so not professional."

She laughed. "I have a photographer I shoot with all the time but he's just a dude from Craigslist."

"So is this guy," I whispered.

Daphne smirked. "You know, I thought he seemed a little dodgy. Like he's definitely shot at least one porno in his life."

"And he thinks he's shooting one right now." I looked to the group for encouragement. "She's got this, right everybody?"

"Yes! Fuck yeah!" They cheered.

"Meg, can you splash her up a bit?" Seth asked. "Throw some suds back and for—" Before Seth could finish the sentence, Daphne tugged on my shirt and pulled me into the tub with her, clothing and all. I fought back viciously, splashing her face as she tried to dunk me under the surface. The room burst into hysterics as we struggled like fools.

"We got it!" Zed finally declared. "That's a wrap!"

Michael and Nicky didn't hesitate before grabbing their kits and fleeing the scene. "That was FIRE!" Susan declared, handing Daphne back her phone. The second the device touched her fingertips, her eyes widened, and her face contorted into a delirious grin. She held the device high above her head and made a face I'd memorized from hours of scrolling through her page.

She turned and flashed me the photo she'd just taken. "What should I caption this?" Daphne began reading off a list she'd saved in her email drafts.

"Can I see it again?" I asked.

In the picture, Daphne looked sultry with wet hair, smoky eyes and wearing nothing but a bathrobe.

"What about, something like *Is this a good look for drop-off?*"

"I'm dead!" Daphne looked back down at the photo and shrieked diabolically. "Do I dare?"

Even Lauren couldn't help but let out a chortle from across the room.

"Well, you look too hot," I said. "And when you don't call it out, you just seem like an asshole." I was starting to understand that the more blunt I was with Daphne, the more she seemed to respect me.

She laughed as she typed. "I'm going with your caption." When she was done, she looked back up at me. "Hey, are you coming to that dinner? Say yes. I need to see you drunk."

I clocked Lauren looking slightly shocked.

"Maybe!" I said. "I just have to check with... my family." For some reason, I didn't want to say the word "husband."

Daphne didn't seem to register any of it. "What do you do for workouts?"

I shrugged. "Stress. That's my primary cardio."

"What do you have tomorrow at nine-thirty?"

"I'm technically supposed to be working." I glanced over at Seth and Vigo, remembering that they still hadn't given me a dime.

"Have you ever heard of Tramp Stamp?"

I shook my head, pretending not to already know everything there was to know about Amy, pronounced Ah-Mee, the former Tracy Anderson instructor who'd gone rogue and created her own method of movement, a dance and trampoline hybrid that, according to the website, gave women the ultimate "booty-pop."

"Give me an hour and I'm going to change your life," Daphne promised.

As if she hadn't already done just that.

CHAPTER FOURTEEN

The following morning, I tried to tamp down the anticipation coursing through me as I entered Tramp Stamp's Tribeca studio. Daphne was nowhere to be seen. A currant-scented candle burned next to bowls of complimentary apples and hair ties on the white lacquer counter. Behind it sat a dewy pixie of indeterminate age wearing a name tag that said "Swae." I told her which class I was there for.

"Nine-thirty is for members only. Are you a member?"

"No... but I'm friends with Daphne Cole."

"Megan?" Swae looked me up and down again.

"That's me." I smiled.

She didn't crack one in return. "Wait over there."

I walked to a white sofa and pulled out my phone, my go-to move whenever I was feeling out of place or uncomfortable. In the few moments since I'd last checked, Daphne had managed to make her third post that morning. This one was of her kids having a pillow fight on her bed while she sat on the edge doing her makeup. "Just winging it. My motto for life and eyeliner." I laughed to myself. She really did have the most corny captions.

"Morning, sunshine!" I glanced up to see Daphne beaming at me. She was wearing shiny purple leggings and a tank top that looked small enough to belong to one of her twins.

"The caption." I laughed, flashing her the post.

"Do you approve this time? Or still too cheesy for your taste?" she asked coyly.

I gave her a look.

"Hey, make for the masses, take Tramp Stamp classes," she joked, rubbing her fingers together as if she were a strip club patron doling out one-dollar bills to the entire room.

Daphne led me down a corridor and waved at someone through a window that overlooked a studio filled with women jumping up and down on mini trampolines. Tanya dripped in sweat as she bounced on the lone trampoline on the raised platform in the front of the studio. Ever the Tramp teacher's pet, Tanya had been chosen to lead the rest of her classmates as an instructor paced around the room, calling out moves on her headset. When Tanya saw us, she threw up a peace sign, then stuck her tongue through the middle of her raised fingers.

"I can't believe that bitch! She said she was only taking the nine-thirty but now she's in the eight-fifteen too," Daphne scoffed. "Such a workout whore."

Before I could think of a witty response, Swae appeared behind us.

"We have to do an intake for you if you're going to take class today," she said with zero enthusiasm.

Daphne wished me luck and disappeared into the depths of the locker room. I followed Swae into a tiny office that smelled of lemon disinfectant and half-eaten Sakara salads.

"One class isn't really gonna do anything," she said plainly. "It takes time to learn the routine, sculpt your skin into a shape we think would look best on you. We'll see how today goes."

After filling out an endless digital form that asked everything from my marital status to when I last ovulated, I passed Swae back her iPad.

"Great, great," she said, reading over my answers. "Now take off your clothes and tell me everything you hate about yourself."

I hesitated for a moment, unconvinced that she was serious. Swae picked up a digital camera and waited for me to reply. She was dead serious. Standing in front of a blue wall and posing awkwardly, I felt the need to make excuses for my body. "I just had a baby, so everything is a little saggy."

"Turn around. Arms out to the side." Swae sounded like a bored TSA agent. "Do you like your ass currently?"

I knew that if she was mentioning a body part, it was obviously one that she wasn't into.

"I never see my ass, so I don't really think about it," I replied. "It probably sucks, though." I was eager to find some common ground.

"It's not optimal," she agreed. "Don't worry. Amy is a pro at eradicating math teacher ass. You know her story, right?"

"She was a math teacher?"

"Very funny," Swae said, not laughing. "When Amy created the method, she drew inspiration from a lot of different places. Obviously, Tracy Anderson, Body by Simone, The Class." Swae clasped her hands together and leaned forward. "She was a backup dancer for Justin Timberlake for years. So the technique is rooted in hip-hop cardio. But Amy isn't just interested in achieving that long and lean muscle look. She believes in booty."

"Just not math teacher booty."

Swae couldn't spare a smile. "That's why we bounce. Okay, let's see the numbers." She pointed to a state-of-the-art digital scale. I gingerly stepped on and held still while Swae affixed a panoply of wires to various parts of my body. "OH MY GOD!"

"What?!" I asked.

"You are like thirty-five percent fat! How are you even standing up? Average body fat for a woman is typically between twenty-five to thirty-one percent. It's like you have rickets."

"You know I just had a baby, right?" I reminded her, still hoping for a little leniency.

"So did Amy." Swae pointed at a picture of Amy taped to a bulletin board. Her curly hair was tamped down with a Rosie the

Riveter-style bandana, and she looked chiseled as could be in her jean shorts and cropped tank. "That was, like, two weeks after the baby," Swae intoned. "She's bounced back now… Literally!" It was the first time I'd heard Swae laugh. She reeled herself back in and effected a humorless expression. "So, the deal we usually offer influencers is unlimited classes in exchange for one video story per class and an in-feed static post monthly."

"I'm not an influencer," I clarified.

"Daphne said that you were." The lines on Swae's forehead grew more pronounced. "Well, then it's fifteen hundred."

"Dollars?"

"No, pesos," Swae joked. "I just need a card number and we can put you on a monthly renewal." She was growing angry. "Do you need to think about it?"

"Yeah… I should probably think about it."

"First class is complimentary." After handing me a bottle of water that retailed for thirty dollars, Swae pushed me through a heavy soundproof door and into the studio. Rap music was blasting through two large subwoofers and the instructor, Bambi, a smolderingly sexy woman with fire engine red lips and a fishnet bodysuit, bent over as she did some sort of ass smack move.

"Thirsty thot! Thirsty thot! *Thiiirsty*! YAS, ladies!" she cried, dropping to her knees. "You're hot. You're smoking!" She screamed into the sea of middle-aged white women flailing in the air like so many aerodynamic rag dolls.

With sweat glistening on her chest and arms, Daphne mouthed every lyric of the NSFW Azealia Banks song, as she kicked her legs high above her head. *"I guess that cunt getting eaten, I guess that cunt getting eaten, I guess that cunt getting eaten."* There was something so primal about her, so aggressive and intense. I focused on bouncing. Anything to keep myself from staring at Daphne. Within three minutes, I was sopping wet and could hardly breathe. After the class, Daphne and her friends infiltrated a corner of the locker room that they claimed had the best selfie lighting. Lauren took a gulp of lemon water from her jug, toweled herself off, and then began crawling around on the floor like a dying seal.

"What are you doing?" Tanya stopped snapping photos of her ass. She looked at Lauren, horrified.

"What does it look like? Stretching out my sacrum!" Lauren shot back. Various unfazed Tramp Stampers stepped over her on their way to the showers.

"So? How did you like it?" Daphne locked eyes with me. "I told Swae that you were an influencer. Did you go along with it?"

"Um, no. It was pretty obvious I'm a member of the *influenced* class."

Daphne scoffed. "I was trying to hook you up. Think faster next time."

"Haven't you hooked her up with enough?" Lauren said from her spot on the floor.

"What are you talking about?" Daphne shot back.

Lauren stood up and took another swig of lemon water. "Never thought it would be harder to get Silas a kid's pool membership than it would be for a complete rando to score an invite to Daphne's house."

That was enough to make Daphne snap. "If I hear one more comment out of you about who I invite anywhere, I'm gonna shove that jug down your fucking throat."

Nobody in the entire locker room dared move.

"I didn't mean it like that," Lauren tried backpedaling, but it was no use.

"APOLOGIZE," Daphne demanded. I'd never seen this side of her. It was scary. It was also a little hot.

"I'm sorry," Lauren stammered. "Geez, it was a joke." As Lauren gathered her belongings and slinked out of the room, Tanya couldn't help but comment, "That was pretty intense, Daph. I probably would have gone with something more casual, like carving 'slut' into her locker —"

"Careful," Daphne warned.

Tanya tried to lighten the situation. "I should do doubles more often. The nine-thirty is clearly where the action is!"

Daphne turned to me, her eyes filling with tenderness. "I'm sorry about her. You okay?"

I nodded, hurt but also touched. Daphne Cole was my protector.

"Lauren will chill out," she promised.

"I'll work on the pool thing," I said, knowing that Lauren wasn't going to make my life any easier until I helped her with hers.

"Who cares about whether Silas gets to swim," Daphne said, still peeved by Lauren's poor form. "You're coming to that damn dinner."

CHAPTER FIFTEEN

When a high-profile fashion influencer capable of impaling someone with a jug of lemon water tells you to do something, you do it. When that thing happens to be attending an exclusive all-women supper club at her fancy Tribeca apartment, you buy yourself an outfit for the occasion. Unfortunately, I couldn't afford a new outfit. I still hadn't been paid and even if I had, that money needed to go toward more important things, like cobbling enough cash together for my children's exorbitantly priced lives.

If I mentioned any of this to Iliya he would have given me shit about working for free and followed up with more shit about my need to impress a bunch of vapid strangers. Under normal circumstances, I might have agreed. The supper club was the last thing I should have been thinking about. It was also the only thing I could think about.

I managed to convince Marina to stay late on Thursday night while I attended a "work function" by promising her an extra fifty bucks and a spicy tuna roll with tempura flakes from Blue Ribbon. "I'm literally sabotaging my relationship with Lastrelle over this and all I'm getting is one spicy tuna roll?" Marina kvetched as I gave myself a final once-over in the mirror by the door. "I should at *least* be getting the sashimi platter."

When she wasn't driving her wing mobile, babysitting for us, sexting on Tinder, or lying to her mother that she was still enrolled in nursing school, Marina was hustling. Her most ingenious way of obtaining extra cash was by scheming her way into focus groups for anything from pharmaceuticals to breakfast cereals. She was registered on some lists as a female between the ages of 18 and 25 and others as a female between the ages of 35 and 45. Over the years, she'd pretended to have cats, be allergic to wheat, and even suffer incontinence — whatever it took to make it to the final round. While she signed up for the money, Iliya and I suspected she stayed for the validation. If she wasn't going to be America's Next Top Model, she was at least going to be America's Next Top Survey Taker.

"Lastrelle was only going to give you another twenty-five bucks," I said, evening out my under-eye concealer with my pinky finger. "This is a better deal — even without the sushi."

"You're missing the point, Meg. I was supposed to show up. My reputation is at stake." As she spoke, she took a shot of her cleavage and uploaded it to her Snapchat.

"Fine. You can get two rolls. But not the sashimi!" I backed away from the mirror and ran my hand down my outfit in an effort to banish any creases.

After hours of rummaging around my closet, I'd settled on my black maternity trousers that I belted high on my waist. On top I wore one of Iliya's nicest dress shirts and a vintage cropped blazer that I'd originally bought for an eighties-themed birthday party back in LA. Using one of Ken's dull bread knives, I unceremoniously tore out the cartoonish shoulder pads.

"Why do you have to leave? I don't want to go to bed without you!" Roman whined from the couch. He was distraught, but not enough to take his eyes off the TV. Marina had made her way to the kitchen, where she was searching for pre-sushi snacks.

"I'm not going to be gone that long," I said, carrying Red out from my bedroom and setting him down next to Felix's bouncer. Red waited all of two seconds before shooting me a "fuck you" look and scurrying away.

"I'm really feeling this dentist by the way," Marina said as she followed me toward the door with a mouthful of peanut butter Puffins. "He's playing games, which you know I love."

While she was desperate for a relationship, Marina never seemed to like guys who liked her back. If they were too nice or too normal, she was immediately turned off. It was only the guys with emotional baggage and unexplained eye patches that seemed to hold her attention.

"I think he might be the one. Won't send me a photo." She wistfully shook her head and leaned against the deadbolt. Crumbs were trickling down her shirt.

"Wait. You've never *seen* him?" It suddenly occurred to me that she might be talking to some kind of child predator who could be endangering my kids.

"He's not divorced yet so he's cagey about posting online."

"Can't he just privately text you a pic?" I inquired as I moved into the hall. I was running late and could not afford to let Marina lure me deeper into the conversation.

She shrugged. "It's more fun this way."

"We'll talk more later!" I assured her as I scurried, toward the elevator.

I heard the door slam shut and then I heard her exclaim, "Who wants to build a fort?" It sounded like Roman cheered in response, and I wondered how much of his anxiety was his own and how much of it was mine that I'd managed to project onto him.

It was still warm outside, and the slightest breeze was coming off the Hudson. The trees were in full autumnal glory, shades of aubergine and blood orange blazing overhead.

Daphne lived in an apartment building on the corner of Vestry and Greenwich Street. It was one of those addresses that always had

fresh floral arrangements and no fewer than three doormen standing vigil at all times. The men on duty watched me as if they'd made
an unspoken pact to mace me if I dared wander anywhere past the
front desk. A concierge wearing a tightly tailored black suit did a
bad job concealing his surprise when he heard that I was heading
to Daphne's apartment.

The elevator delivered me to a foyer whose walls were covered
with black and white wedding portraits. I keyed into the sounds of
the party and took a deep inhale.

"Welcome!" A plump woman in navy slacks and a white polo
materialized and asked if she could take my jacket.

"I'm fine," I said hesitantly, not wanting to reveal the surgery
marks on my jerry-rigged outfit.

"I'm Rosamie," she said sweetly. "Do you want anything? There's
a beauty closet for guests."

Trying not to be offended, I shook my head. "I'm not really a big
makeup person," I told her. I followed Rosamie past a seven-foot-
tall sculpture of a weeping woman I recognized from art history
class as a Lichtenstein, and into a living room grander than any
I'd ever seen. A pair of all-white leather sofas wrapped around
the room like snow-covered train tracks. In the center, a mar-
bled coffee table groaned with silver towers of exotic fruits and
cheeses. The shelves held art books and small precious objects
that could serve as instruments of violence if wielded the wrong
way. The room was warm and noisy, as the assembled women
competed to be heard over the surround sound's sultry jazz.

Walking out onto the terrace, I could see clear from the Brooklyn Bridge to the Empire State Building. I tried to maintain my
composure as I gawked at the sweeping view.

"I was standing behind this weirdly hot guy at Sweetgreen today," I overheard somebody say. "He was half my age but *still*, I felt like we had this cosmic sex connection. Then he just took his blackened chicken salad and left. Barely ever looked at me." The woman telling this story was a Barbie-bodied brunette wearing a sweater whose embroidery let the world know that it was Balenciaga. "If I had been ten years younger, a guy like that would have been begging to drizzle his cashew dressing all over me," Barbie lamented. "I know as women we're not supposed to want to be objectified anymore, but don't you feel like being invisible is even worse than the alternative?"

A slightly older woman wearing silk pajamas with feathered fringe was nodding in fervent agreement. "I face-tuned a photo of myself so much yesterday that when my daughter saw it, she asked if it was her."

Stifling a giggle, I rounded a corner to see Lauren sitting on a lounge chair, wearing a floral smock dress and smoking a cigarette. I'd take Barbie over her any day, and I turned back around. "Oh, come on, we are still hot!" Barbie reminded the group. "We've got at least ten more years before facelifts."

"They say that 40 is actually the best time to get a facelift," the older woman countered. "I'm having this vaginal rejuvenation procedure done in Midtown that is supposed to increase libido. Apparently, you go in and get banged by this metal probe that rebuilds your collagen. My friend Dina had an orgasm the last time she was getting it done and the nurse told her to just let go and embrace it." She drained her drink. "I don't know if I'd be able to have an orgasm with some nurse staring at me."

Now Lauren came over and took a seat between the two. She tugged on her necklace that read Mommy in diamond pave and stared through me. I didn't know how to enter the conversation, so I just pretended to be busy studying the view like I planned on painting it.

"Are you talking about Dina Sarcoski? The six-sentence poet? I'm really good friends with her!" Lauren said. "She told me about her magical doctor's appointment. I'll have what she was having any day."

"Dina? You're kidding. She's never mentioned you." The older woman cocked her head.

"I mean, we've never met in real life but yeah, I consider her a *pretty* close friend. We've had some late-night DMs that get deep. I actually think we're profiling her on the blog next month." Lauren shifted her tone and looked straight at me. "Meg, can I help you with something?"

All three women turned my eavesdropping way, and my stomach did a twist. "Is Daphne out here?" I asked, unable to think of something better.

"No." The woman in the pjs was staring at my outfit like it was a math problem she couldn't solve.

"This is Meg, Daphne's new Alek," Lauren supplied. I had no idea who Alek was, but it was clear from Lauren's tone that she was being disparaging. "Her husband is head of membership at Chelsea House," Lauren added.

The women with Lauren brightened. "Love Chelsea House," the woman in pjs said. "I'm Tabitha."

"And I'm Karla." Balenciaga Barbie waved and smiled at me, until she was distracted by Tabitha's micro purse. "Le Sac Chicito? What actually fits in it?"

"Nothing. It's empty," Tabitha replied giddily. "I've heard next season they are going even smaller! I can't wait until it's practically invisible."

"Daphne is upstairs with Tanya," Lauren informed me. "Bitch has been here less than fifteen minutes and already lost her phone. They're combing the place trying to listen for a vibration." She rolled her eyes. "Hey, any movement on those pool memberships? I'm getting nervous that we aren't going to have them in time for summer."

"It's still October," I reminded her. "I think that they are just making their way through all the applications before they sit down for a proper powwow. Sort of like at private schools. Speaking of…" Lauren hated me, it was obvious, but I wasn't going to let that get in the way of my trying to secure an amazing opportunity for Roman. "I heard that you are on the board of Abington. I'm getting ready to send in my son's application."

It was Tabitha's turn to weigh in. "My sons went to Collegiate but if we'd gone co-ed, it would have been Abington, hands down," she said. "That rooftop garden!" Tabitha trailed off and stared at her empty glass in confusion, as if trying to recall if she was the one who'd drunk the contents.

"It's pretty impressive," I beamed.

"Well, for that price tag it should be," Tabitha murmured.

"Collegiate is the same price," Lauren reminded her.

"Is it? I don't remember. It's been a minute." Tabitha signaled to a waiter for another cocktail.

"Yeah, the finances are still something we need to figure out," I said, forgetting my audience.

"She can't afford it. Or can you?" Lauren aimed a venomous smile at me.

"Can I what?" I stammered, taken aback.

"Afford it?" she stopped. "I just assumed. Based on… you know… All of it." She waved her hand down my body, dismissive.

"It doesn't matter to me either way. I'm still happy to help. There are a handful of families there on scholarship." Her smile widened. "But it's gonna cost you pool memberships."

"You can't be serious!" It appeared that Karla was getting off on Lauren's cattiness.

"Of course not." Lauren laughed. "Or am I?" She winked at me.

A waiter who was probably two seasons away from being the next Bachelor appeared beside us with a silver tray full of Michelin-starred maki. Half tempted to dump the entire tray into my purse to bring home to Marina, I took a single toro roll and ate it.

Tabitha looked at her watch and made a sad face. "I'm intermittent fasting," she said. "I can't start eating until nine."

"There she is! The queen bee herself." Lauren pretended to bow as Daphne descended an outdoor staircase. She looked majestic in her tight-fitting black sweater dress that had open crocheting down both hips. Tanya was close behind her in red leather leggings and a cropped tartan blazer. "We found it!" she declared proudly, waving a phone in the air.

I wanted to go join Daphne but a bald guy in a tight suit covered in Gucci logos and snakes got to her first. "Hell-o GORGEOUS!" he squealed. I was left to read the words on the patch across his shoulders: "I'm super famous."

Daphne gave him a few minutes of attention, then got lost in the sea of people, exchanging kisses and pleasantries. At last, she raised her voice. "Shall we eat?" she asked, motioning toward her dining room.

When I entered the fabric-walled room, I was relieved to see name tags discreetly folded into the linen napkins on top of each place setting. I didn't want the pressure of choosing where to go or the awkwardness of being asked to scoot so far down the table that I ended up in the kitchen.

"Meg, you're next to me," Daphne called out.

"Love it," I said stupidly, feeling dizzy and a little scared.

I was next to her! OMG, yes. But also, OMG, NO! Sitting next to Daphne meant that I couldn't slink into a corner and hide. It meant that I needed to be on, and that I had to be funny, and that I couldn't slip out early in order to relieve my impatient, sushi-mongering sister-in-law. Sucking in my stomach, I sat down beside Daphne.

"Thank god you made it," she said sweetly. "You look beautiful, by the way."

"I had nothing to wear." I shook my head, embarrassed. "I knew trying to keep up with this crowd would be impossible but… wow. These women are next-level."

"Meg, you could be in a paper bag and you'd still be the hottest one here."

"Said the woman who was literally the hottest woman in all of Manhattan," I replied.

"You aren't vegan, are you?" Daphne asked as a waiter interrupted us, placing a small plate in front of her.

"Oh, no! I love meat!" I said, wanting to seem as low-maintenance as possible.

"I don't eat meat," Daphne replied. "Just fish."

"Me too," I faltered. "I mean, if I have the choice, I *always* choose the fish."

"Fish is always a good choice." She smiled a wry smile. I averted my eyes, glancing down at the smoked salmon that had been placed in front of me. The sliver of fish was folded in a way that made it look like a tiny vulva. As if reading my thoughts, Daphne looked at the amuse-bouche and started giggling.

"This is a female empowerment dinner. But I thought we were going for a Georgia O'Keeffe vibe, not Penthouse Pets." Daphne cast a look at the waiter.

"I'll let the chef know," the waiter said.

"No need," she told him. "It's funny."

"What's wrong, Daphne? I thought you ate vagina," Gucci dude teased.

"I thought you didn't," she shot back.

Ever the hostess, Daphne leaned in close and provided bios of my dining companions. If they weren't CEOs of real companies, then they were CEOs of fake companies that still managed to afford brick-and-mortar storefronts up and down Bleecker Street.

"You see, it's no longer cool to just have a jewelry line or be an interior decorator," she said. "*Ladies who lunch* was our parents' generation. These are ladies who *launch*." Daphne regaled me with tales of when all these women were just girls, when they were interns and styling assistants living in studio apartments in Bushwick and Murray Hill and playing musical chairs with their career paths and romantic partners.

"Before Lauren was with her husband, she and this girl, Harley, once serviced Kip under the table at Florent. It was a dare, and they were on coke but like, how tacky? I always bring it up whenever we go on double dates because it makes her husband furious," Daphne cackled. "Oh, and Karla was a bottle service girl at Tao before she met her husband and built that palace south of the highway in Bridgehampton. She was always such a founder hounder. I think at one point she was dating a Winklevoss. Oh, and for her fortieth birthday, her husband rented out the Ziegfeld and she entered the party from the ceiling suspended by wires."

I looked over at Karla and tried to picture her flying. "That sounds absolutely amazing," I said.

"Oh right, you're the purported theater geek!" Daphne said in a teasing tone. "Maybe you guys could do some wire work together? Sing some Pippin to the group?"

Before I could respond, Lauren started tapping her Champagne flute. "EVERYONE, *shhhh!*" Lauren continued clinking. "Ladies, goddesses, welcome to Mompire, our third power mama supper club of what I hope will be many! I will have you know that this table was meticulously curated by Daphne and myself, and each of you is here because we consider you a BOSS BITCH. I hope tonight will be filled with inspiring conversations and ideas that we can apply to our daily hustles. So first, I wanna do a little trust exercise. If that is cool with you girls?"

Everyone in the room nodded trepidatiously.

"Pull out your phones," Lauren said. "Now open your text messages and pass your device to the woman on your right." Lauren's eyes were growing big, like a cartoon cat that had swallowed a canary. An uncomfortable energy fell over the room. Guests turned to each other, preparing one another for what they might be about to learn. "Ladies! We have to promise not to be offended. No matter wh—" Lauren's instructions were interrupted by Tabitha, who was already seething with anger. She'd seen something unfortunate.

"Karla!" Tabitha wailed. "You bendy little bitch!"

"I wasn't body-shaming you!" Karla gasped. "I just meant that you looked fuller... in a good way... weight makes your face look younger!"

"Oh, so I'm old now too?" Tabitha threw her hands in the air.

Daphne tutted and turned to me, offering up her phone. She extended her palm, ready to receive mine. Wracking my brain trying to think of what or who I'd texted last, I had no choice but to let her take my sacred device.

I watched as Daphne read through a panicked conversation I had with Iliya about Roman's obsession with me dying, then a half-baked rant from Seth that was mainly turkey emojis, and finally a brief exchange with my mom where she pretended to be curious about how we were adjusting to New York and then never responded to my answer. I was so relieved that Daphne's name hadn't been featured in any of the threads that I almost forgot I was holding her phone too.

"Go ahead." She motioned to her device.

The first message was from Lauren bitching about where I was seated. Apparently, there were "way bigger people" that Daphne was slighting by switching the seating chart at the last minute. The second was a back and forth with Susan about a Target deal falling apart because the client wanted an "actual celebrity like Chrissy Teigen's mom." The third stopped me in my tracks. It was a fight between Daphne and Kip. She accused him of being indiscreet with his extramarital affairs and he called her a total fraud.

My stomach bottomed out. "Thank you for sharing," I said at last. I couldn't think of anything else to say.

"For the record, next to me was the only place I would have ever seated you," she said, as if the other texts didn't exist.

"So, what did Daphne's texts say?" Lauren called across the table, eager to embarrass Daphne in front of the guests.

"Yeah! I wanna know that too!" Gucci guy slurred. His shirt was suddenly unbuttoned down to his navel like he was my dad in the seventies.

I looked at Daphne, who looked at me, aware of what I'd seen on her phone but not betraying any worry. It almost felt like it was a test.

"Just a text from you about me…" My tone was all syrupy innocence. "Want me to read it?"

"That's okay," Lauren backed down, knowing she was busted.

"BORING!" Gucci man groaned. "Go to the next thread."

"All right, everyone. Forget that exercise!" Lauren said. "It's time to go around the room and introduce ourselves. But look, instead of talking about our triumphs, let's talk about something we are struggling with. I want to remind you that this is a totally safe space. Feel free to open up. I guess I'll go first." Holding up her butter knife in lieu of a microphone, Lauren dropped her head and took a deep breath like she was Barbra Streisand giving a farewell concert. "So, most of you already know me. I'm Lauren. I run MommybearTribeca." She paused, waiting for applause that didn't come. "I don't need to tell you guys that multitasking isn't easy, running back and forth between fittings and shoots and soccer practice," she continued. "But we make it work. Sometimes with chipped gels and only a half hour of cardio— but we get by… I guess what I'm struggling with right now, as I watch my business grow and all these AMAZING opportunities come my way, is balance. Yes, that's right, balance." Lauren repeated herself like she'd said something worthy of being etched on a slab of limestone.

Daphne pretended to listen to Lauren while glancing back at me every now and then.

"Bread?" A waiter appeared beside me holding a basket of brioche.

It smelled delicious. Trying not to salivate, I shook my head no. Not indulging in the breadbasket was one of the cardinal rules of being a woman, right up there with wearing flats to a concert and always carrying a backup tampon.

Lauren was only getting started with her woes. "Last weekend we were out at the Amagansett house," she continued. "I was on the phone arguing with Harry over at Mecox about the turkey I reserved for Thanksgiving when the boys started fighting. I got off the phone expecting to see one of my Rogan Gregory sconces shattered on the floor, or one of their iPads floating in the swimming pool, but there was nothing. When I asked what the problem was, they said that they were upset because they both want to marry me when they grow up." She let off peals of laughter. "I tried explaining that I was already married to Daddy and that it wasn't really an option. Which maybe I shouldn't have said, because it only seemed to make them want me more. They are just like their father. They refuse to take no for an answer." She snorted. "So eventually, after my blowout, we set up a mini ceremony on the tennis court. I gave them both flower bouquets and had Jehan take the train back to the city to pick up my wedding dress. It gave me a good excuse to see if I still fit into it." She paused for dramatic effect. "Which I do!" Color rose to her already-rouged cheeks. "We took so many pictures and had so much fun. Silas got one shot of me, silhouetted on the bluff and was like, 'Mommy, this is too good not to post!' There's gonna be a whole story about it on the blog next week. It was really sweet, and well," she smiled coyly, "I guess I'm a polygamist now."

The point of Lauren's story might have evaded the entire room, but it didn't stop them from applauding. Lauren was the co-host, after all.

My nervousness grew as the knife slowly made the rounds. There were so many things I could have said, so many ways I was feeling inadequate, both as a woman and as a mother. But it was doubtful the crowd would have understood.

As the tales piled up, with their ample mentions of designer clothes, private schools, big city apartments, second homes out East, weekday nannies, weekend nannies, interior designers and exterior groundskeepers, I burned with shame. I hated that I didn't have any of these things, and I hated myself even more for wanting them.

My feelings of inadequacy didn't stop at all the things I didn't have. What hurt most was the person who I wasn't. Coming on five years into having kids, I was only getting worse at the juggle. I still hadn't figured out how to be the woman who I dreamed of becoming and the mother I never had. I was forever trapped, a slave to two masters.

The knife was in the hands of the woman across from me, Heidi Glick. Buttoned up with a slicked-back bun, Heidi looked like she belonged at a law office rather than a swanky New York dinner party.

"I have to have a D and C tomorrow," she started slowly. "I was pregnant, or am pregnant, sort of… hence why I've been back and forth to the bathroom all night. Anyway, my OB says there is nothing inside the sack so technically I'm not pregnant, but my body thinks it is…" Tears ran down her face and Mr. Gucci rubbed her back. "It's a blighted ovum, which I guess is quite common, but this is my second miscarriage. And my hopes of having a third child are really starting to dwindle." She paused to wipe her eyes. "Back to the drawing board, I guess." Heidi nodded stoically as people began chiming in with recommendations on acupuncture and IVF clinics.

Her story was more moving than any that had come before it. There was no way I was going to follow Heidi. *How, after a series of vapid shares, did I happen to be sitting across from the one woman in the room who just brought everyone to tears?* Before Heidi could pass me the knife, Daphne leaned over and asked if I wanted to sneak out.

"Please!" I looked at her, desperate.

"We'll be right back, small emergency," Daphne told our end of the table as we slipped out of the room. "You want to meet my roommates?" she asked in a conspiratorial tone as she led me upstairs.

"Sure," I said, assuming we were going to check on her kids.

I followed Daphne down a hallway lined with vintage Italian sconces and a giant art photograph of bathers on a European beach.

"Heidi really sucked the air out of the room, didn't she?" Daphne shook her head. "I mean, don't get me wrong. It's great content and she does need to have another baby if she's so determined to keep up with the Joneses. Three is the new two, after all." She said this in the tonal equivalent of an eyeroll. "But talk about a heavy drop. Made me want to stab myself with that butter knife."

"It was heavy," I concurred.

We made our way upstairs and rounded the corner past a spotless playroom and an all-white office, finally arriving at her bedroom. An epic four-poster bed draped in camel-colored cashmere stood tall in the center of the room. There were no stray containers of Pirate's Booty, no striped pajamas piled up on the floor. "I don't get it," I marveled. "It's like you don't even have kids."

"The maids were just here," she explained as she shut the door. She seemed more relaxed now that we were away from the party. "Lauren always insists on doing these weird activities instead of letting people just enjoy their meals." Daphne kicked off her heels.

"Last month she hired the Medical Medium to come and tell us who at the table had Epstein-Barr. She thinks it's bonding, but it always just ends up getting weird. Next time, we'll do a normal dinner. Maybe a double date? I'm so curious to meet your husband..."

"Iliya," I said, hoping I didn't sound as awkward as I felt. "He wants to meet you too."

"Let me show you my favorite room," Daphne said, leading me through a door at the far end of her bedroom. We found ourselves in a massive walk-in closet that had been converted into one of those beautiful French fashion house-type sitting rooms, filled to the brim with taffeta, tulle, and silk. With powder pink walls and a matching mohair lounge chair, the space was a shrine to some otherworldly fashion god, a temple graced with the wisdom of Anna Wintour and the strength of a thousand Hermes horses. I tried counting the Birkins but kept losing track.

"These are my closest friends," she said with a light laugh.

It suddenly dawned on me that the roommates she'd referred to weren't her kids but the clothes.

"It's a lot," Daphne admitted, sounding mildly embarrassed. "But it's not like I bought it all."

"Is that supposed to make you more relatable?" I teased her.

"Organizing closets was one of my first jobs. That might explain why this is my little retreat."

"Little?" I looked around, still mesmerized. This was a candy shop of cashmere sweaters and denim, shoes in every heel height and color imaginable.

"I'll tell you a secret. It starts to lose its excitement when it's free."

This made sense. "A friend of mine actually did his dissertation on the religion of luxury," I told her. "His central thesis was that when you sacrifice an exorbitant amount of money on something it's sort of an offering to the gods, and the item is instilled with this religious importance."

"So I guess that explains how I've lost my religion." Daphne let off a rueful laugh. "The truth is, it's hard for me to spend a cent on anything. I come from nothing. I'm not from this world, Meg." Daphne met my eyes and paused. "I'm more like you than you realize."

"It's impressive," I told her. "What you've built."

"Thank you. Everything I have is because I busted my ass." Her accent was starting to warble. It did that when she was overcome with emotion. "Kip does fine. But this life that we are living? This is my creation. You know, I didn't even go to college."

"College isn't everything," I said.

True. Especially in New York, all anyone wants to talk about is where you went to High School. I usually tell everyone I graduated from Bronx Science. She paused. "I mean, I did go to school in the Bronx. And I took science." She gave a wicked smile. "You need a good story if you ever plan on getting anywhere. This town treats you how it meets you."

I wasn't sure what surprised me more: That she'd lied about such a trivial part of her backstory, or that she was confiding in me about it.

"You look like you just saw a dead body. Do you hate me?"

"Not at all," I stammered. "I just can't believe you're…." I tried to think of a nice way to put it. "You're basically the Great Gatsby. I love the way you're writing your own story."

"Oh my god, Meg. I think I love you," Daphne shrieked. "Speaking of stories. Did you write your Abington essay yet?"

"I started and stopped about three times," I confessed.

"Just be creative. That's my unsolicited advice." Daphne walked closer toward me, and my palms began to sweat. I cut through the awkwardness the only way I knew how: by asking more questions.

"What is going on with all these clothes? Do they just magically show up on your doorstep?"

She laughed. "You want to know how that all works? You worked in advertising, I'm sure you have some idea." She bent over to pick up a Dior bag. "There's no real money in the luxury brands because they don't need to pay for publicity. But I end up getting deals with the Kate Spades and Reeboks of the world. And they pay a ton. I got a hundred thousand dollars to announce my pregnancy with Clearblue Easy. The trick is to mix it up, high and low. I show you all this stuff you can't afford," Daphne said, playfully pulling things off their hangers and throwing them at me. "Then I post a pair of New Balance shorts that are verified cute but also within your budget and you don't think. You just add to cart!"

"I hope you weren't totally insulted by the NBD offer," I said, suddenly self-conscious. "I know you took less than your quote."

"I wanted to do it," Daphne said. "How else was I going to see you again? She stopped for a second, staring at me. "Have you ever considered doing your own account? You would kill at this."

I laughed. "I don't think I have anything anybody wants to see."

"You have the commentary. And you're adorable."

Oh my god. She was serious. And calling me adorable.

Daphne handed me a gown that weighed roughly fifteen pounds. "Try it on."

I looked at her in confusion. "Now?"

"It's going to be big on you. I'm like twice your size. And your age."

"No you aren't."

Daphne touched the dress. "I wore it to the royal wedding. Not to the church but one of the parties. There were so many parties and after-parties, I couldn't keep count. They took our phones so that we couldn't document. Shame." She laughed as she walked over to the bar and poured two glasses of brown liquid from an Art Deco decanter. She waited while I climbed into the dress. It was basically a giant trench coat and five inches too long on me.

"Wow. Fire." Daphne pulled out her phone and snapped a pic. "Okay now what would you caption this?" she asked, flashing me the image and taking a swig of her drink.

I tilted my head to the side, thinking. I looked absurd. But cute-absurd. "I'd probably go with, *Hamburglar but make it fashion*?"

Daphne spit out her drink. "Why is nobody funnier than you?"

"I'd like to thank the competition," I said, pointing to the floor. "I can only imagine who's holding Lauren's knife now."

"Good point," she said, rolling her eyes. "I mean it, though. You would be such a breath of fresh air. You actually have talent. You're a real artist."

I'd never been called an artist in my life and tried to savor the words for as long as possible.

"Look at Lauren," Daphne said. "I guess she's sort of a micro-influencer at this point, with like forty or so thousand followers. I would kill for you to have more than her. God, that would be so satisfying. Let me just get you to fifty?"

I imagined what Iliya would say if he could see any of this. "You're crazy."

"Actually, that would be you. For not taking me seriously." Daphne helped me onto a pedestal in front of the full-length three-way mirror. She took a step backwards. "Jesus Christ."

"What?"

"You're fucking beautiful."

I felt a prick of sadness. It had been so long since anyone other than Iliya had made me feel attractive. I shouldn't have cared about that sort of thing, I knew. A mother's mind was supposed to be on more pressing matters. But I couldn't help mourning the days when I felt more seen.

I turned to look in the mirror. The ball gown was supposed to be snug around my breasts but ended up gaping with a low-cut V-neck that dove straight down to my navel. And yet, it was gorgeous.

"The piece was a one-off, made originally for the Met Gala and then never put into production," she said. "It's Zoe. That's who I'm flying to Paris for in December. Ever since Salvatore Firenze took over as creative director, their vision has gotten so good. I think he drops a lot of acid. Enjoy the dress. It's yours."

"I'm not taking your things!" I protested.

"I've already been paparazzied in it so I can't wear it again."

"Daphne, there's no way. The sentimental value alone. You wore it to the royal wedding after-party."

"The *after*-after-party," she corrected me. "Take the gown or I'm never letting you out of my closet. All it needs is a little tailoring. I have a woman you can call."

She turned me back toward the mirror, holding the dress in place with her hands. Our eyes connected in the reflection when I suddenly heard a man's voice. "Looks like I found the real party."

I turned around. It was Kip, looking past me the way men do when they meet women they don't want to fuck. He was shorter than he looked in pictures, with bluish eyes and a Keebler Elf nose. His workout shirt was dripping with sweat.

"Meg, meet ball and chain," Daphne said, turning to her husband. "Soul Cycle?"

Kip grunted. He never really smiled in the pictures that I'd seen on Daphne's feed. I'd always assumed that was his resting bitch face, but now it was clear that he just hated his wife. "Playing dress up?" he asked disinterestedly as he opened a drawer and pulled out a large Ziploc bag filled with weed. "Don't you have guests downstairs?"

"I do," Daphne replied. "Maybe you should go say hi."

He glared at her as he lit a joint. Kip finally looked at me for a moment, taking a long drag. "Careful," he said. "You're her type." He blew a ring of smoke into the room as he walked out.

"It's getting late," I told Daphne. "And I need to be up early with the kids. And you have your fans who must be missing you."

"You're not staying for dessert?"

"I really can't." Things had gotten weird enough for one night.

"You're a good girl." Daphne smiled, visibly disappointed. "You almost make me want to be better."

I tried not to make too much noise as I crept into the apartment lugging my gargantuan party favor.

"So how was it?" Iliya was sitting up in bed, still working on his phone.

"Good. Yeah, I think it was really good that I went," I said, trying to make my way toward the garment rack in the corner of the room before he questioned what I was carrying. "Everyone there wanted pool memberships for their kids."

"So does everybody everywhere." Iliya looked up. "What is that?"

"What is what?" I played dumb.

"Meg, you have a dead body in your arms. Did you kill someone?"

"It's just a dress," I said airily.

"That's a dress?" Iliya gave me an incredulous look. "For what? Your coronation?"

"My second marriage," I shot back.

"Very funny. Where I come from, women who try and leave their husbands get stoned to death."

"So you've told me." I laughed.

"I hope you can stuff that in a drawer because we don't have enough space to hang it."

"How about you go to sleep and let me worry about the dress."

"I will. But first, we need to talk," he croaked. "Something happened."

I tensed, preparing to run straight back to Daphne's if he said that he was having an affair.

"Ken's dead," He said, pulling his hair the way he did when he was stressed.

"He's dead?" I stared at Iliya in disbelief.

"Not Ken. The character. He got killed off." He was barely able to get the words out.

I looked at him, still in shock. "Dysentery?"

He shook his head. "Typhoid."

"So when will he come back?" My head started to spin.

"December... or... I don't know. Sometime soon after Christmas. He met a girl. They're going to Kona-"

I cut him off. "Iliya, it's October. What are we going to do?"

"We're going to try and find another place. Is your start-up compensating you for your time yet? Because it really makes no sense to keep paying my sister if you aren't actually working."

"I AM actually working," I barked back, years of resentment rising in me. "I was just at a WORK DINNER!"

Furious, I walked into the bathroom and closed the door behind me. After brushing my teeth and washing my face, I checked Daphne's feed to calm myself down. She'd posted another photo, a close-up selfie. I recognized the closet in the background, and the vulnerability in her eyes made me fairly certain the picture had been taken soon after I'd left her. "The *after*-after-party misses you," she captioned the picture. It was a message for me. I couldn't help but blush.

I got into the shower, letting the hot water run down my back. I leaned against the tile wall and took some calming breaths. I closed my eyes and tried to relax by thinking of nice things. A purple flower. A beach. Daphne's face when we'd locked eyes in the mirror. That's when I reached between my legs, rubbing myself slowly until I climaxed into the steam.

NAME: ROMAN CHERNOFF
GRADE: KINDERGARTEN
PERSONAL STATEMENT

My son Roman has always had a noticeably high EQ. He is asser-tive, enthusiastic, social, and more than a little persuasive. He is being raised bilingual, speaking both Russian and English in the home, has been playing piano since before he could walk and seems to under-stand the game of chess without ever having had formal instruction. As his mother, I would never be so bold as to call him a genius *but his pediatrician has thrown the word around once or twice.*

We recently moved across the country from Los Angeles, and Roman's ability to adapt to his new environment has been seamless. While he isn't keen on the fact that his parents both work full-time, he is grateful for the access and opportunity that our high-powered jobs have afforded him.

Even at his young age, Roman is ambitious. We have only been in the city for a few months and he already has a monopoly on apple cider stands at Pier 25. Originally he wanted to sell lemonade, but I told him that he was off season. Roman accepted the information and wasn't afraid to pivot. The cider is only lukewarm as Roman is acutely aware of the liability that comes with serving hot beverages to tots.

Aside from being an entrepreneur, Roman is also a lover of music and a young patron of the Met, the Whitney, and the Museum of Natural History. This year he hopes to start attending more theater as well as joining the Junior Fencing Society at Chelsea Piers.

I graduated from college summa cum laude and was blessed with a plethora of options for my master's. Wanting to stay on the West Coast because of a sick grandmother, I passed on the opportunity to attend Harvard and resigned myself to staying in-state. While I am satisfied with my education and am immensely proud of the work I do, I will always wonder where I would be if I had taken a different path.

As my Olympic track coach used to say, "A man is only as good as the people he surrounds himself with." We want to surround Roman with the very best, and we want to give him all of the opportunity he deserves.

Where I feel my son is the weakest is when it comes to creating his own boundaries. Roman has a need to be liked and often compromises his own needs in order to put others first. Roman wants to save the world and his idealism is infectious. He reminds me so much of our close family friends Tom Hanks and Rita Wilson. He is a true humanitarian with a selflessness that I lack the eloquence to articulate. He has a deep need to do the right thing. Fifty percent of the proceeds from his cider stands go to Jessica Seinfeld's Good+ foundation.

I am excited about the opportunities Abington offers not only in the way of scholastics, but also in its understanding that the world is getting smaller and smaller and participation in a global community is imperative. Being alive now requires a curiosity about others, a willingness to see things from a different point of view, an ability to be flexible, and a generosity with knowledge that can extend beyond country lines. (If this generosity could also find a way to extend into our apartment — more specifically, Roman's toy box, which is still off-limits to his baby brother, Felix — that would be the icing on the cake!)

With great thanks and warm wishes,
Megan and Iliya Chernoff

CHAPTER SIXTEEN

One week after I submitted Roman's personal statement, Abington invited Iliya and me for a highly sought-after applicant meeting with Marilyn. Not every applicant lucky enough to be invited into the school got to sit down with the queen bee. Some parents were relegated to various guidance counselors or even the school nurse, Chickie, as Sari had told me.

A meeting with Marilyn meant one of two things: We were either of great interest to the school and actually in contention, or Daphne had pulled some strings and Marilyn was simply humoring her. Either way, I was thrilled. I spent too long getting dressed for the appointment, and finally settled on my black jeans and a boatneck sweater that was presentable, if a tad too small thanks to a dryer mishap.

"I must say, your essay was impressive. Quite impressive indeed." Marilyn flipped through her notes as I held my breath, praying to God that she wouldn't read what I'd written aloud. I glanced at Iliya. He was clueless about the creative license I'd taken with our application, and I desperately hoped to keep it that way.

"Do you two have any questions for me?" This was the moment of truth. I'd read enough message boards to know that what we asked at this precise moment would define us and cast Roman's fate, for better or for worse. I tried to think fast but Iliya was faster and had started talking before I could open my mouth.

"I work in the private club business, which isn't dissimilar to what you have going on here," he said with a chuckle. "I'm curious; how are you making sure you aren't raising a bunch of — I won't mince words — privileged douchebags?"

Marilyn blinked up at Iliya, taken aback by his candor and crudeness. "Douchebags?"

"Iliya went to public school," I jumped in, my heart pounding. "And so did I and we just want to be sure that if we were to get this opportunity, which would be beyond amazing, we will still be raising a good person with the right kind of values. I know values are very important to the administration here." I smiled, trying my hardest to undo the damage Iliya had done.

Marilyn cleared her throat and folded her tiny hands on the desk. "Let me start by assuring you that this is a different kind of education than what you are going to get at any of the public schools in our area. We are on a different level in terms of academics, cultural exposure, and teacher-student ratio. I'm not going to lie and tell you that our demographic is outrageously diverse. Roman would be one of several kids here on scholarship, were he to matriculate, but we also have children who spend their winters in Aspen and summers aboard yachts and whatnot. That being said we treat everyone the same. Our entire ethos is based on raising well-rounded, open-minded citizens of tomorrow."

I did a fist pump in my mind. "That is so good to hear, right honey?" I turned to Iliya, hoping he was swayed. I could tell he wasn't. But he smiled anyway.

"What really speaks to us is how much support you are able to offer the children emotionally," I said to Marilyn. "Not that Roman has any serious emotional issues," I was quick to add, "but so many kids his age are still working on sensory development and self-regulation. Your school feels like a place that really knows how to give each kid the individualized attention that they deserve."

Marilyn nodded. "That's true. That's what we do best. All kids have their strengths and weaknesses and believe me, we have dealt with them all. I have no worries about Roman on that level."

"Neither do we." I squeezed Iliya's hand.

When our meeting wrapped up, Marilyn escorted us through the halls, which were now fully decked out for Halloween, and led us to the front entrance where I'd originally seen Daphne and her posse.

"This is fun!" Iliya smiled, touching a fake cobweb stapled to a mahogany door frame. It was always the most random shit that impressed him.

"Oh, by the way," Marilyn said, reinserting herself into our conversation. "We still need your payment for the application fee."

"Of course." I turned to Iliya. "Do you have any cash?

"Or card? We accept any and all forms of payment." Marilyn pressed her lips shut.

Iliya pulled out his credit card and handed it to Marilyn. She smiled, clocking the wallet's frayed edges and missing stitching, then walked off to run the card.

"Great! Now she thinks we can't afford this!" I hissed under my breath, watching Marilyn disappear behind a door draped in fake caution tape.

"We can't afford it," Iliya calmly reminded me. "And why don't you have any cash on you?" Iliya hated when I wasn't carrying cash almost as much as I hated it when he walked into our bedroom wearing his outside shoes.

"I just need to go to the bank," I said, eager to move on. "By the way, what should we go as for Halloween? I'm thinking we should dress up as *The Incredibles* now that we have a baby Jack Ja—" Iliya took me by the arm and stopped me again.

"Is this because of your job? Tell me the truth. Are they not paying you?"

"I just don't have cash on me! Can we not do this here?" I looked around, embarrassed.

What I still hadn't told Iliya was that not only had Vigo and Seth failed to pay me a penny of my retainer fee, they also managed to max out my Mastercard buying the entire crew pizza the day of the shoot. The bill was around three hundred and fifty dollars, which put me over my thousand-dollar limit. Vigo had promised to pay me back as soon as possible, and I took him at his word. Besides, I was invested in NBD. I believed in the product, as much as anyone can "believe" in a bath bomb. More than that, I believed in Daphne.

"I really hate that you are walking around without cash." Iliya couldn't let it go, emptying out the fifty dollars remaining in his wallet and stuffing it into my purse like I was his teenage daughter.

It was early afternoon, and we were closer to Chelsea House than Matcha Pitchu's office. I had my laptop on me, so I decided to join Iliya and work remotely for the rest of the day. What were they going to do, dock my pay?

"So, what did you think?" I probed as we walked away from the school.

"I liked it more than I thought I would."

"And not just because you liked all the decorations?" I teased.

"If they could offer Roman a scholarship, I think it would be worth considering."

"Right?" I said, excited by his moderate enthusiasm. "Did you feel like she was into us?" I was replaying the interview in my mind.

"Sure. She seemed to like our essay."

The minute Iliya brought up the essay, my stomach dropped. He was staunch in his belief that one should never come across as too braggy or arrogant. His only advice to me before writing the essay was to keep things humble and real. Which probably precluded my lying about being besties with Tom Hanks.

But Daphne had advised me in her closet that being real wasn't what these people actually wanted — even if they claimed that they did. The truth was boring. At this age, all kids were pretty much equal. So I did with Roman what I would have done with any other product I was trying to sell: I hyped the shit out of him.

A gust of wind passed over us. The weather was finally starting to turn chilly.

"You need to start wearing a real coat." Iliya wrapped his arm around me.

"I'm fine," I lied. Trying to savor the occasional pockets of sunlight, I hurried along the streets, stopping when I noticed the Zoe flagship store. The mannequins in the window were wearing skimpy zipper dresses and cradling headless baby dolls.

"Nobody does the whole Madonna/whore complex better than this guy," I said, parroting what Daphne had told me. "I hear he drops a lot of acid."

"That's great," Iliya said. "Do they have coats?"

"Sure, for like five thousand dollars." I shrugged, still drooling over the display.

"I haven't seen you look at clothes in years." Iliya smiled.

I shrugged. "Check out those totes!" I pointed at a row of bags rotating the space on a giant conveyor belt. The bag leading the charge was a large carry-all embroidered with a serpent eating an apple.

"That's cool," Iliya said. "I could see you with that. You could probably fit your laptop inside it."

"In my dreams." I shook my head thinking about how Daphne walked into places like this like they were her local drugstore. I, on the other hand, would be afraid to pick something up for fear of being mistaken for a shoplifter.

Iliya checked his watch. "Do you want to go in?" he asked sweetly.

"No," I said wistfully. "It's just fun to look."

CHAPTER SEVENTEEN

Chelsea House was buzzing with activity when we arrived. Every table in the cafe was filled with a member accompanied by either a latte or a laptop. Most had both.

"Take one of the bar seats," Iliya told me. "I can't sit with you anyway. We have a special meeting."

"A *special* meeting? Sounds romantic." I scanned the room looking for a hot waitress to be jealous of.

"Super romantic. Founding members are here. We're finally going through the kids pool memberships."

My eyes lit up. "Oh, are you?"

"What?" He clenched his jaw. I could tell he was already on to me.

"Nothing… it's just, I know this mom who happens to be on the board at Abington and she *really* wants to get her kid up to the pool."

"Yeah, I think you've mentioned." Iliya seemed annoyed.

"Well, if we could help her… maybe she could help us."

"You know I don't do that." This was the Iliya who would shame me for letting our four-year-old son cheat at Uno.

"Not officially," I countered. He loved to play prim when it concerned others, but I knew that he bent the rules on occasion, accepting Lakers tickets in exchange for fast-tracking a friend off the waitlist at the Malibu property or upgrading someone's hotel suite if that someone happened to be Russian. "Please," I said quietly. "For Roman."

Iliya frowned. If I had said any word besides *Roman*, the conversation would have already been over.

"Can I just come along and offer a verbal recommendation?"

Iliya looked aghast. "Not happening."

"I'm a member. I'm allowed to recommend someone." I turned around and saw that my seat at the bar was gone.

"In writing," he reminded me. "And you aren't a founding member of this house, so you aren't allowed to sit in on meetings."

"Well now there's nowhere to sit so it looks like you have to let me come."

"You're not coming in," he protested.

"I'll behave," I said, the smugness rising.

The conference room was dark, save for a projection screen flashing faces of Chelsea House pool applicants. Bubby walked in and insisted that I join them. A trio of founders sat around a long table with notepads and mini bottles of sparkling water.

"Meg has work to do," Iliya said. "She just wanted to pop in and say, hello."

"Do it here," Bubby said. "There's literally nowhere to sit in the dining room and it's too cold on the roof."

I shot Iliya an I-told-you-so smile. Allowing me to sit in on the meeting was completely in character for a group of people who adored breaking their own rules. It was a way of flexing their power.

I took a seat near a man-bunned founder and checked my Instagram under the table. At the top of my timeline was a paid post from Daphne. She'd just built the most perfect gingerbread haunted house. It had three levels, a pool, stained glass windows, and even a two-car garage. "Halloween is my favorite time of year. And nothing is scarier than SUGAR!" her caption read. "Impress all of your little ghouls and boys with this wacky activity that the whole family can enjoy! Building these babies is a family tradition over at our place. Pair yours with a cauldron of hot cider or a super spooky snack board and you've got yourself a KILLER night in! Link in stories to purchase all the fun!"

I took another look at the gingerbread house. It belonged in a Harvard Design School graduate's portfolio. I didn't understand how Daphne had the time or patience to pull off all of the crafty projects she shared with her followers. She was a skilled chef, floral arranger, calligrapher, balloon twister, origami expert, and even a face painter. I thought about her kids, and how lucky they were to have a mom who could do everything.

"Where are all the cute kids?" Bubby was saying as she flipped through a facebook on a projection screen. This snapped me back into the moment. A few more members of leadership had dribbled into the room.

"Sorry to be so blunt," Bubby said, "but how did the tank get filled with so many bottom feeders?"

"What, you want models? These are the only kids we got. If their parents aren't members, they can't apply." This was Mona, an artsy forty-something with neon green nails and hair that looked like it was cut by her cats.

Bubby clicked past several more underaged applicants. "I get that, but if the kid isn't cool, we aren't letting it in."

"It?" Iliya furrowed his brow.

"You know what I mean! This isn't coming from me. It's coming from corporate," Bubby insisted.

"I thought *we* were corporate," Iliya said. "Why are we gathered here if not to make the decisions?"

"I don't even have health insurance," Bubby fumed. "Not to be a bitch but just because they're minors doesn't mean that our entire aesthetic goes out the window. We need to curate a specific look and vibe that's on par with the caliber of adults we have in the house. We can't just have a bunch of brace faces floating by on inner tubes and trying to kill each other with water guns. This isn't the goddamn YMCA."

"I hate to say that I agree but… I do," Nir, a soft-spoken man with wire-rimmed glasses, chimed in. "We need the right kind of kids."

"These are kids. Let's not lose sight of that." Iliya was shaking his head in disbelief.

"Easy for you to say," Bubby said. "You were probably a hot child." She glanced at me, and I shrugged in agreement. I detected Iliya cursing in Russian under his breath. Bubby continued going through photos. I spotted Lauren's son, Silas. He was dressed in a Vineyard Vines-style bow tie standing next to what must have been his grandfather's yacht.

"Yes!" I blurted.

Iliya shot me a look.

"Ew! Noooo!" Bubby made a cringe face. "He's a total Chadtucket. He looks like the kind of prick who accidentally roofies himself and then wraps his dad's Porsche around a telephone pole."

"Wow. So visual." Mona widened her eyes.

"It's a hard picture," Man Bun shared.

"I have a nonbinary sort of punk-rock-looking teen from the East Village. The dad is the bassist for the Sunday Sauce, and he's a member," suggested Emmanuel, a portly Frenchman who went by his DJ nickname, La Poubelle.

"What does the mom do?" probed Mona.

"Not a member," Emmanuel replied. "But she's a wellness influencer. She's into cauliflower smoothies."

"You know why we don't serve cauliflower smoothies on our breakfast menu anymore? Because people were complaining that they tasted like fucking cauliflower." Bubby shook her head.

"You hid cruciferous vegetables in the smoothies? No wonder I was always getting gas," Mona said, as if she'd just discovered the Fibonacci sequence.

If I planned to act, this was my moment. I looked at Iliya nervously. He was pretending I didn't exist. "Can I just say one thing?" My voice cracked.

"By all means," Bubby said.

"Okay, so I know this kid's mom and she's...nice." I lied.

"*This* kid?" Man Bun asked in disbelief, gesturing at Silas.

Bubby looked down at her stack of applications, reading. "MommybearTribeca? She sucks balls. You know how I know that she sucks balls?" Bubby asked.

"How?" I tried to tamp down my nervousness.

"Because she literally signed her application "MommybearTribeca!" Lauren wasn't making this easy for me, but I refused to give up.

Iliya looked at me and I took a deep breath. "I thought she sucked at first too." I racked my head for a moment, remembering the universal defense for all assholes the world over. "She's just painfully shy."

"She doesn't seem shy to me." Man Bun was onto me.

"She's in therapy," I told him. "She's been working through a lot of... trauma. And she's actually been really helpful to me, with all the mom stuff. She's different once you get to know her privately." The lying got easier as I kept talking. It wasn't like I was hurting anybody. It was a stupid social-club pool. "I've met this boy and he was lovely. He's much edgier and more creative in person. He knows everything about nineties hip-hop and he's really into...

freestyling." I'd never actually met either of Lauren's sons, but now I was the one freestyling.

"Meg isn't on the committee," Iliya reminded the room. "So I don't want us making decisions that we are going to be blaming her for later."

Bubby looked around the table. "Are we accepting the kid or waitlisting him? And by waitlisting I obviously mean never letting him in ever."

"To be honest, I don't really care. I just want to get through this meeting. Anyone opposed to giving him a shot?" Emmanuel asked the room.

"And his brother," I added, sheepishly. "I mean, you can't just take one."

"Fine." Bubby slammed her fist on the table like an auctioneer's gavel. "They're in."

Feeling flush with victory, I turned to Iliya and grinned. He barely blinked.

My spirits soaring, I shot Daphne a text from under the table. "Guess who just got their pool memberships?"

CHAPTER EIGHTEEN

"We're moving *again*?" Roman asked at school pickup the following day. There was never a good time to break bad news to Roman, so I'd kept it to myself, but he'd overheard Iliya bitching while surfing apartment listings the night prior. Roman was impossible with transitions. He'd just gotten used to living at Ken's, and we were already getting the boot. "But will Santa know where I went?"

"First Santa is gonna come. *Then* we're going to move," I explained. "But it's going to be great. Everything is working out." I held onto his backpack, trying to keep him from darting into the road.

"Can we get ice cream?" he asked at the sight of a passing food truck.

"Honey, that's a kebab truck." I shook my head. "Besides, it's too cold for ice cream."

"Okay, then what isn't it too cold for?" He gave me a look to let me know that whatever I suggested better be equally decadent.

"I have an idea," I said, suddenly inspired. "You want to make an enormous gingerbread house?"

Fifteen minutes later, Roman sat in my Whole Foods shopping cart as I wove in between professional grocery shoppers on scavenger hunts for other people's pantries and depressed housewives looking for Chardonnay. I typically didn't shop at places where a pint of strawberries cost over seven dollars, but it was the closest grocery store around. Standing in the dairy aisle and scanning the egg cartons, trying to determine which illustration of a farm looked the most like a Club Med, I heard someone call my name.

I spun around to see Sari, her basket heaving with probiotics and melatonin gummies. "Girl, you're everywhere I turn!" she exclaimed.

I grabbed a random carton covered in hens wearing red bikinis and smiled at her. "Hey!"

Sari's expression shifted to something a little darker. "Congratulations," she said. "So how did you do it?"

"Do what? Are you talking about my interview with Marilyn?"

"I'm talking about Daphne Cole, dummy." Her eyes bore into me. "The post."

My head was swimming with confusion. "What post?"

"Can I set this here while I run and grab some It Chardonnay?" Sari smiled at Roman, who accepted her basket. "Check your phone."

Once Sari disappeared, I reached into my bag and pulled out my phone. What I read made me gasp. "What happened?" Roman asked. "Is it from Santa?"

Daphne hadn't just tagged me on her page. The post was a picture of me. Just me. In her closet. Wearing her clothes. She even used my caption, "Hamburglar but make it fashion." The picture had over four thousand "likes" and the comment section was too long to scroll through. I felt dizzy.

"Who is that?" wrote @PriceisnoSnobject, Vogue's accessories editor. "What designer is that?" wrote @Bagsforally, a well-known handbag consigner. "Are you able to share deets on who designed your closet?" another follower commented. It went on and on.

"Next level, right?" Sari said, reappearing with two armfuls of Chardonnay. "And when are we having drinks, by the way?"

I cocked my head ever so slightly. Sari had never initiated drinks before now. She still hadn't gotten back to me about coffee.

"Is now a bad time?" she asked, resting her bottles in her basket. "I could also do it later this evening." She sounded hopeful, almost desperate.

"I'm supposed to be decorating a gingerbread house tonight," I said. "But soon?"

"I'm going to hold you to that. I know I'm small potatoes compared to Daphne Cole, but I'm still fun." She smiled, grabbing two bottles and pretending to chug them simultaneously.

When Roman and I got back to Ken's building, the grocery bags hanging from my wrists were cutting off my circulation and turning my hands a cyanotic shade of blue. Fingers still tingling, I pushed open the front door and I saw a stack of packages blocking my mailbox.

"Did you order me something?" Roman sounded excited.

Assuming that there was either a mistake with the post office or that Marina was shopping on Ambien again, I picked up a box and examined it. It was addressed to me.

After two elevator trips, I'd managed to bring everything upstairs. Roman sat at the bar peering over me as I opened the first box with a pair of scissors. "Is it a new Ben 10? Is it a Kevin 11?"

Marina, who'd come out of the boys' bedroom holding Felix, was equally transfixed.

"Is it a LuMee light? Is it something from Kim Kardashian?"

Tuning them out, I tore through an inordinate amount of tissue paper to find a note from Susan, Daphne's agent. "Daphne thought you'd enjoy! Xo Susan and the team at SLAY!"

"It's a beach ball," I announced, confused.

Typed on a postcard taped to the inside of the box were instructions. "Hey Meg, wanted you to be the first to hear about @PlantainBaby, the all-natural sunscreen for little ones that now comes in a variety of bright fun colors. Paint on your face, get into a bikini, and use this beach ball in a quirky yet sexy pic you share with your followers. Don't forget to tag @PlantainBaby so we can see your silly style."

The next package contained seven boxes of chickpea crackers and a note that read: "Toot your heart out with these gluten-free, nut-free, dairy-free, sugar-free, vegan, organic, paleo, Tootchips. Show your love by tagging @TootChipsUSA."

I ripped open a bag. "Not terrible," I said as I tasted a chip.

"These aren't yummy!" Roman exclaimed, spitting a mixture of chickpea powder and vegan cheese all over the hardwood floor.

Marina dove into another box filled with Styrofoam noodles and branded water bottles. "This is what happens when you're an influencer," she told me excitedly. "You just get sent free swag all day long."

"I'm not an influencer!" I assured her. "Daphne just had this stuff sent here." I was baffled yet amused.

Marina snorted. "My brother is going to kill you, you know..."

"Why?" I asked even though I already knew the answer.

"Because he hates this stuff." Felix was getting buried under all the wrapping paper on the floor, and Marina picked him up.

"What stuff? Chickpea chips?" I watched as Roman chased Red around the couch with the Plantain Baby beach ball.

"Strings-attached stuff." Marina took a flat stone from my hand and started running it over her forehead. "It's called a gua sha, it's a beauty contouring tool. They're like thirty bucks at Sephora. Consider this part of my payment for today."

I stared at her, still not satisfied with her response. "What strings are attached exactly?"

"These companies want you to post this stuff. And if you want more, which you will, you'll have to post more. That's how it works. How am *I* the one telling *you* this?"

"Yeah, I get it but I'm not even public!" I reminded her.

"Duh! That's the first thing you have to do," she said, rolling her eyes. "Fix that shit."

It was past ten o'clock when Iliya finally got home. He smelled like booze and perfume, which was not uncommon but never failed to stress me out. He headed into the bathroom to wash off.

When he was fresh out of the shower, Iliya stood in front of me wearing nothing but his towel. He gestured toward the boxes in the kitchen. "So..."

"My friend Daphne. You know, the influencer I told you about."

"Who?" he asked.

I glanced away, then back at him. God, his abs were so annoying. "The woman I met at Chelsea House," I said. "I've told you all about Daphne, no?" I'd managed to avoid saying her actual name aloud to my husband for nearly three months. I was too afraid that if it slipped off my tongue, he'd be able to read every thought I'd ever had about her. "She has kids at Abington," I added.

"The pool membership lady?" he asked, still not following.

"No! That's Lauren, her cousin. I've been working with her on the NBD campaign," I continued, trying to seem nonchalant and professional as I rummaged through a drawer for nothing that I actually needed.

"NBD?" he looked at me perplexed.

"The mommy bath bombs? I told you that I made them change their name."

"No, I don't think you did. Just like you didn't tell me they hadn't paid you yet."

"I told you everything," I insisted. "You probably just weren't listening." I'd had enough petty fights with Iliya to know that if I stuck to my story long enough, he would eventually give up and agree with me.

"Okay, maybe you did. I have a billion things on my mind at the moment."

"It's fine. Anyway, she had her agent send a bunch of products over," I said. "It's just random junk they send influencers. They probably had extra," I added nervously. "And don't worry, it was free."

"Nothing is free," Iliya mumbled. "So are *you* an influencer now?"

"No, but it would pay a hell of a lot better than copywriting," I said with a sigh. "Marina suggested that I should make my account public." I waited for him to reply.

"She also said you have over ten thousand friend requests," Iliya said, two steps ahead of me. I was a fool to think that my sister-in-law could keep a secret. She'd probably called her brother the minute she'd left our home.

"I'm not really sure how the whole thing works," I said, knowing that I was at exactly eleven thousand two hundred and twenty requests the last time I checked. Five minutes ago.

"If you are seriously considering accepting all those people, you need to delete the kids," he said firmly.

"I'll delete them," I agreed. "That's your only thought on the subject?"

Iliya shrugged. "So you're really going to do it? You're going to put yourself out there for all the criticism… all the judgment…"

"All the Toot Chips," I said, trying to make light of it.

"It doesn't seem very *you*." He looked at me, skeptical.

"What does that mean? I already do it for other people."

"Yeah, for other people. But for yourself? I don't see it. You're not the kind of girl who needs all that attention. And I mean that as a compliment." His phone vibrated on the dresser. The name Anna popped up. I'd never heard him mention anyone named Anna.

"Actually, a little more attention would be nice." I motioned to the phone. "Do you need to take that?"

"No, I'm off work. They can survive without me."

"Can Anna?" I asked archly.

Iliya was getting flustered. "You know what? Go for it. Maybe it will make you more secure with yourself and you won't sit here accusing me of nonsense."

"Really?" I was too elated to be jealous.

"Sure," he said. "But no pics of me and no pics of the kids."

"That's fine." I watched him pull a clean T-shirt over his head. "We might make some money. The kind that could help pay for wherever we are moving in January, money that could help with private school. Money that could help pay for a lot of things."

"What the fuck am I wearing?" Iliya cut me off, looking down at his chest. The front of his shirt was printed with "How Do You Toot?"

"Oh that," I said, trying not to laugh. "It came in the mail."

I could tell Iliya was annoyed but also a little amused. "It's actually pretty comfortable."

I looked at him and smiled. "I know how to get you more."

CHAPTER NINETEEN

I woke up early the next morning trying to recall if I'd actually pulled the trigger on going public or if it was just a dream. The text from Daphne set me straight: "Proud of you, baby." As I digested her words, I felt a heat building within. And not just because she'd called me baby. This was exciting. It was also quite scary. While I had wanted all the perks that came with shrugging off my private status, I didn't know if I wanted all the attention. Especially this early in the morning.

I glanced across the bed and contemplated waking Iliya up and making my anxiety his problem. But I knew that if I actually admitted why I was freaking out he would say, "I told you so."

I remained tight-lipped about what was going on until I showed up at work. Seth spun in his swivel chair like a child who'd never sat in a swivel chair before. "With those kinds of numbers, we have our own in-house influencer."

"I wouldn't go that far. Twelve thousand is a random college kid with a podcast," I said, brushing off his claim. "I'm by no means an influencer."

"Yet." Seth's eyes widened. "But you will be. And it just so happens that we have a perfect post for you." Seth pointed at Vigo, who was looking at the shots from Daphne's shoot on his laptop. "Hit it, Vigs."

"So, you are going to think we are crazy but..." Vigo looked at Seth, a devilish smile creeping across his face. "The shots with you and Daphne. You're like the yin to her yang."

"We like that," Seth told me as he began nervously braiding his bangs.

"For the campaign," Vigo clarified.

I felt a pit in my stomach. "I was just there to make her comfortable," I said. "I'm not going to *be* in the campaign."

Vigo flashed me a picture from the shoot. My body was halfway submerged in the tub, a leg hanging off the side of the basin. My hair was wet, and my shirt utterly soaked. Daphne, covered in suds, appeared to be completely nude. We were both laughing as she held me by my wrists, trying to dunk me.

I shifted uncomfortably. "This looks like softcore porn."

"I know, right?" Seth nodded in excitement. "It's perfect. She's the trophy mom and you are the..."

"Teething baby?" I offered.

Vigo cocked his head. The vibe is more C-section Blues here."

"Look, Meg," Seth said, softening his tone. "This was a happy accident that none of us could have seen coming. But that's how these things usually work."

"Daphne is never going to go for this." I shook my head and started to worry about how Iliya would react to seeing my nipples standing at attention on a poster.

"If we want to take this campaign national, we can't just have some New York socialite as our spokesperson," Vigo explained. "We need someone approachable."

"You mean poor?" I laughed in disbelief. "Speaking of which... maybe if I were actually getting paid for the work I'm doing here, the class divide wouldn't be so big."

"It's coming," Vigo promised.

"For real, when am I getting paid?"

"Let's not make this contentious." Seth used his hands to call for a time out. His braid now looked like a broken unicorn horn flopping back and forth on his forehead, which made it even harder than normal to take him seriously. "The money is coming. And tell us how we can help you, Meg. We want you to be happy."

I raised an eyebrow. "First of all," I said, pulling my credit card statement from my purse and slapping it down on the table. "You need to pay this off before my husband sees it and has a fit. Second, where is my retainer fee? And third, *Daphne* is your brand ambassador. Not me. She signed a contract to be *the* face of this campaign. Singular. We are launching at the beginning of November. To start changing things now is just —"

"For what it's worth, she looks way thinner in the shot with you than the rest of the shots, and that seemed to be an issue," Seth said.

"That's ridiculous," I retorted. "You sound sexist and body-shaming."

"I'm just saying what she said." He shrugged. "I'm a good listener."

I clenched my teeth. I didn't want to be in the NBD campaign with Daphne. I was meant to be the Cyrano de Bergerac of the operation, putting words in other people's mouths, lubricating the wheels for the talent to shine.

Just then, my phone started vibrating. I glared at it, annoyed that the day was blowing up and I still hadn't even helped myself to a free hot beverage. I had made it a goal to drink as many as possible on the job, at least until my payment came through. When I saw Daphne's name light up the screen, I motioned for the other two to pipe down.

"Hello?" I answered nervously.

"Hi, stranger." Her voice sounded almost sweet. "The world's looking at you. So when are you going to post something?"

"Soon. I'm still trying to think of what it should be."

"Hurry up," she said. "Lauren says thank you for the pool hook-up, by the way. That was really cool of you."

"Oh, of course. No problem," I said, pretending it had not required my bursting into a private meeting and risking all my credibility with Iliya's co-workers. I signaled to Seth and Vigo that I'd be back, and I brought the phone into the hallway.

"So this is going to sound crazy, but Susan's favorite image — and mine too," Daphne said, "happens to be of the two of us. Have you seen them? They're hot. What are the odds of you agreeing to let us use one of them for the campaign?"

"I don't know if that's necessary," I replied. "There are so many great shots of you alone."

"I still just really like the ones of the two of us the best," she whined Veruca Saltishly. "I look skinnier. And happier." It was clear that Vigo had already spoken to Susan. Before I could deflect with another joke, Daphne continued laying it on. "I know that you are afraid to put yourself out there, but you are a total smokeshow. And these are the hottest pics you've ever taken. And I've seen every pic ever taken," she said, throwing my words back at me.

"You're too much," I laughed.

"I just know how talented you are. Not to knock the Matcha Pitchu guys but you're too good for them. You could be big time. You took the first step. You can't spend your life just taking care of other people. It's time to be the hero of your own story."

I glanced back at my purported bosses. They were playing a violent game of thumb war. To each his own foreplay.

"I'll think it over," I told her.

"Think about it," Daphne replied. "But just so you know, there's only one right answer."

CHAPTER TWENTY

The following weekend, Daphne invited the kids and me to join her at the Museum of Cookies for a "content shoot." The museum was an interactive art exhibit with themed rooms that celebrated the invention of the cookie. Maybe it wasn't the hottest ticket among the Guggenheim Museum crowd, but in Daphne's world it was. Even Roman had heard about it somehow. When I told him I'd be taking him, he went berserk.

We showed up a few minutes before the doors opened. The line to get in already stretched around the block. Daphne had told me to text her when we arrived. A young woman wearing an apron and a pink lab coat scurried outside the building and introduced herself to the kids and me. Helping me with Felix's stroller, she led the three of us to the front of the line, pushing people out of the way as if I were Lady Gaga.

Inside, she affixed nametags on our shirts and opened a sliding door that brought us into a room covered in pink wallpaper with giant fake clouds hanging from the ceiling. A sulky teen boy who could have been a stand-in for Claire Danes stood behind a counter pulling small sugar cookies out of an electric oven. His nametag read Simon Snickerdoodle.

"Welcome to the other side of the rainbow," he said in a rehearsed and unenthusiastic mumble. "Would you like a super sugary sugar cookie? Heads up: They were made in a facility that uses nuts."

"YES!" Roman screamed like he'd just won a game show.

Just then, another door slid open to reveal Daphne. In full hair and makeup, she was wearing a crisp color-blocked suit that appeared to be made of taffeta.

"Meg!" She waved me over. "Thank fucking god that you're here because I'm at a total loss for captions."

"You're so dressed up," I said, flooding with insecurity over my disheveled appearance.

"I should have had something sent over for you," she replied, taking in my cropped sweatpants and Nirvana T-shirt.

"I was on my own this morning. Iliya had to go to work. And I lost track of time," I said.

"Iliya," she repeated. I detected a tinge of prickliness in her voice. "We still need to do that double date. Otherwise I'm going to start feeling like your side piece."

"Totally," I said, looking around the room. "Where are your kids?"

"Oh, they got a better offer." she said, rolling her eyes. "But I'm so glad you brought yours."

Daphne awkwardly knelt down and patted Felix on the head like he was a macaque on a chain in the Marrakesh Medina. She rose back to her feet and introduced me to her photographer, Rodrigo, an NYU film student rocking a faux hawk. Then Daphne turned to me with puppy dog eyes. "Can I trouble you for one itsy bitsy caption? Please? I know. You'll figure out something good." Before I could ask what picture, she dove into a fake swimming pool filled with chocolate chips.

"This one," Rodrigo said, flashing me a shot of Daphne luxuriating in the pool with her eyes half closed.

I thought it over for a moment, then waited for Daphne to return to my side. "How about, *My muscle relaxant just kicked in*?"

Daphne looked at the image on Rodrigo's camera and snorted. "Oh my god. Earmark that."

She was far more in her element with Rodrigo than she'd been with Zed, and it wasn't just because her clothes were on. The pair had a rapport. She trusted him. I watched Daphne work her angles, all the while lecturing me as people trickled into the room. "I look at the world in terms of backdrops," she said somewhat grandly from her corner of the chocolate-chip pool. "Everywhere I go I think to myself: Would that make a hot photo on my grid or is that just some throwaway for my stories? What did I post last? What is getting the most traction? It's all a rather complex equation, and sometimes you have to let your instinct take over."

I nodded and listened like I was James Lipton listening to Sir Anthony Hopkins break down his craft on *Inside the Actors Studio*. She was sexy and confident when she talked shop. There was a method to the madness. And she'd chosen me, of all people, to mentor.

"There are tons of copycats out there, so in a week every Becky With The Long Hair is going to have this exact shot," she said. "That's why it's important to act fast. You always want to be the first 'grammer to capture whatever the next cultural phenomenon is."

"And this week it's cookies?" I smiled unsurely.

"Along with PopSockets, plant-based eggs, and shackets."

"Shackets?" I repeated.

She fixed me with a stare. "Shirts that are also jackets."

"Aren't those just shirts?"

"Not exactly. You'll know when you see one."

Daphne and Rodrigo both looked at me with equal parts patience and pity, as if I were a foreign exchange student who'd just been introduced to her first pumpkin spice latte. Daphne resumed cavorting in the pool, alternately blowing kisses and throwing chocolate chips into the air, while Rodrigo captured every moment.

A lifeguard perched on a graham cracker diving board informed us that we should try and finish up. As Rodrigo snapped his final shots, influencers of varying ilk wandered into the room and took turns diving into the chocolate-chip pool. They, too, wanted their money shot.

There were prematurely sexualized TikTok tweens, a twenty-something Rock-a-Billy who wore head-to-toe magenta, a K-pop princess, and a German dude with a selfie stick.

Roman was enjoying himself but mainly because he was being plied with sweets at every turn. I pushed Felix through the crowd as I followed Daphne and Rodrigo into a darker room that had been designed to look like a subway car.

I told Daphne the place reminded me of an article I'd once read about underground sex clubs in Japan, where perverted businessmen could go into fake subway stations and feel up all the actors posing as passengers.

Daphne looked at me. "Are you coming on to me?"

I laughed, trying to think of how to respond when Daphne's attention abruptly shifted to the top of my head. "So what are you thinking about your hair?"

"Umm... I wasn't really thinking about it," I said, confused.

"I love it. But did you notice it photographs a bit harsh?"

"Really?" I asked, trying to swallow the blow.

"It makes you seem slightly unapproachable, and you are anything but that," she assured me. "I'm just thinking ... should you lighten it?"

"I mean, I could," I said, feeling completely destroyed by the criticism.

"I think you'd look stunning. Not a huge change. Tiny. Maybe even let it grow out a bit. Get your bangs looking a little less *Amelie*. It's cute and all, it's just a little 2001." She slowed down when she spotted a woman on the opposite side of our car taking photos with a gaggle of kids. "The Mormons kill it on the 'gram," Daphne said. "I guess it's mostly through affiliate programs, but that chick is making a million bucks a year just from swipe-ups. It's all about the kids." Daphne turned to Rodrigo, concerned. "Should we get some kid shots? Where's Roman?"

My son was waiting for his turn at the top of the slide.

"I think you are fine without kid shots," I offered, suddenly worried she might try to pick up Felix and use his body as a prop.

Luckily, Daphne seemed to forget about kids. She was distracted by a knapsack attached to a stroller in the corner of the room. "That's a dope Chanel backpack," she told me. "It's from their pre-fall collection! You should take a picture with that. They don't come around often."

"Don't you think that would be weird? Considering it's not mine..."

Daphne rolled her eyes, then looked at Rodrigo, who shook his head and chuckled. "Meg, you have to fake it till you make it, remember?" she reminded me. "If it makes you feel any better, the bag I'm carrying doesn't belong to me either." She held up her rhinestone-encrusted Oreo cookie-shaped clutch. "This is borrowed from the Judith Lieber showroom. And this suit is a sample too. It's getting picked up by Alice + Olivia later this afternoon."

I guessed it made sense. Daphne changed at least three times a day and never repeated pieces, aside from her Teddy coat. I'd seen her closet, which was already bursting at the seams. She couldn't possibly keep everything, and why would she when more was always coming?

Her eyes held mine. "People don't follow you for the truth, they follow you for the fantasy. They want to believe that if they just owned a pair of Celine sunglasses and a two-toned Rolex Daytona, their lattes would taste sweeter, their Sunday scaries would evaporate, and their personal life would come together like the last fifteen minutes of any Nancy Meyers movie. I mean, who doesn't want that?" Daphne walked up to the unattended stroller and lifted the Chanel off the handlebar. "These women who follow us, they might not ever make it to New York City or the Museum of Cookies." She was referring to the Museum of Cookies as a bucket-list destination. I tried to keep a straight face.

"It's our job to take them there, Meg!" she went on. "Our followers rely on us for all that is missing in their lives. They need us to break them out of their monotonous, thankless jobs, their fucked-up marriages, their dysfunctional families, and all the depression that comes with age and mounting responsibility." Daphne gazed into the distance like a Union soldier who'd just won the Civil War surveying the Great American Plain. "I take what I do seriously because I know that I'm not just selling cookies or handbags. I'm helping women all around the world live their best lives. I'm a humanitarian, for god's sake."

"They would love you at Coca-Cola," I said under my breath.

Daphne held the knapsack in front of her and dangled it like a hypnosis pendulum. I tried to be discreet as I made my approach and swung the bag over my shoulder. As soon as Rodrigo started snapping shots of me and "my" Chanel, Roman came bounding toward me with another small boy with bright blue fingers and lips.

"They have a cotton candy cookie!" Roman exclaimed. He was jumping up and down.

"We have to get you out of here." I shook my head, already dreading bedtime.

"Hey, that's my mom's purse!" The little boy was pointing his sticky fingers at me.

"Oh my god!" the woman accompanying Roman's new friend exclaimed, and my stomach bottomed out. She was going to call security on me. Then I realized she was staring at the back of Daphne's head, her eyes growing bigger and bigger. "I knew it!" she gushed when Daphne turned around. "Wow. Such a fan." The woman did not seem to be remotely worried about her purse. "I have a whole text thread with my girlfriends simply titled *Daphne Cole's post-baby abs*," she told Daphne. "Speaking of, where are Vivienne and Hudson?"

"Oh, you know, probably off with the woman who actually carried them." Daphne laughed and took the knapsack from my hands.

"You crack me up!" the woman howled.

"Your bag is phenomenal," Daphne said, touching the leather before returning it to its rightful owner. "It's so hard to get a sense of the scale of these things in pictures."

The woman nodded. "I love it because it's just so easy with my city lifestyle. I mean don't get me wrong, I loved cruise collection but where am I wearing that see-through life preserver bag? Even the vanity cases just don't work when you're a mom."

Daphne erupted into hysterics, then masterfully tied up the exchange by offering the woman something even more desirable than another Chanel bag. "Shall we selfie?"

CHAPTER TWENTY-ONE

I posted the picture of myself holding up the Chanel backpack and captioned it: "Chanels like teen spirit." Not everyone got the joke, which led to hours of insecurity and self-doubt. And I wasn't just kicking myself for making a Kurt Cobain reference in a Coco Chanel world. The picture was so basic and bougie that no matter how witty the caption, I felt like a douche.

Daphne assured me that the post was funny even though I'm not entirely sure she was telling the truth. She tended toward captions like "when life gives you lemons, put them in your vodka." But she warned that if I spent too much time thinking about a post it could be paralyzing. It was far more important that I commit to churning out content at regular, ideally constant, intervals. I was up to 16,000 followers. And I did start to post more. Stupid signs I'd see around the city. Pictures of my bra on the floor. My overflowing Diaper Genie. Things that I found funny and that I felt other moms might relate to.

I didn't want to mimic Daphne, who shared photos of herself hanging from the side of the Brooklyn Bridge in a Bottega bodysuit or waltzing down Times Square in plastic pants and eight-inch platform high tops. I didn't want to present my life like it was somehow perfect or easy. Because it was anything but easy. I still didn't even know where I was going to live by the end of year.

"I am the mom your kids warned you about," I wrote on a post of myself holding up a botched pancake that looked like Gene Simmons from KISS. "Like for Like" @Sheshootsforthemoon replied. "OMG MOM FAIL!" @Victorialovespolo exclaimed. "Been there!" @Apple234 assured me. "Are those gluten-free?" "Where do you buy your dish towels?" "Where do you buy your dishes?" "Where do you buy your pancake mix?"

I didn't know these people, but I felt obligated to answer them like I was their primary-care physician. They asked questions about everything, from organic toothpaste and eco-friendly cleaning products to ski resorts and breast implants. I didn't know why they wanted my opinion, or why they trusted me as an authority on any of these subjects. They just did. So I went with it. And just like that, I was up to 20,000 followers.

As my career started to veer in two separate directions, so did my daily life. There was the path that I was on with my family. And then there was the path that I was on with Daphne. They both required so much time and maintenance. It was nearly impossible to keep everyone happy.

Busy as she was, Daphne was hyper-invested in my success. "What is going on with your outfit?" "Did you call my hair guy yet?" "Why aren't you posting more?" she'd write to me. Despite how much she had going on, she responded to my every move. She never missed a thing, which meant that I couldn't let go of the wheel either.

On Halloween, Iliya was losing patience with me. "Can we put our phones away for a bit?" he asked, taking off his Mr. Incredible mask to do a safety search through Roman's Halloween bucket.

"Sorry, it's NBD stuff," I lied. "These guys need so much hand-holding," I said, answering a message from Daphne about a "sick" sample sale she wanted me to attend with her.

"Daddy is trying to steal my candy!" Roman cried, fending off Iliya like he was some kind of Grendel figure attacking his village.

We were all dressed as the Incredibles with a sexy pirate cat in tow (Marina), making our rounds through Tribeca and up into the

West Village. Daphne was in Midtown dressed as the Tin Man at some Wizard of Oz-themed Heidi Klum event she'd been paid to attend. She was clearly bored out of her mind.

"Do you and your husband want to go to this new restaurant in Chelsea where we have to fish for our own dinner?" "I'm considering getting the bags under my eyes removed. Do you think I have bags under my eyes?" "Can you tell that I'm bored here and hate my husband?"

Her texts kept coming. Every few blocks, I pretended that I needed to pee so that I could sneak off to a restaurant restroom and answer them.

We were ambling down Barrow Street when Iliya sprung something on me. "I think I might have found us a place," he said. We were at the foot of a brownstone stoop while Marina led Roman up a flight of stairs.

"Really?" I said, filling with guilt that I hadn't so much as clicked on a single link to aid in our apartment search. I justified this by telling myself that I didn't know the first thing about the city, and I was handling everything else. "Where is it?"

"Long Island City," Iliya said. "It's not a terrible commute."

"Where is Long Island City?" It sounded more than a couple blocks away.

He pointed his finger in the direction of the health food store on the corner. "Queens," he said.

"But what if we get Roman into Abington?"

"That would also be a commute," he admitted.

"Are you sure this makes sense?" I was starting to panic, knowing that Daphne would find my moving so far away from her wholly unacceptable. "I thought we wanted to try and stay in the area," I added.

"Meg, look around you. We can't afford this area." I scanned the block we were on. It was all Land Rovers, twelve-million-dollar townhouses, and an overpriced soap store.

Before I could come up with a retort, I noticed Marina snapping a picture of us.

"Sorry to interrupt your little spat," she said from the top of the stairs. "But with your costumes on, it was too good. I'm sending it to you both."

Iliya would not let me post pictures of him online. But since we were both wearing masks, and also because I was so frustrated with him, I took it upon myself to upload the picture to my feed. The caption was: "Great shot of my husband and me communicating. #HappyHalloween." Before I could stuff my phone back in my jacket, Daphne fired off a text. "SHOW YOUR GODDAMN FACE. Don't be an amateur."

"Don't you have a party to be focusing on?" I wrote back, obstinate. But she was right. The majority of the photos I was posting were just random things I snapped without much thought. If I really wanted to legitimize myself, I needed to make more of an effort. I needed to become the main character of my feed, not just the narrator. And to do that, I needed a freaking photographer.

Later that night, I approached a promising candidate as we waited for Roman to finish brushing his teeth.

"So what exactly would I have to do?" Marina asked.

"Just help me take the pictures," I explained.

Iliya popped his head back into the bathroom. "Just checking to see if I'm hearing what I think I'm hearing. Because if so, it sounds pretty warped."

"This is hard for me to ask! Please don't make it any worse," I said. "You said you would support me," I reminded Iliya, annoyed.

"I never said that I wouldn't make fun of you." He waggled his eyebrows.

Ignoring him, I turned back to Marina. "It will be a creative project! Daphne said that she has tons of props that I can use. And clothes. Things that she's already shot in. Last season Gucci, Prada, and even a couple Marni pieces that she claims actually have a shape."

"Who *are* you?" Marina stared at me, turned on by my growing lexicon of high-end designers and the perks of being my sister-in-law.

"Thank you," I said, giving her an arm squeeze. "You won't regret this."

CHAPTER TWENTY-TWO

Marina's virgin white Mercedes GLA 250 peeled out of its tight parking space on Watts Street like it was being commandeered by a band of Muppets. I checked that my seat belt was securely fastened. "This thing is a fucking stick shift?" I looked out the window, making sure the car parked in front of us still had its bumper. How were you ever an Uber driver?"

"A Wing Woman," she corrected me for the gazillionth time, flipping a U-turn in a street thronged with pedestrians. "And my clients were all drinkers, so they were much more relaxed than you'll ever be." She was having fun teasing me, but not as much fun as she was having zipping through streetlights like they were mere suggestions.

"How's your dentist?" I inquired, reaching into the back seat and resting my hand on my sleeping baby's lap. Felix felt so tiny and warm.

"I finally got a photo. He's a little bald, but doesn't that mean he's well-endowed?" Marina said as if there wasn't a baby in the back seat.

"I think it just means he has an excess amount of testosterone."

"Whatever, that's not what I care about. We've been getting super hot and heavy over text. I told him that I wanted a mold of my mouth made by next week."

"Mouth mold," I said. "Sounds hot."

"It's always good to throw out a couple ultimatums to see how serious someone actually is."

Before I could respond, I glanced out my window and saw a cluster of NBD posters plastered down the side of a building on Canal. My stomach dropped.

Just then, my phone started vibrating. It was Daphne.

"THEY ARE UP," she wrote. "Do I look old?" "Why am I older than you?" "Do I look fat?" "Why am I fatter than you?" "Don't let me eat again." "BTW I booked our double date at the fish restaurant." "Fuck, I guess I'm eating again." "You better start typing back or I'm coming to find you."

"CHILL! I'm literally on my way to your house, bitch!" I wrote back, accidentally talking to Daphne the way that I talked to Marina.

"I'm not home," she finally responded, leaving me wondering if she was telling the truth or just pissed that I'd called her a bitch. "Wynne is bringing stuff down." I'd never heard of Wynne but told her that sounded great.

"Jesus Christ, my brother is going to shit a brick when he sees his wife's nipples plastered all over downtown!" Marina exclaimed, snapping me back to attention.

I said, gritting my teeth. "And now you're my right hand. You're supposed to tell me that it's art and he will understand and it's going to be all good."

Marina threw the car in park and turned to me. "It's art and he will understand and it's going to be all good."

"Do you mean that?"

"Not even a little bit."

When we arrived at Daphne's address, a preppy woman in her early thirties was waiting outside the building. She introduced herself as Wynne as she barreled toward me, her arms full of boxes. "Daphne said you were taking all this?" she asked.

"If that's okay," I said, getting out of the car to help her.

"Fine by me." Wynne laughed as she loaded the boxes into the trunk.

Marina looked at Wynne and did a double take. "I know you!"

Wynne looked at Marina. "Lastrelle!" they said in tandem.

"Oh my god!" Marina said. "Are you still in the study?" I detected a smidge of jealousy in her voice.

Wynne shrugged. "I have rosacea, so I sort of had an advantage. They wanted to make sure it worked for sensitive skin."

"And does it?" Marina inquired.

"Not really," Wynne admitted. "But I made an extra hundred bucks for saying so in a testimonial video."

"Congrats." Marina nodded solemnly as if she was an actress who'd just learned that she'd been beaten out for the lead role in a new Warner Brothers franchise.

"I hate lying," Wynne confessed. "My boyfriend is in law school studying to be a public defender, but you know how it is. They get you in there and next thing you know you're telling them what they want to hear simply because you want that money." Marina nodded along. "Anyway, they were stupid to cut you. You are so pretty, you would have made an amazing spokesperson."

Marina smiled, and then looked at me. "You ready to unbox these fuckers?"

I glanced at the trunk of the car, which we'd barely been able to close. "Let's ride."

From the second we opened up the first box of Daphne's belongings, Marina no longer cared about surveys or sexting. I'd never seen her so focused on anything that wasn't her horoscope. She had a new purpose: to make me over. "The best years of your life were wasted in sweatpants and Mavi jeans!" she told me. "If you don't wear the shit out of this stuff, you are doing a disservice to women everywhere."

I learned quickly that in order to build my following, I had to feed it. Every one of them — a number edging close to 25,000 — wanted to feel heard, and I needed to take the time to let them know that I was listening and that I cared. That was what made Daphne so successful. She wasn't just a pretty picture or silly video to swipe past. She was your friend.

The pictures I took with Marina's assistance weren't as serious as Daphne's. And the captions I threw up were mostly nonsense that happened to make me laugh. I couldn't keep a straight face sipping coffee at Sant Ambroeus or looking lost and lonely as I crossed the cobblestone street. Instead I played in the produce section at Trader Joes, climbed trees in Battery Park, and rented paddle boats down by Pier 26. Marina and I were just two girls playing dress up. And I had to admit, it was kind of fun.

By the time I had 30,000 followers, Seth and Vigo finally ponied up and gave me half the money they owed me. They were probably scared that I was going to post about their cavalier attitude toward labor laws. They promised me that the rest of what I was owed would be in my bank account by the new year. The posters were up, and the bath bombs were online. My work was ostensibly complete. But Seth wanted me to stay on past the holiday push to help them develop a line of adaptogen-infused shower gels for the "trophy mom on the go," whatever that meant. There was only one issue. Vigo was looking for investors for their second round of funding, and until he had a better sense of where the company was going to land, he couldn't renegotiate my contract. This was more than annoying. If I didn't start pulling in more cash, we were going to end up living with Iliya's mom and her fake Faberge egg collection.

My part in the NBD campaign gave a bit of a boost to my Instagram account, but Daphne was the real reason it kept growing. She kept tagging me and reposting my shots on her stories with little stickers and thumbs up emojis. For all intents and purposes, she had made me, and she wanted to show me off.

I wasn't seeing dollars, but the products kept rolling in. Boxes of everything from veggie-flavored ice cream to serums made out of pig placentas started showing up at my door. I switched from almond milk to tigernut milk because Daphne claimed it was better for gut health. I started eating collagen gummies from some company called Goo and put Red on a grain-free diet that showed up monthly on dry ice. My nightly beauty routine grew from ten minutes long to an hour and a half once I factored in the glycolic peels, vitamin C drops, hydration pellets, and the red-light mask. These things were mine for free as long as I posted them.

I was already up to 40,000 followers when I met up with Daphne at her hair salon. The space was wide open with poured concrete floors and steel-framed windows. Styling assistants scurried back and forth, mixing colors and fetching diet sodas for the thirsty clientele.

Daphne stood over my chair, scrutinizing my tresses. "So I don't want you to mess with the length," she told the stylist, Javier. "We're letting it grow. And for the color…" Daphne cocked her head, pretending to think even though it was obvious she already knew exactly what she wanted. "Just softer. More like mine." She looked up at Javier, who nodded.

"I know what you like," he told her.

"Of course. This isn't your first rodeo." Daphne picked up her phone so she could film us. "Javi. Sorry… Can you start your bit again? Tell me what you want to do and then I'll come in with my thoughts."

"And what should I do?" I laughed awkwardly.

Daphne smiled from behind her phone. "Just sit still and look pretty."

CHAPTER TWENTY-THREE

Shoppers had started lining up in the middle of the night. Some of them brought folding chairs, and I even spotted a couple of tents. It was ten a.m., and the queue snaked around the block, teeming with women waiting to ravage the L'Orangerie sample sale once it opened to the public. Daphne, Marina and I were already past the warehouse gates, since Daphne got early access. Not only did she get to assess the wares before they were picked over by the hoi polloi, but she could take whatever she wanted, free of charge. So, for that matter, could her entourage.

Marina could barely contain her excitement. "We can just help ourselves to *anything*?" she confirmed.

"Pretty much," Daphne said. "This is all last season's inventory. There's nothing they can do with it besides take the hit and sell it off to Nordstrom Rack. We're doing them a favor if you think about it."

"Does every designer do this?" I asked.

"Except for the top ones. The Guccis and Louis Vuittons of the world set their shit on fire in Piscataway." She sounded nonchalant.

"NO! You're kidding!" Marina gasped. "But… Why?" Marina's face took on the expression of a child who had just been told that Santa Claus wasn't real.

"Two reasons," Daphne said, sauntering down the aisle. "One, they don't want to flood the market and mess up the exclusivity of their brand and two, they are imported products, which means that they paid an import tax to get each piece into the United States. So if they destroy their product and then report it to customs, they get some money back. Kind of brilliant if you ask me."

"Louis Vuitton bags… burning in New Jersey," Marina said, her voice quivering. It sounded like she might cry.

This was the first time Marina had been around Daphne. And aside from their shared love of European luxury cars and liposuction videos, the two women couldn't be more unalike. Daphne had ascended to an enchanted place where everything was handed to her, whereas Marina made it her life's work to shamelessly scheme and haggle and grab as much as she could take. They were both beasts, but from wildly different animal kingdoms.

"I think I'm going to have a panic attack," Marina said.

"Relax, this should be fun." Daphne smiled. "What are you in the market for? Going-out looks? Vacation? Work clothes?"

Marina puckered her lips. "All of the above!"

We followed Daphne over to a rack and stood back as she loaded a shopping cart with leather bombers. It felt like a fever dream or some sort of hallucination, watching Daphne fill our cart with garments that she had no intention of paying for. It was a Vegas buffet where we could consume as much as we wanted. Daphne rattled off commentary as she went. "This is great!" "Take it!" "You don't need it, but with the right top…" And while she didn't pay Marina much mind, she was never dismissive, as I had feared she might be. "Meg!" Daphne held up a turquoise mohair sweater. "I've been wanting to see you in more blue. How good does she look in blue?" she asked Marina, who was too busy sniffing a buttery leather pant leg to register that she'd been called on.

After our two-hour bender, a PR rep checked us out, if you could call it that. The receipt stapled to the side of my shopping bag was at least two feet long. At the bottom, the subtotal was zero.

Marina was on cloud nine as we made our way back home.

"I should really start influencing too," she said as she sped down the FDR.

"Would you want to?" I asked. "You totally could."

"Not yet," she said. "I wouldn't attract the same demo as you. I'm too young and hot. I'd just have an inbox full of dongs."

Her delivery could have been more tactful, but she wasn't wrong. "Scantily clad sexpot" was its own Instagram subgenre. And while those sexy accounts bolstered big followings, they rarely made any money. They didn't get the big deals because they had the wrong demographics. Their followers were creepy men, not women who were in the market for skinny teas or diaper bags. It was the moms who had the buying power. And Marina was right. The moms would hate her.

"Maybe once I have a baby…" she said dreamily, gunning her car over a nasty pothole.

The truth was it the moms who had the buying power. The moms would hate her.

CHAPTER TWENTY-FOUR

My adventures in influencing didn't trouble Iliya as much as I'd thought they would. He was more freaked out about my new hair, which he said glowed in the dark. He was also troubled by the fact that it was hard to walk around our apartment now that it was filled with cardboard boxes.

Or maybe he was too distracted with the apartment search to notice just how consumed I'd become with my life in pictures. He was still angling for the Long Island City apartment that was more affordable than anything he'd seen in Manhattan. Iliya showed me a video, and while it looked lovely, I had reservations. Moving to another borough wasn't ideal. I certainly didn't mention the possibility to Daphne, who saw anything further than Bergdorf's as another country she'd only travel to for a CO2 laser.

I hoped Iliya wouldn't bring it up on our double date. The long overdue outing was finally happening. We'd made plans to meet Daphne and Kip at PESCE, a new "concept" from the guys behind Matador, one of Daphne's favorite restaurants. Iliya didn't have time to come home after work, so we agreed to meet at Chelsea House and walk to the restaurant from there.

I could feel the tension between us as we started down the street. It was one of those nights where a fight was imminent. It was just a question of when. We'd already gotten into it that morning, bickering over where we were going to spend the winter holidays. I wanted to get away and go somewhere pretty. He wanted to stay close to his mother and sister, now that they were finally in the same city.

"But you guys are Jews! I don't know why we have to spend Christmas with your mom when she doesn't even celebrate it."

"Where we grew up it was illegal to be Jewish," Iliya said. "So yeah, we do Christmas even if we don't do Jesus."

"I just feel like everybody is going somewhere but us!" I said, none too proudly.

"Stop looking at your phone and maybe you won't feel that way." It was a low blow, and I was still smarting twelve hours later.

"I'm freezing," I muttered, trying to keep up with Iliya in a pair of Daphne's old knife mules.

"I told you to wear socks. It's winter."

"Technically it's still fall. And I'm suffering for fashion." I tried to make it sound like I was joking.

Iliya stopped and cocked his head. "Those shoes are fashionable?" He was trying not to laugh.

"Yes, they are."

"They're also way too big for you," he noted. It was true, Daphne's feet were a size bigger than mine, but I was usually able to cheat it in pics. Before I could respond, Iliya picked me up and flung me over his shoulder.

"Put me down!" I was kicking and screaming. He paid me no mind and lugged me like a disgruntled sack of potatoes the rest of the way to our destination.

The restaurant was behind a nondescript door. Iliya rang a bell and smacked my ass while we waited. "Ow!" I shrieked, fighting my way to the ground.

When a man in a gondolier hat opened the door, I rushed inside, trying to shake off the chill.

"I think we have a reservation," Iliya told him.

"Do you have a password?" the man asked.

"I'm sorry?" Iliya's eyes narrowed.

"We text all our patrons a password an hour before their reservation. If you want to check your cell?" He motioned to Iliya's pocket, but Iliya didn't budge.

"We aren't using our cells," Iliya said plainly. "It's date night. The last name is Chernoff. Iliya Chernoff."

Hearing Iliya's name, the man snapped into hospitality mode. "Mr. Chernoff! Of course. I'm Serge. Danny mentioned you were coming in and to take good care of you. Can I take your jackets?"

"This is my wife, Meg," Iliya said, handing Serge his jacket.

"We are actually meeting Daphne Cole," I added.

"Yes, of course. She hasn't arrived yet but let me show you around."

"Meg was just on the verge of shoeicide, so if there is a booth she can kick her legs up in," Iliya started.

"A booth? Didn't Danny tell you?" Serge looked at us, surprised. "You're in boats tonight."

"I'm sorry?" Iliya coughed.

We followed Serge past a bar filled with bankers out for their monthly bro-makases down a long hall covered in sea grass and vertical veggie gardens.

"Up front we have our crudo bar where we do more casual dining," Serge said, leading us into what looked like a man-made grotto with a giant pool of water in the center. "And this is where we have the main event." Serge motioned toward the gondolas filled with foodies fishing for their dinners. The boats floated past in every direction. "All you need to do is catch a fish. Chefs are floating by and ready to clean, grill, and garnish," Serge said.

"This is wild!" I said.

"Actually, all the fish is farm-raised," he whispered under his breath.

"Your secret is safe with me." I nodded as the bellowing voice of a baritone singing Pavarotti echoed through the cave.

Iliya held his tongue as we stepped into our boat. Once Serge was out of earshot, he turned to me. "You've got to be fucking kidding me, Meg. What is this, Disneyland for douchebags?"

"This isn't my fault. She picked the place. And you spoke with Danny beforehand. Did he not mention anything?"

Iliya struggled with an oar and pushed us away from shore. "Do you think I asked him if we were riding in bumper boats? And how are we expected to eat with anybody? We're in a two-seater," he pointed out, flustered.

Just then a small dude covered in neck tattoos rowed his way up beside us. He poured Iliya a kombucha and delivered me a glass of prosecco, then handed us both fishing rods and a tackle box filled with bait and bibs.

"At least you're getting the vacation you wanted," Iliya said a moment later. "If you squint your eyes almost shut, you could tell yourself you're in Italy."

"Are you going to be making fun of me all night?"

"Meg!" A voice came from across the grotto. It was Daphne, dressed in a bustier and spray-painted jeans. Kip stood next to her, talking on his phone. They were still on land.

"Come here!" She waved us over, like a Siren beckoning a ship of sailors to their death.

"You've got to be kidding me. You guys have matching hair," Iliya said under his breath as he rowed.

"Hiiii," Daphne cooed, instantly sizing up Iliya. I could tell she was impressed by his good looks. "So I finally get to meet my competition," she said. "I feel like we should arm wrestle or something."

"You might be stronger than me," Iliya said. "I've seen the videos of your trampoline workouts." This was news to me. I wondered what else of Daphne's he'd seen.

Daphne laughed. "Hey, I like your shirt. It looks better on your wife, though."

I looked at Iliya again, realizing that he was in his favorite button up. The same one I'd worn to the Mompire dinner. Iliya shot me a look.

"Hey, man. Nice to formally meet you." Kip looked at Iliya. I clocked that they recognized each other from somewhere.

"Nice to meet you," Iliya said, playing along. A dock worker helped Daphne and Kit into their gondola, then tied our two boats together.

I was waiting to see how long it would take for Kip to acknowledge me this time.

"So!" Iliya said, placing his hand on my knee. "Should we fish?"

"This place is so crazy!" I smiled at Daphne. I wanted to let her know that she still had my undivided attention.

"What? Sorry, I'm a little distracted," she said. "I'm getting emails from Instagram telling me that my pictures go against the platform's guidelines. And that if I continue, they are going to shut me down!"

By the look of Kip's face, this was a topic he was sick of hearing about.

"That's impossible," I said. "You haven't posted anything inappropriate."

"Well I must have because certain posts of mine are missing. They took them down!" Daphne pulled out her phone and scrolled through her grid, trying to remember which shots had vanished. "You know what? Fuck that! Let's make some more inappropriate content," she said, changing her tone. Daphne held her phone in my face and motioned for me to smile as Kip engaged Iliya in the kind of ritualistic small talk that men reserve for other men. "I think if I get another notice telling me that they really are deleting me," Daphne said, "the move is to just post a full nude saying, 'bye bitch!' " Daphne cackled.

"Give 'em what they want," I laughed.

"Speaking of posting, I was thinking that you should talk to Susan," Daphne said, now aiming her camera lens at her tackle box.

"About what?" I took out a gummy squid and attached it to my pole.

"About her repping you. She's expressed interest. That dog food company has money and Cha Cha hates their food so I'm out. If you had someone in there who could negotiate on your behalf, I know that they'd pay you."

"But Red is like a thousand years old. He's not exactly a cover model," I reminded her.

It wasn't my dog Daphne wanted to talk about. "You're already posting for them anyway. You should be getting something more than just free food. You're at what? Fifty-five thousand followers now?" she said, pretending not to know.

"Something like that," I said.

"You are no longer micro, Meg. You passed the 50k mark. You can start demanding a fee. Especially with that hair."

I blushed, watching Daphne struggle with her pole. Eventually she gave up and took Kip's.

"Hey!" Kip protested. "I was getting a nibble!"

"You have the following, but you need an agent if you want to make any money." Daphne glanced at Iliya to see if he was listening. "Oh shit! I think I have something!" Daphne yanked so hard on her pole that our boats disconnected.

"Slow it down!" Daphne kept yelling.

"I'm trying!" Kip shot back, annoyed.

I watched as Kip and Daphne floated away. There was something strangely cute about them. They were similar in a certain way, like siblings who spent too much time together or two actors who hated each other but were stuck playing love interests on a hit TV in its seventeenth season.

"Well, this is fun," Iliya said facetiously.

"We have to go get them."

"Do we?" Iliya looked at me. "I can't spend another minute talking about Ben Roethlisberger. You know I hate American sports."

"I know. But we still haven't even eaten anything," I reminded him.

Iliya continued to bitch as we rowed our boat back to the other side of the grotto. We found Daphne and Kip tied up to another gondola. I was taken aback to see Tanya and her husband riding in it. I thought this was supposed to be a double date, not a party.

"Long lifeline," Tanya said, hanging off the side of her boat reading Kip's palm as we approached. In the boat beside them, a chef tended to sea bass cooking on a Roboto-style grill.

"That's not the only thing that's long," chimed in Tanya's husband, Howie. He was a super tan, well-preserved man of about fifty-five with curly salt and pepper hair and a wrist full of kabbalah bracelets. Tanya gave her husband a for-shame look. "What?" he said. "I've stood at a urinal next to this guy. I know you aren't supposed to peek but I'm a doctor so I'm just looking out. Kip, free scrotox when you're ready, bud."

"I'm going to vomit," Tanya said.

Daphne must have sensed my discomfort. "Meg!" she cried out. "Kip caught a bass! And look, I caught a bass! And a crab!" she pointed to Tanya and laughed.

"I'm not a crab, I just don't want to talk about nut sacks while I eat."

Howie shook Iliya's hand like they'd just pledged the same fraternity. "Who is this handsome Dan?" Howie slurred, drunkenly.

"Howie!" Tanya hit her husband on his non-braceleted hand.

"Easy, princess. That's my injecting finger!" Howie pointed his crooked finger into his wife's face, scolding her. "And I'm secure enough in my heterosexuality to be able to appreciate an attractive man when I see one. Let me ask you something," Howie said, scrutinizing Iliya. "Your nose, made by the knife? Or life?"

"This is why I didn't want to do the wine pairing." Tanya looked at Daphne, frustrated.

I could feel Iliya's judgments flying. There was nothing he hated more than a sloppy drunk. Actually, there was: a whole sea of them.

"You don't mind if they join us, do you?" Daphne batted her eyelashes.

"Of course not," I said, elbowing Iliya.

"I'm so glad we bumped into each other! Literally!" Tanya laughed then turned to Iliya. "So, what do you think about your wife becoming an influencer?"

"I have a lot of new visors and sleep shirts." Iliya said, clearly fading out. He was done with these people.

"Kip, why don't you ever sleep in any of the swag I get?" Daphne picked up her phone, seizing the moment to film.

"Why would I wear anything to sleep when I'm next to you?" Kip was cranking up the charm. They were a different couple when the camera was on. It was almost sociopathic.

"Oh Kippy! I love you!" Daphne said. They kissed for the camera, then went back to eating in silence.

"What do you do, Iliya?" Howie asked.

"I'm in the private club business," Iliya said, trying to stay vague.

"Like strip clubs? I put tits on half the dancers in this town. You ever been to Happy Endings in the Financial District? They've got some very talented young ladies."

"Howie!" Tanya shouted.

"What!? They do! They're excellent dancers. Very flexible."

"I'm so sorry about him." Tanya shook her head, mortified. "He doesn't get out much."

"It's fine." I smiled.

Before there was time to order tiramisu, Iliya was asking for the check.

"Oh, don't be silly," Daphne said to him. "It's comped. Because we posted."

Iliya nodded, then steered our boat over to the dock and helped me back onto land. I was embarrassed that we were rushing out, but I knew that if we didn't, Iliya was going to lose it. He gave zero fucks what Daphne or any of the people floating around us thought. And he would have no qualms sharing that information with them if given the opportunity.

After tipping the waitstaff, we hopped in a cab, damp and smelling of fish viscera. The second the taxi meter started running, the fight I'd been anticipating all evening finally broke out.

"*That* is who you got pool memberships for?" Iliya shook his head, disgusted.

"No! That girl wasn't even there!"

"Are you claiming that the woman who you hooked up is any different from the sampling of people I just met?" He gave me a long, hard look. Now was not the time to tell Iliya that Lauren was actually worse than the people we'd just dined with.

"You're just annoyed because they were tipsy," I said. "You don't even know them."

"I know enough. Did you see how they were sizing me up? Wanted to know what I did for a living? I'm sorry but I refuse to associate with a bunch of arrogant, status-obsessed, drunks."

"Um, sorry but there is no difference between these people and all your drunk Russian friends except for the fact that my friends can actually afford the Hermes belts they're wearing!"

Iliya ignored me. "And that Kip guy? Do you know how many times I've seen him in the club with other women? Does your friend not know, or does it not count in your world if there aren't any pictures to post?" This took the wind out of me. I couldn't cobble together a response fast enough. "Seriously, Meg. I'm asking. Tell me how it works. Now that you're such an expert."

"Wow, Iliya. I take you out to meet my new friends — something you sure haven't done since we came to New York — and this is the way you want to act? I'm glad you're so superior to everyone else on earth. It must feel pretty awesome. You know what else would be awesome?" Tears were pricking my eyes and I could hardly see anything. "If you would kindly fuck off."

CHAPTER TWENTY-FIVE

There was no exercise on earth more annoying than bouncing. It hurt my knees and every time I jumped, a little bit of pee seemed to escape me. But Tramp Stamp was where Daphne went. And that's where I found her two days after our dinner. Before I could talk to her at the end of our session, Lauren cornered me.

"Meg, I keep seeing your face all over my walk to school. Congrats on the NBD launch. It's a pretty BD!" she laughed. "We should do a feature with you on my blog. Maybe we could shoot you at home with the kids and husband? I heard he's hot. At some point I should properly thank him for getting me those pool memberships." She was being nicer to me than she had ever been. Daphne and Tanya came over to join us.

"I don't show the kids' faces on social media," I said almost apologetically. "And Iliya is pretty private."

Lauren buried her sweaty head in a towel. When she looked back up, half of her face had smeared off on the terrycloth. "Well maybe we could do something just you and me," Lauren said, looking to Daphne for her approval.

"You and Meg?" Daphne cocked her head to the side. She seemed dubious.

"Yeah, like a fireside chat for mom-trepreneurs. Maybe even stream it….," Lauren spitballed. Before she could continue, I felt a tapping on my shoulder.

A glistening twenty-something in a spandex hot pink workout bra was standing inches away. "Knew it! From behind I could have sworn that you were Daphne."

"It's the hair!" Lauren and Tanya said in unison.

"I'm right here!" Daphne waved her hand.

"Duh. I know. I'm just saying that you guys are like twinning," the spandex girl said, then turned back to me. "You're Meg Chernoff, right?" She sounded nervous. "My friends and I are obsessed with your feed. *Chanels like teen spirit*? I died laughing!" she gushed. "Would you mind if we took a selfie?"

"Sure," I said, feeling anything but sure.

"Sorry I'm so sweaty." I could feel the girl shaking as I wrapped my hand around her waist and smiled. I knew that people were following my account, but this was the first time I was face to face with a "fan." It felt surreal.

"Thanks so much!" she said. "Keep doing what you are doing. And Daphne, you know I love you too, obvi!"

"Thanks, girl." Daphne waved as the girl pranced off.

Lauren's eyes widened, unable to hold back her shock at my ascent. Having 60,000 followers was one thing. But IRL fan girls bum-rushing me after gym class?

"So, about our fireside chat," Lauren continued, talking faster than before. "I'm out east for Thanksgiving and then I have a couple of non-negotiables, but how about mid-December?"

Daphne interjected as she led us out of the muggy studio and over toward the juice bar. "She'll be with me in Paris."

"What?" I stopped and looked at Daphne.

"You're going to Paris with me in two weeks. Did I forget to tell you?"

Lauren looked at me, clearly seething with jealousy.

"This is the first I'm hearing of it," I told Daphne.

"I asked Susan to try and get you a fee!" Daphne announced.

"A FEE? For WHAT?" Lauren couldn't help herself. Her face was growing redder by the second.

"For her time. You should really be offering her something too if you're gonna use her to promote your blog, Lauren. Even her dog is commanding fees these days. Right, Meg?"

Daphne handed us each a pea green wellness shot. Lauren looked like she was going to be sick, and not because of the wheatgrass.

CHAPTER TWENTY-SIX

Thanksgiving in Tribeca was quiet. According to my feed, most people were either cuddling under cashmere blankets in the Hamptons or flouncing around in flannel upstate. Iliya insisted on hosting dinner at our place even though we barely had a functioning kitchen. We ordered in and invited my mother-in-law, Dasha, whom I'd successfully avoided since our move back east.

Dinner had been ready for a half hour, but we were still waiting on Marina. She was supposedly on her way but not picking up her phone.

"We can't keep Red on that disgusting food," Iliya said. "He's had blood in his stool for the past two days."

"I know, but we need to pretend he's on it because they just started paying us," I said, watching Iliya cut up a scrap of turkey and toss it into Red's bowl. "And why are you giving him more meat? He's clearly reacting to the protein. We need to just have him on a pumpkin and rice diet for a few days." I snatched the meat out of Red's bowl and excused myself to go to the bathroom. There was a frantic text from Daphne waiting for me.

"THEY ARE GETTING RID OF LIKES!" she wrote. "Do I still have them? Will you check my page?"

Before I could reply, she continued typing. "Some accounts have already lost them. ARGH!! And I have a weird feeling that I'm being targeted."

I'd read about Instagram removing "likes" and as a parent, I felt that it made sense. Kids were killing themselves based on how many people hearted their photos. But Daphne didn't see it that way. "Kids have no place being on Instagram to begin with!" she'd proselytize, then post a picture of her twins doing an ASMR video.

"Your likes are still there," I assured her.

"Thank god," she replied. A second later, a video of Kip and his buddies doing a cheer pyramid on the beach with the caption, "Get a load of these turkeys! #HappyTurkeyDay" appeared on her feed.

Before returning to the living room, I freshened up in the mirror. Then I pulled my old bottle of half-eaten placenta pills out of the cabinet. "I was in charge of the stuffing," I wrote, followed by Daphne's hashtag, #HappyTurkeyDay

I laughed out loud at my own joke but then instantly worried that Daphne might think that I was spoofing her and quickly deleted the hashtag.

"Mommy! Are you pooping? Come OUT!" Roman screamed. "I have presents!"

"Is Marina here yet?" I inquired, secretly hoping that her tardiness would buy me a few more minutes alone with my phone.

I knew that my family was on the other side of the door, and that it was a holiday and that these moments with my kids were limited. They wouldn't be this young forever. I would eventually regret not savoring every second of their youth. But I just couldn't stop scrolling, pulling down on my screen to refresh the content like it was a slot machine.

Finally, I came out to find Iliya's legally blind mother sitting on a hemorrhoid pillow on the couch and pulling age-inappropriate gifts out of a Rite Aid bag. "There is no Kevin's," she grunted to Roman. "When you die, you die."

"What are we talking about?" I looked at Iliya, who clearly wasn't keeping an eye on his mother in my absence. "Nobody is dying. These are adult topics that we don't need to be discussing with a preschooler."

"Mama, *perestan' govorit' o!*" Iliya called out from the kitchen.

"No death talk, fine. I'm gonna die first, you know," Dasha added in the same breath. "And what is happening to your wife's body?"

"What do you mean?" I asked timidly.

"You're getting too thin!" she scowled.

"Can she even see me?" I asked Iliya under my breath, scattering pecans on a salad.

"Of course, she can," he insisted, his hands covered in butter.

"From this far away?" I squinted at Dasha from across the kitchen island.

"I can hear you, too!"

It was true, I had been losing a bit of weight. It was a side effect of following along with whatever fad diet Daphne was on. Some days it was no dairy, some days no gluten, some days it was something called a GG cracker, which was basically just a high-fiber crispbread that tasted like tree bark.

"Yeah! A gun!" Roman exclaimed. "Thank you so much, Nana!" he said, pointing the pistol straight at his little brother.

"Hang on! No guns!" I stopped him. "We aren't a gun household."

"It's not a gun! It's a water gun," Dasha clarified, annoyed. "You people are so uptight. Live a little. Jesus."

"Jesus?" Roman said, having his eureka moment. "Mommy was saying that when the house was on fire!"

"When was the house on fire?" Dasha asked, picking Felix up from his playmat and placing him on her lap.

Iliya shook his head, pleading for me to disengage. "We don't have to do Christmas, okay?" he negotiated under his breath.

Even before kids, my relationship with Dasha had been a struggle. I respected all that she'd been through and all that she'd sacrificed for her children. But she was difficult to be around. She was a master at finding a way to make herself the victim in any circumstance. She simpered and pouted and glared like nobody else. I'd once been to a restaurant with her where she pulled out her Weight Watchers scale to weigh an eight-ounce petit filet. When the steak came in at two grams under, she complained until her meal was comped. And she wasn't even the one buying.

There was nothing any of us could do to make her happy. Sometimes she'd laugh or smile at the boys, then catch herself and retreat back into her gloom, disappearing into her bedroom to sneak a cigarette and contemplate how her husband died of lung cancer when he never smoked a day in his life.

"It's time to eat!" Iliya called out.

"But what about Marina—" Roman reminded him.

"It's time to eat anyway." Iliya took Felix from his mother and brought him to the table.

Just then Daphne texted: "So are you coming to France or what?" She hadn't mentioned Paris since Tramp Stamp and I hadn't brought it up. It was almost as if she telepathically felt my attention shift toward my family and needed something to reel me back in.

"You're not serious, are you?" I wrote.

Iliya shot me a look. "Honey?"

"I get two tickets and you know I don't want to take Kip. His French is abominable. He pronounces the T in Merlot."

"Honey?" Iliya intoned again, this time less softly.

"Can I think about it?" I asked, typing as quickly as I could.

"THINK about what? It's fucking ZOE!"

As far as Daphne was concerned, there was no greater honor than being invited to a Zoe anything. And I understood enough to know it would put me in a different echelon of influencers. I wouldn't just be part of the downtown mommy 'grammer scene, I'd be part of the global luxury market.

"MEGAN! We are about to eat dinner. Can you put the damn phone down?" Iliya snapped.

I looked up at my family seated around the table. Roman blinked at me. Dasha looked at me with an air of superiority and judgment. Felix just babbled to himself in his high chair and Red slowly crept out of the room to go post a want ad for a new family.

"Sorry," I said sheepishly.

My phone vibrated again, and it took every ounce of self-discipline I had not to look down.

Later that night, once the kids were asleep, I walked into the kitchen to find Iliya still tidying up.

"Daphne invited me to Paris," I told him.

"Okay." He didn't sound surprised. "Are you going to go?" He didn't look up.

"Can I?" I was waiting for him to make eye contact.

"You can do whatever you want," Iliya said, grabbing a loaf of black bread and making a turkey and pickle sandwich. "How many days?"

"Like, three!" I said.

"I didn't ask *like* how many days. I asked *how* many days."

"I'd fly out late next Thursday night and be back Sunday.

"I have the Chelsea House holiday party next Friday. It's all the investors. There is no way I can get out of it."

"Well, maybe your sister —," I started.

"Maybe." He shrugged. "But those things go late..."

"If it's too much right now I understand. Red is going to need to go to the vet if this rice doesn't help him. And you'd have both kids…." I trailed off, feeling guilty. While I wanted to go more than anything, I knew that it would be a logistical nightmare.

Iliya stared at me. I could tell he was trying his hardest to stay even-tempered. "Do you want to go with her?"

"I mean, it's Paris!" I said. "You know I've always wanted to go to Europe. And when are we going to be able to afford a trip like that?"

"Just you and her?" I could see him grit his teeth. He reached for a stack of mail.

"I don't know why you don't like her. She's been so good to me."

"I don't not like her. I just don't like what she does to you."

"What does she do to me? She thinks I'm talented. I don't know where I'd be right now if it weren't for her." I shook my head.

"You'd be here," he said bluntly, then passed me an envelope with my name on it. It was my credit card statement. I steadied my breath as I ripped it open. Of course, Vigo hadn't paid my balance. Those guys didn't give a shit about me. I was just a cog in a wheel, useful but replaceable. If I wanted my life to change, I needed to do it myself.

"Thank you," I said to Iliya. "I'm gonna go."

CHAPTER TWENTY-SEVEN

The Air France A380 departed JFK for Charles de Gaulle at 9:55 p.m. I questioned my decision to board up until the minute I took my first sip of complimentary Champagne. I knew that I wasn't leaving Iliya in the best position but opportunities like this one only came around once in a lifetime, if that. I'd arranged for Marina to watch the kids Saturday night so that Iliya could make his big work event. And I'd made them both promise to contact the vet if Red's condition worsened.

Vigo had assured me that his assistant had sorted out my outstanding pay and promised that he'd settled my credit card bill. He even swore that he'd gotten the late fee waived. Unfortunately, I could only check on my account from my laptop, so I had to hope I was in the clear to score a few small gifts to bring home to the boys.

With muted shades of palomino leather and warm pink lighting, the first-class cabin was a capsule of serenity. Daphne sat to my right wearing Gucci sweatpants and gigantic designer dad sneakers. Her Birkin was filled to the brim with rose water facial mist, digestive enzymes, satin eye masks, fashion magazines, iPhone chargers, and collagen protein bars. Aside from a cashmere hoodie that used to be Daphne's, I looked like an imposter cocooned in my pod with a hiking backpack and Ziploc bag full of raw almonds.

Thankfully, a dividing wall separated our seats, relieving me of the anxiety that had been building up all day long. I had no idea how I was going to be my chattiest and funniest self for seven hours straight. I was browsing the movie options on the TV in front of me when Daphne's head popped over the privacy divider. She was taking my picture, I realized after the fact.

"Look natural," she said, sounding disappointed.

"Okay," I said, resituating myself into a position that she approved of.

"Your hair looks so good. Did I tell you that already?"

"Yeah, I'm getting used to it now. Javier did a great job." I smiled.

"He's the best!" she cooed. "I think next time we can even go lighter."

Daphne reached her arm over the divider. A bottle of Ambien was in her palm. "Want one? I like to take mine before the meal comes."

I tensed up. "I don't like to take anything just in case something happens to the captain and I have to land the plane."

"Do you have a lot of experience landing planes?" She cocked her head, amused.

"If my life depended on it, I'm pretty sure that I could figure it out."

"Take half." She bit a pill in two and fed one half-moon to herself, handing its mate to me. I inhaled deeply and swallowed the medicine.

After a dinner of foie gras and brioche (Daphne passed on the brioche) followed by filet mignon and risotto (Daphne passed on the risotto), I tried to stay coherent by making small talk about how cute I found the mini bottles of olive oil and balsamic vinegar.

"These would have been perfect in your Feast of San Gennaro-themed lunch," I said.

"Which lunch?" Daphne asked groggily. "Can you pull it up?"

"I don't think I have service." I checked my phone for bars.

She looked at me, half-smiling. "Babe, you know I don't actually make any of that food, right?"

"You don't?" I stared at her, confused and fading.

"Do I *look* like I can cook? I'm afraid of food!" She laughed. "I have a chef who does all those meals. It's not even my kitchen! Haven't you ever zoomed in on the marble? It's so obvious."

I looked at her in disbelief.

"Do you think I'm a bad person now?" she whispered, leaning closer to me.

"What? Of course not," I said, trying to seem unfazed. I felt like an honor-roll student being offered a blunt under the bleachers.

"You're so innocent, Meg. I'm a curator. I'm not sitting in the kitchen making my own sourdough and shit. When would I have the time? *You* don't even have the time."

I forced a smile, trying not to take offense. Instead, I asked about her epic gingerbread house, even though I already knew the answer.

"Did you see that thing? It wasn't even edible. It had running water and electricity. Who do you think I am, Bob fucking Vila?"

"And… The cardboard Paw Patrol vehicles that the kids drove trick or treating around Tribeca?"

"Meg!" She leveled her eyes at me. "That was a sponsored deal with Michaels. It *said* #sponsored in the post. Have I taught you nothing?" Daphne shook her head with mock disappointment. "You are my favorite person, you know…"

"Don't forget your kids," I reminded her.

Daphne continued as if she hadn't heard me. "This trip is going to be so good for you. You are going to meet so many people, and they're all going to love you." She smiled. "Aside from the fall show, this is Zoe's biggest event of the year. Being a part of this is going to get you everything you want. Do you even know what you want?"

"I guess I want to be able to keep living in Manhattan. To get my kids into great schools… maybe write something real one day." I flinched at my own honesty.

"Like a book or something? You could totally do that." Daphne squeezed my hand, and a wave of warmth rolled over me.

"And you? What do you want?" I asked, curious if she had a master plan.

"I want what everybody wants…" She smirked, reclining deeper into her seat as her eyelids grew heavier.

I looked at her lying there in her three-thousand-dollar track suit with her perfectly highlighted hair. In this soft lighting, I could almost tune out the metal bead extensions peeking out between each strand.

Daphne closed her eyes and her lips parted into a dreamy smile. "More followers."

CHAPTER TWENTY-EIGHT

It was morning when we landed in Paris. My heart skipped as the plane made its descent. I stared out the window at the Eiffel Tower, almost unable to believe it wasn't an Epcot Center reproduction. Daphne's Ambien had worn off and she was back to her more coherent self. She'd managed to expertly apply a full face of makeup in the lavatory before landing, if only to cover it up with a large hat and oversized shades.

After an Air France liaison escorted us through customs and helped us get our bags, a Mercedes S-Class ferried us from the airport to our hotel. I gawked out the window the entire ride. I'd always wanted to come to Paris. I had to keep pinching myself. It was all too good to be real.

Daphne was giddy as she led me by the hand into the lobby of the Plaza Athenée. A white-gloved bellhop whisked away my fifteen-year-old duffel bag along with Daphne's custom-painted Louis Vuitton trunks.

"Madame Cole! So lovely to see you again!" an immaculately coiffed woman with a name tag that read *Cosette* said. "We have a gorgeous suite waiting for you."

"Merci. *Je ne peux pas attendre.*" Daphne smiled, reminding Cosette that she spoke French.

After pointing out the courtyard with its red window awnings and equally red geraniums, Colette walked us past the Alain Ducasse dining room, insisting we order the patisserie tower for brunch.

On the elevator up to our room, Daphne switched into work mode, ignoring Cosette and walking me through the next forty-eight hours.

"Okay, so this morning we shoot content in the room, then I go to my product shoot with a few other bloggers. I'll get into which ones to avoid later — there are some doozies. Tomorrow is the actual show. Oh, and *tonight* we have the welcome dinner. The dinner will be fun."

"What are you promoting by the way?" I asked.

"Hiking sandals. They're like Tevas, but twelve hundred dollars," she said, straight-faced.

"Diva Tevas!" I joked.

"Exactly!" Daphne nearly spit in amusement.

Long-legged Cosette led us down a carpeted hallway that smelled of vanilla and cigarettes.

"No way! You guys are giving us 361?" Daphne gushed. "This is my favorite suite in the entire hotel."

Cosette suppressed a smile and opened the door, revealing the most breathtaking room I'd ever seen. Just beyond the grand piano and chandelier decorated in black tassels was the kind of view of the Eiffel Tower that compels people to drop down to their knees and propose marriage. A ring of velvet sofas and upholstered Louis XIV chairs surrounded an antique coffee table laid out with fresh fruit, a chocolate cake, a bottle of Champagne and the Zoe tote that I'd seen in the store window with Iliya. Daphne's name was embroidered on the side of it.

"Oh my—," I gasped, collapsing into a plush loveseat.

"Don't get too comfortable," Daphne said under her breath. "This isn't the room we are sleeping in. This is just where I'm shooting all my hotel content. Check out this view. And the bathrooms...," Daphne said, trailing off as she walked into the large marble bathroom. "I hope they still have the Bulgari soaps."

"If there is anything else you need, please don't hesitate to call," Cosette said, standing by the door.

"You got the tote!" I marveled.

"Yeah, but I already have one in red." Daphne sounded bored. "Why don't you take it?"

"It has your name on it!"

"All the better." She laughed. "It's like the new letterman jacket."

"You're insane." I smiled, picking up the tote and walking toward an antique full-length mirror. "I never thought I'd hold one of these bags in real life."

"It's a great tote. You can fit your laptop in it," Daphne said with a fraction of the enthusiasm I had for it.

"Honestly, I couldn't. They want you to have it." I handed the bag back over.

"No, they want me to *post* it," she corrected me. "After that, I think they could give two fucks. No more discussing. It's yours." Daphne dove onto the king-size bed like a six-year-old girl at a slumber party. Apparently the don't-get-too-comfortable rule only applied to me. "I'm already having the best time ever! Are you?"

Before I could figure out a way to gracefully fall down onto the bed beside her, there was a knock at the door.

Daphne looked up. "That's probably the clothes,"

With my new tote on my shoulder, I walked to the door with confidence. A bellhop stood next to a rolling rack filled with standout pieces from Zoe's upcoming spring collection. Two stacks of shoeboxes teetered on either side of the trolley. The attendant wheeled it into the room and vanished before I could tip him.

"I thought you meant *our* luggage," I called out to Daphne.

"Yeah no, those bags are going straight to our real room. Although I might need to run down there for a belt or two." Daphne took her time moving from the bed to the trolley, sifting through the deliveries with laser-like focus. "No. No. This was way cuter in the look book." She held up a pink suit with matching gaucho pants. "I really had no idea what it would look like in person." She sighed. "I still don't know how they expect me to pair this stuff with hiking sandals." Daphne opened a shoebox and pulled out a pair of bedazzled hiking sandals with large white rubber soles and two-toned snakeskin straps. Aside from the flashy rhinestones and the word "Zoe" printed all over the heels, the shoes looked like something one of my mom's ex-husbands would have bought at a camping store and paired with cargo shorts and a Cliff bar.

"These are trending?" I asked incredulously.

"They will be," Daphne assured me. "And apparently they're edible. Made out of sugarcane and coffee. Smell."

I did as I was told. They did smell delicious, like breakfast in bed.

Daphne examined the clothes, arranging and rearranging them next to various pairs of shoes. "THIS! Now this is chic. You should wear this to the dinner," she said, walking toward me with a green sequined dress. She held my gaze, and I felt a blissful weightlessness. Maybe it was the jet lag, but I doubted it.

Three hours later, I woke up dry mouthed and groggy in our much smaller hotel room. Daphne was gone. My nerves settled when I saw the note she had written on the hotel stationery. "Please don't make other plans. I want you to come to my "Teva Diva" shoot at the Eiffel Tower. P.S. I have exciting news." Checking her stories, I saw that Daphne was already there. She looked beautiful and dewy as she posted about her #nonstop day.

Wearing one of Daphne's full-length sheepskin coats and one of Iliya's old soccer scarves, I headed to the Eiffel Tower, the place I'd nurtured dreams of going my entire life.

The city was already decked out for Christmas with fairy lights and poinsettias lining every block. The sky was pink, and the air smelled of roasting chestnuts and mulled wine. Cheesemongers sucked cigarettes outside their fromageries, and young couples canoodled at cafe tables on every corner. Each building I passed was more charming and historic than the last, and every passerby looked like an extra from one of the Jean-Luc Godard films I'd studied in college.

From the crosswalk at Avenue Gustave Eiffel, I could already see the flashing of cameras. The shoot was well underway as Daphne and a couple of fellow influencers walked arm in arm toward a photographer and steadicam operator. Here, in the shadow of the Eiffel Tower, Daphne looked a million times more confident than she had in Seth and Vigo's bubble bath.

"Meg!" Daphne called out, looking ready for spring in a floral sundress and denim jacket.

"Hi!" I waved. "You must be cold!" I said, noting her bare legs.

As I made my approach, I recognized two of the other women from Instagram. In a tank top and painted mom jeans was Rebecca Silva, a former Brazilian model who went by the handle @ FashionTravelPancakes. She always showed up on my explore page chowing down on a lamb skewer in Chefchaouen or eating crickets at a night market in Bangkok. Wearing a long pleated black skirt paired with a cropped neoprene vest was Kiki Chu, a pint-sized heiress from Hong Kong who went by the handle @ Kikachu.

"Come over here!" Daphne demanded during a break. "Guys, this is Meg, one of my most favorite people ever!" Daphne exclaimed. "Meg, this is Kiki, Rebecca, and Dagmar." Now I noticed another member of their pack, ridiculously tall and dressed in head-to-toe camouflage like she'd just returned from Operation Desert Storm.

"Hi," Dagmar said. "You're pretty. Are you a fashion girl?" She spoke in a thick German accent, like a villain from a James Bond movie. Dagmar continued to fire off questions while the photographer resumed taking pictures. "How do you guys know each other?" "Are you on Instagram?" "How many followers do you have?" "Are you going to the dinner?" "How old are you?" "I'm at the George V but I hate it and want to move. The turn-down service is a joke and the honeymooners in the suite next to me won't stop bonking." "Where are you staying?"

Daphne shook her head "no" behind Dagmar's shoulder, implying that I shouldn't answer Dagmar's question.

"You're with us at Athenée, aren't you guys?" Kiki turned to Daphne, oblivious.

"Yeah, but it's also not great," Daphne lied. "The Dorchester group really needs to step up their shit. It's also not a good look, considering the Sultan of Brunei isn't exactly an LGBTQ ally. But Le Bristol was all booked sooo..."

"I might be joining you later," Dagmar informed her.

Daphne shot me a look just as a stylist stepped in front of her to take her jacket and adjust her shoes. I looked down and noticed all four women had on the same atrocious sandals, each in a different color.

At the next break, when the others dispersed, I stole a minute with Daphne. "So what's the exciting news?" I asked.

"Oh!" Daphne plopped down in a director's chair with her handle painted on the back. "Can you hear the wedding bells? Susan wants to know if you would be willing to let your dog get married."

"Red can get married?" I looked at her in confusion.

"It's a whole collab with this new doggy detangler brush and they want two dogs to 'tie the knot.'"

"But aren't they anti-knots?" I was struggling to follow.

"Yeah, the pitch is that they get married, then they get groomed during the reception, and at the very end, the whole thing is annulled. It's a cute publicity stunt. *The New York Post* is going to cover it. Cha Cha is the bride, but they need another dog and I asked Susan if it could be yours. Anyway, we'd be doggie in-laws!" She smiled. "You'll only get twenty grand, but it should be easy for you. The dogs do all the work."

I coughed. That was a semester of private school. "Are you serious?"

Before Daphne could respond, the director, an older Frenchman with salt and pepper hair and enough ego to land a girlfriend far out of his league, screamed that he was ready. "Think about it," Daphne said.

Twenty thousand dollars. That was what Seth and Vigo had offered, and I still had only seen half of it. There was nothing to think about. "Red's in," I told her.

"Goody!" Daphne clapped her hands and smiled. "I'll get Susan to email you all the deets." And with that, she rushed to join the other girls.

I stood in place, watching the foursome laugh and pose as if the best of friends. Zoe brand reps swarmed the talent the moment the director yelled "Cut!" While Daphne said her goodbyes, I crept off to a private area where I could FaceTime with my family.

I was waiting for Iliya to pick up, aiming my phone at the Eiffel Tower, when Daphne slithered up from behind and rested her chin on my shoulder. "Let's go get a drink!" she said. "I need something strong if I'm going to get through tonight!"

"Yeah, sure," I said shakily. "I was just checking in with the boys. I wanted to catch Roman before he went to school," I explained, distracted by her head and wondering if she was going to move it before Iliya appeared on my phone.

"Did you do the math? It's already ten there," she informed me. "I've learned not to check in when I'm away. It's too easy to get sucked into whatever drama is going on at home."

There was still no answer on the tenth ring, so I hung up. I'd try again later.

"You haven't posted anything since we landed," Daphne informed me. "Zoe is expecting you to. They are hosting us, after all."

"Of course!" I said, caught off guard. How naive of me to think they were just operating out of the kindness of their hearts.

I held my phone up to the Eiffel Tower and took a shot. I posted the pic with the caption, "I was starting to worry that there weren't enough pictures of this tower on the internet," followed by all the Zoe hashtags I could think of.

Seeming pleased, Daphne wrapped her arm around me. She was in a chatty mood as we walked back to the hotel. "See what I mean about Dagmar! If you give her an inch... And what the fuck with asking how old you were? She's so weird. We can't let her wind up at our hotel because we will never be able to get rid of her." Daphne sighed. "How did I look in the shoot?"

"It was great. You looked gorgeous," I gushed. "The shoes are going to take a while to grow on me but —" A flock of young schoolgirls was heading toward us, with matching blazers and bobs straight out of a Madeline book. Daphne was too distracted to take note.

"Did I seem comfortable?" she asked. I told her she'd been in her element. "Good, I thought it went well too. Now at least you know that I'm not always a disaster." She went on, "I know there's room for improvement. I'm shooting my capsule collection for Revolve in February, so I really need to figure my shit out before then. The pieces look so good. I can't wait to get them on you." She paused to raise her finger. "And you will not forget to post them."

"I'm planning my rollout already," I told her.

Back at the hotel bar we ran into Kiki, the tiny heiress, and her entourage. Along with her personal makeup artist, a square-jawed blue-haired girl who looked like a Minecraft character, were a nerdy web designer who ran her blog and three gay BFFs she paid to keep her company.

The two of us sat at a nearby table sipping martinis as Daphne scrolled through her phone. A post Kiki had just uploaded revealed that she had suffered a seizure.

"It's so fucked up of her," Daphne said. "She gets everything. There isn't an issue this girl hasn't revealed. She's been ADD, OCD… had a UTI, a DUI… and even an SUI… although I suspect that one was a sponsored deal."

"SUI?"

"Stress urinary incontinence. She pees when she laughs. WHO CARES!"

"And now she ticks seizure off her list!" Daphne popped an olive in her mouth. "I suppose I'm just being jealous," she finally admitted. "I just don't get her appeal. Her style isn't even that original!" I glanced back at Kiki again, who I saw was wearing a unitard made entirely out of bottle caps. "Her grandfather is like the Sumner Redstone of Singapore, so visibility for her is easy. She hosted this show called *The Fake* where five strangers are thrown into a dinner party and have to pick out whose handbag is real and whose is a knock-off. It ran for sixteen seasons!" Daphne rolled her eyes. "I'm just internet famous. Not even... I'm app famous." Daphne sulked. "I need to get a third kid. It's really the only way to stay in the game."

"I still haven't met the two you *do* have," I said, trying to lighten the mood. "And you don't need more children to stay in the game. You *are* the game!" I protested. "What you've already done, most women only dream about. You didn't have any of this given to you. You built it with your own two Photoshopped hands," I said, swigging what remained of my overpriced cocktail.

Daphne laughed. "How do you know I Photoshop my hands?"

"Because you're a perfectionist. You don't let anything slip."

Daphne smiled at me like a guru pleased with her disciple's spiritual progress. "You're really learning how all this works."

I felt two large hands pressing down on my shoulders. For a second, I thought it was Iliya. "Meee again!" Dagmar's Teutonic singsong caused me to jump. "What are you guys going to do before dinner? Should we all go somewhere for drinks?"

Daphne looked up and smiled a fake smile. "I have to do an interview. There's a reporter coming from *Marie Claire*."

"Online or for the actual magazine?" I could hear the competitive streak in Dagmar's voice.

"They said both," Daphne replied.

"That usually means just online." Dagmar pressed her mouth into a frown. "*Argh*, they were giving me such a hard time up front about Helmut." She looked down at her purse and I realized the fluffy lining was actually a terrier. Helmut had milky eyes and a *Hedwig and the Angry Inch* bouffant.

"They thought he was a possum! Can you believe it? This guy who has three hundred thousand followers was mistaken for a rodent!" Dagmar announced loudly. "He could tell they were giving him no love and he was NOT happy. And you know how Helmut gets when he isn't happy."

As Daphne and I walked toward the elevator, she told me about Helmut's better days. In his younger years, back when he didn't look like a rat pumped full of formaldehyde, Helmut had been quite an Instagram sensation. At one point he even had a sister that looked just like him, but she was killed in an unspeakable gender-reveal accident.

"Now he's just scary to look at," Daphne said with a shudder. "That's why they didn't approach Dagmar for the doggy detangler deal. She is going to shit a brick when she finds out that we're doing it." She clasped her hands diabolically. "I can't wait for dinner!"

"Please don't bring it up," I said. "She scares me!"

"Oh, she's harmless. She's just weird."

We entered our room to find a bouquet of flowers sitting on the desk in the corner. There was a note. "Thank you for a successful day!" Daphne read out loud. "Can't wait to see you tonight. Love, Your Zoe Family."

Daphne uncorked her gifted bottle of Champagne and poured us each a generous glass. "They are so classy." Daphne mused, setting down her drink and snapping a pic with her phone. "I have to post these." She stalled. "What would you write?"

I pretended to be thinking, too buzzed to be of any real use.

"I already know that this post is going to underperform. If you've seen one bouquet of flowers you've seen them all." Daphne walked around the bed and came toward me slowly. My neck went warm, and I gulped.

"Why not write something ridiculous like, "My husband is too cheap to ever spring for bouquets this fancy. Thanks for always raising the bar @Zoe!" I said, looking out the window, scared she might be able to detect my nerves. She was standing so close to me.

A bright smile broke across her face. "You're just fucking brilliant." She shook her head typing.

"I'm just awkward, is the truth," I corrected her. "I'm terrible with sentimentality." I could hear my voice catching. "Maybe I'm just scared of vulnerability."

"Or maybe you're just fucking funny."

Our faces were now so close that I could see the congested pores on Daphne's chin and the slight creases around her eyes. I wanted to kiss her and be her all at once.

"I..." I hesitated, as if standing on the ledge of a building deciding whether or not to jump. Before I could say anything else, my phone started ringing. My stomach lurched when I saw who it was: Marina.

I immediately answered.

"Meg." Marina coughed. "I have food poisoning. I've been vomiting my brains out all morning. Bodega sushi. My body is rejecting these toxins."

I was screwed. Iliya had his Chelsea House holiday party that night. Investors were going to be there, Saro was going to be there, everyone was going to be there. This wasn't just bad. This was really fucking bad.

"Where are you now?" I asked.

"I'm at my place," she replied.

"Wait, then who is with Felix? I double-checked the time.

"Iliya. I told him that I had a survey thing I had to go to because I was hoping that with enough fluids I could beat this, but it's not happening," she continued. "You have to tell my brother."

"Me? But you're the one who's sick!"

"If I do it, he's gonna think I'm lying," she countered.

"*Are* you lying?" I was pacing around the room, trying to sober up.

"I'm really sorry, Meg. I have to go hurl."

I stood there for a moment thinking about my options. It was six-thirty in Paris, so that meant that it was twelve-thirty in New York, still early enough to find someone. But who? Iliya's mother could barely see, Seth and Vigo knew nothing about children, and Bubby had the same obligation as Iliya. "Fuck." I let off a long exhale.

"What?" Daphne asked from the other side of the room, finishing the last of her Champagne.

"My sister-in-law is sick and Iliya has to be at this event he can't miss. We have no sitter." I started running through different scenarios in my mind. "He could put the kids down before he goes at eight. But that's if Roman actually goes to bed at eight. And even if he does go to bed at eight, who the hell is going to stay with them after? I have nobody."

"There's no nanny?" Daphne looked at me confused.

I shook my head.

"No weekend babysitter?" she asked.

"Nope." I tried to take a deep breath.

"A housekeeper? An intern? An au pair that you pay under the table?"

Daphne ran down the list as she started shooting off texts. Moments later, she looked up. "Okay, I got you someone. My girl Wynne can do it."

"Wynne! The girl who gave us the clothes at your building that day?" I remembered liking her. I hoped I did anyway. "Can I trust her? Can she stay late? He's not going to be able to leave until his boss does."

"She's outstanding," Daphne said. "I've known her for at least ten years. Super trustworthy. And yes, she's a big girl, she can stay up late." I tried not to watch as Daphne changed into a tailored two-piece suit, ditching her bra and buttoning the jacket at her navel. "You can trust her, trust me. I just shared her number with you." Daphne pulled her locks into a clip, then dropped to the floor. "Where are my Manolos?" Daphne giggled. "Where the fuck are they? Did they walk away?"

I looked over at the bar and saw the Champagne bottle was empty. I'd only had half a glass.

Just then, the phone rang. The interviewer from *Marie Claire* was waiting in the lobby. Daphne was in no condition to be talking to anyone with a recording device, but I knew better than to stand in her way.

"Be downstairs in an hour," Daphne said, grabbing her bag. As she stumbled into the hall, she had more instructions for me. "Do the sequined dress. And wear your hair up."

"At your service," I called after her.

As soon as I was alone, I texted with Wynne and explained my situation. If she could drop whatever her plans for the night were and watch my kids while I cavorted with Instagram stars halfway across the world, she'd be saving my life (I didn't get into the cavorting part). The second she agreed, I called Iliya, who was too frazzled to put up a fight.

"And you know her?" he double-checked.

"Of *course*, I know her, Iliya. And your sister loves her," I said, stress-eating all the Jordan almonds in the mini bar.

"And what about the kids?"

"The kids aren't even going to see her. This is Daphne's nanny of over ten years. She's practically part of their family. Just order her a pizza and tell her to make herself at home." I was now standing in front of the wardrobe rack, deep in a staring contest with the incredible sequined dress.

"How is everything else?" I said, thumbing through the other dresses on the rack. I stopped to process a not-so-classic LBD with a built-in bustier for three breasts.

Iliya was still unloading about the stress of single parenting when I tuned back into the conversation. "He doesn't want to wear clothes and if he does, he wants them to be matching but what is the problem with mixing navy and gray? I'm no fashion icon but what the fuck?"

"And Red?" I asked.

"RED? He won't even wear black!"

"Not the color, our dog!"

Iliya grunted. "Same as when you left. I called the vet and she said to bring him in but I was waiting for you to schedule."

"Is it urgent? Because if it's urgent, Iliya, just take him. I have a deal where he is going to make us twenty-grand, so I need him healthy."

"You want me to take him to the vet for one of your *deals*?"

Shame churned through me. "No, he's clearly sick and I want him to get better. But that's a lot of money," I pointed out. "Can you just call the vet and see what options are available?"

"Can *you* call? I'm trying to do a lot of things here, Meg. I didn't even go to work today!"

"I get it, you're a big deal. But it's not my fault that your sister ate shitty tuna rolls. I'm trying to help. And I'm halfway around the world."

"I'm well aware of that," he said, his resentment oozing through the phone.

I took a deep breath. "Look, I don't want to fight. I appreciate you letting me take a weekend trip."

"Thursday's not really the weekend," Iliya pointed out, then changed gears. "So how is it?"

I walked to the window and drew back the curtain. The view of a brick wall wasn't exactly on par with the one offered by our first room, but it was still a brick wall in *Paris*. "It's been flying by," I told him. "We've been so busy I haven't really seen the sights. But it's magical here and the city looks so gorgeous with all the likes."

"Stop," Iliya said. "Did you just say, 'with all the *likes*'?"

"No. I said *lights*. It looks gorgeous with all the lights. For the holidays."

"What time is it there? Have you been drinking?" he asked judgmentally.

"Not really…. A bit," I admitted.

Iliya didn't say anything for a moment. The silence was worse than hearing whatever thought about me was running through his mind.

After we got off, I looked at the clock and realized that I needed to get down to the lobby. Daphne was a stickler about time, at least when it pertained to the punctuality of other people.

CHAPTER TWENTY-NINE

The green sequined Zoe dress had a giant slit that ran from the bottom left hem all the way up to my right hip, as I discovered once I'd slipped into it. I'd never shown so much leg in my life. Not even back in the day when my body was nothing but legs. Stepping into a pair of heels, I looked at the woman in the mirror and felt a surge of confidence. The buzz helped, sure, but I felt like a million bucks. Or whatever the Zoe dress retailed for.

When I came downstairs, Daphne was sitting at the bar whispering into a brunette woman's ear. The moment she saw me, she jerked back and stopped speaking. A group of French businessmen turned their heads to ogle me as I walked past them.

"Meg." Daphne smiled, unable to stop staring at the slit up my leg. "What a dress!" She stared a moment longer, then remembered the person to her left.

"This is Alek, she's one of my most favorite people ever."

So she had multiple "most favorite people ever," perhaps one in every port. I tried not to grimace at "Alek," the mystery woman Lauren had compared me to in that unmistakably worrisome tone once upon a rooftop dinner party. Now that I was standing closer to "Alek" (I still couldn't think about her without the quotes), I saw that she looked just like me, only about ten years younger. Same brown eyes, same pretty enough face, same bushy eyebrows. Only difference was her dark hair. I felt a little queasy.

"Nice to meet you," Alek said, clearly having the same thought I was but playing things far more cool. "Love that look. It's a killer."

"*She's* a killer," Daphne corrected. "Anyway, we should get going. It was really good to see you, A."

"You too," Alek said wistfully. "Do you know when you'll be back to town?"

"Not for a while, baby." The second the word came out of her mouth, I felt something inside me burst.

Daphne kissed Alek on both cheeks while clocking my reaction out of the corner of her eye. Alek looked at me too. "I used to have that hair color," Alek said.

"You did... It looked great on you." Daphne smiled. Alek gave a sigh and watched us head out.

Once we were in the car on the way to dinner, I couldn't resist asking Daphne about her friend. "How do you know Alek?"

"We met a few years back. She used to live in Dumbo. Good girl. Super talented writer. But young. Too young for me."

Overcome with jealousy, I turned to the window and gazed at the Seine.

"She brought us party favors." Daphne opened her clutch and pulled out a bag of white powder. She dipped her pinky nail into the bag, shoveling up a bump that promptly disappeared up her nose. "I can't wait for you to see this dinner. Salvatore is a fucking trip. Have some?"

"I... I should probably eat something."

Daphne playfully shoved my shoulder. "Come on, you love it. Cocaine, concerts, and what was the third one?"

"Cult status movies." I softened slightly. She remembered our first text exchange.

"That's it," Daphne said, sliding closer. She excavated more white powder and held her nail up to my nose. I inhaled and could almost immediately feel my heart speeding up.

The car stopped in front of a wide stone stairway leading down to the water. A white riverboat waited at the dock below, with tuxedo-clad men ready to help us aboard. In the boat's lavishly decorated parlor, fashion influencers, VIP shoppers, and a smattering of corporate types bantered, waiting to take their seats at a long table that stretched the length of the ship. Dagmar and Kiki were among the few attendees I recognized.

Daphne pointed to a beautiful man in red leather pants and chain-link shirt holding court in the corner. "That is Salvatore. Isn't he hot?"

With long curly hair, exaggerated cheekbones and kohl-rimmed Jared Leto eyes, Salvatore *was* sexy. He seemed like the kind of guy who might try to suck your blood one night and then make you watch him suck himself off the next. Salvatore smiled lasciviously as we approached. He then pointed at me and kissed his fingers. "*Très magnifique.*"

"I think he likes your dress." Daphne laughed.

"Thank god," I said, my heart still pumping faster than I was used to. "He definitely seems like someone who wouldn't hold back if he didn't."

"You okay?" Daphne asked. "You seem a little off."

Before I could respond, a waiter rang a bell signaling for everyone to be seated. As soon as we sat down, large towers filled with oysters, shrimp, and tuna tartare materialized on the table. In front of each plate was a gift box, neatly wrapped in white paper with a sterling-colored bow. Several photographers circled the table like fish swimming in and out of a coral reef, documenting the proceedings from every angle.

Sitting across from me was a wacky-looking designer chick from Silver Lake named Jane who went by the handle @JanesAddictions. She had aqua hair and wore a necklace that informed people she was bipolar.

"I hope it's the Chinese handcuff bracelet! I've been coveting one since last year." Jane tore into her box and pulled out a keychain. "Really?" She turned to Dagmar, waving the gift in her face. "Is he kidding with these? What are my kids going to say?" Hanging from the sterling silver key loop was what looked like a tiny mold of somebody's cock and balls.

"I wanted to share a piece of my heart with you but found the 'heart' thing a bit of a cliché so instead decided to give you an organ I liked better," Salvatore shared with a glint in his eyes. "They are my body!" He paused for effect. "We did a limited number, and these will NEVER be available for purchase! Only for my most beloved."

Daphne looked at me. "I told you we'd need drugs for this."

The Champagne continued to flow as a sixteen-course meal unfolded before us, each plate more decadent than the next.

"The service sucks here." Dagmar stared at me like it was my fault. "And I was in the middle of fishing." She went on to explain what she meant. Fishing, it turned out, was sending messages to the Instagram accounts of random companies in the hopes that they might send products in exchange for a post. "Sometimes they don't even respond, they just leave you as 'seen.'" She sighed. "But that's half the fun. It's strangely therapeutic. Like biting your toenails."

After several vodka shots, Jane started waving her new keychain in the air. "So seriously, whose keychain do I need to suck to get seated front row at the show tomorrow?"

Daphne did a spit take, Champagne spraying everywhere. She couldn't contain her laughter. I pretended to think Jane's joke was just as funny as Daphne did. But I wasn't a good enough actress.

I had to give it to her. Jane was quick. And I was feeling slow. I tried to look for openings where I could and remind Daphne that

I was the funny one, but I was too off my face. I could feel myself spinning out of conversational relevance as Daphne slipped
through my fingers.

Salvatore clinked his glass and gave a toast. "Each of you is here
because of your dedication to fashion. I am honored that you have
supported Zoe for all these years and stand with me as we revolu-
tionize the hiking sandal. You are all — how do you say? My little
cabbages."

I looked down at my keychain again. "These are cabbages? I
thought they were supposed to be testicles."

I was louder than I'd realized. Salvatore shot me a look. He wasn't
amused. "I love your guyliner!" I squeaked.

I scurried off to the bathroom as soon as Salvatore's remarks had
concluded. Trying to get a hold of myself, I splashed cold water
on my face. A knock came at the door. At first I didn't answer, but
there was another one, this time more urgent.

I cracked open the door and Daphne pushed her way in. I
thought she was going to berate me or slap me back to my senses.
But instead, she grabbed my body and began kissing me. Her
tongue pressed into my mouth as she pushed me up against the
mirror. She pinned one arm against the wall as she moved her
hand up my dress, groping between my thighs. I'd envisioned
this moment so many times, yet I was paralyzed with fear. Did I
want to do this? Before I could practice restraint and tell her that
I loved my husband or join her in her passion, she stopped and
pulled away. "That's better. Now you look a little more relaxed."
I stared at her, out of breath. "Do you want another bump?"
she asked casually, cutting up a line and snorting it straight off
the sink.

I was shaking. "I'm fine."

Daphne smiled, as if nothing had just transpired between us. "You feel better? You okay?" She patted me softly on the cheek. "That was hot. Let's do that again sometime." And then she vanished.

I stood there for a good five minutes trying to understand what had just happened. Part of me wanted her to fuck my brains out while the other part of me wanted never to see her again. What game was she playing? Whatever the answer, I was losing.

When I returned to the table, I found that Daphne had helped herself to my seat so that she could be closer to Jane. She was regaling her with the exact same stories she'd told when we first met. Daphne finally acknowledged me, all bubbly. "Meg, you have to keep Jane company at the show tomorrow. You guys are going to be seated together!"

"You and I are the low-level influencers who didn't make the front-row cut." Jane laughed.

"That's not true!" Daphne insisted. "You guys are still in Paris at the Zoe show! Think of how many girls wish they were in your shoes right now."

"You mean our hiking sandals," Jane said. She couldn't keep the annoyance from her tone. "You know only the front row gets photographed. We are just tagalongs. There is a big difference between sitting next to Cardi B and the guy who does her makeup."

Jane was upset but Daphne was cracking up. "You are so funny!" She was squealing. "I can't believe we've never hung out before!"

Daphne was over me. I could see it in her eyes. I knew her better than she knew herself. She'd found a new favorite. Or a new "most favorite" as she was prone to calling us.

The dinner refused to end. And all I wanted to do was to go back to the hotel. But Daphne was still too high to turn in after the boat docked. "We're gonna go to a club by the Bastille," Daphne informed me.

"Who is we?" I already knew the answer.

"Oh, me and Jane and a few of the other girls. But you seem tired. You should go get some rest. Show starts at nine a.m. tomorrow."

Blinking back tears, I looked at Daphne. She was scanning the crowd, trying to find Jane. What point was there in trying to fix things? I just nodded along and told her that I'd see her in the morning.

The hotel phone woke me up. Well, that and a pounding headache.

"Hello?" I answered.

The voice on the other end was speaking French. All I could make out was something about "le glam team."

"Okay," I said, groggily reaching for the lights and looking around the room for Daphne. There was a knock at the door. I rushed to get it and almost tripped over the body splayed out on the floor. It was Daphne's. Her phone was still secured tightly in her hand and one of her shoes was on.

"One second!" I called out as I tried shaking her awake.

"Daphne. DAPHNE!" I slapped her face, but she still didn't budge. With no other option, I opened the door.

"What are you going to do?" Marie, a nicotine-stained makeup artist, asked when she took in the situation.

"She's not going anywhere," said Chuckie, a towering man with dreadlocks and a duffle bag full of hair pieces.

"She has to," Marie said, panicking. "If she isn't there, she will be blacklisted. Nobody will work with her again. Us, too. You know how Salvatore gets. This is going to come back on us. She's in the front row and he's expecting us to deliver her!"

Chuckie hummed ominously as the three of us carried Daphne to the bed.

"Daphne?" I called her name one more time. Daphne suddenly sat up and looked at me, a glint of recognition in her eyes.

"Hi, baby." She smiled, then turned her head in the other direction and vomited all over a pillow. Before I could react, she rolled over and passed out again.

"*Dégueulasse!*" Marie shuddered. "You know what's going to happen. It will all be my fault. I'm good as sacked." She picked up the cordless phone on the bedside table and threw it at Chuckie's shoulder. "We both are."

"*Merde!*" Chuckie exclaimed.

It was already almost eight o'clock. The show started at nine and there was no way in hell Daphne was going to make it.

"You look enough like her. Why don't you just go?" Chuckie suggested. "I have her hair pieces here. We can match the length exactly."

"Are you kidding?" I cried.

Chuckie looked at me. "It's not like she's famous. She's internet famous."

"Worse! She's app famous," Marie added.

"And it's not like these girls look like their posts in real life anyway," Chuckie said, growing excited.

"*C'est genial!*" Marie exclaimed, lighting up a Gauloise.

"This is utterly batshit," I said.

"You have a better idea?" Marie stared at me.

I didn't. I was furious with Daphne, but I wasn't going to let her piss her career away over one drunken night. Thank god Iliya was fast asleep and half a world away. I could only imagine what his advice would be.

"Do you know which look she's supposed to wear?" Marie flipped through the wardrobe rack like she was searching for a misplaced record.

"No idea." I shook my head.

"The Zoe publicist has certain pieces already reserved for bigger celebs," Marie explained, picking Daphne's phone up off the floor and handing it to me. "Well, go through her messages and find out."

I glanced at the clock.

"*Allez-y!*" Marie exclaimed. "We're running out of time."

I pulled Daphne's head toward her phone, using the face recognition feature to unlock it. Scrolling through her most recent emails, I found an update from the Zoe team. I had my choice between the boiled wool tube dress with cut-out nipples or the mustard silk culottes and raincoat made out of what looked like used condoms. I opted for the latter.

I grabbed Marie's cigarette out of her hand and took a drag, psyching myself up. "Okay," I said. "Let's do this."

CHAPTER THIRTY

The Zoe show was held inside a former Yiddish theater in Northern Paris that had been transformed into the Garden of Eden. I was beset with a case of nerves, but the paparazzi lining the streets seemed untroubled by the sight of me disembarking the car. I'd already disabled the lock on Daphne's phone, so it was with ease that I could post "her" updates in the moments leading up to the big event. While Daphne and I had similar hair, especially now thanks to the seven pounds of extensions weighing my head down, we still didn't look alike. She was model-gorgeous, with ample cleavage. I was plain and ordinary, with no boobs and a math teacher ass. But the glam team had done one hell of a job. The people that I needed to dupe — aka the people who didn't really know Daphne — would be none the wiser.

An assistant checked Daphne's name off a list, then escorted me and Daphne's oversized sunglasses to her front-row seat. Every time a camera snapped, I tried to pull my hair over my face or glance down at my sandals.

Kiki scurried in and helped herself to the seat next to me. Dressed in a fur-collared shirt and leather pants with a detachable zebra tail, she looked like some kind of dominatrix-minotaur crossbreed.

"Can you believe Tony, Jhoni, and Tao weren't even allowed to sit on the balcony?" she said distractedly. She was busy on her phone, refreshing the Zoe hashtag.

"That's wild," I said.

Another moment passed before Kiki looked up at me. She gasped. "What the fuck? Where's Daphne?"

My heart pounded and my eyes flared. The lights were starting to dim. "She's still at the hotel sick. Please just go with it." I picked up Daphne's phone and started shooting.

"You even know what you're doing with that thing?" Kiki asked like I was holding a buzz saw.

"I have a pretty good idea." I nodded, adding a filter to the video and tagging both Daphne and Kiki.

The room was pitch black, silent but for the sound of a heartbeat. Gradually, the noise built into a screeching cacophony of animals mating or dying, I wasn't entirely sure. Models strutted down the runway in their Diva Tevas looking hungry and like they wanted to fight. The mud on the catwalk splashed onto the front row with each intentional stomp. The music got louder and more intense. I felt a dollop of mud hit my cheek. And then — no models, no lights, no sound. The whole thing lasted under five minutes.

"That's *it*?" I turned to Kiki, confused.

"Yeah, it's always shorter than you think." She nodded. "That was brilliant though." The lights came back up and all of the models returned to the stage for a victory lap. They were covered head to toe in muck, making it impossible to see any of the outfits. Finally, Salvatore stepped out, in a simple and immaculately clean sweatsuit.

He waved and blew kisses to the audience. It wasn't until he turned to walk off stage that I noticed that his sweats were assless. I snapped a pic and gave it a very Daphne caption. "Suns out Buns out," I wrote, followed by several beach umbrella emojis and Zoe hashtags. Kiki looked over my shoulder. I could tell she was impressed by my work.

By eleven I was back at the hotel, giddy as a cat burglar who'd just cleaned out the Isabella Stewart Gardner Museum. I was eager to tell Daphne all about my success, but when I entered our room, it was empty. I reached for the phone in my bag and tried to call Daphne, only to remember I was calling her on her own device. I then tried my own number. The ringing came from under the bed. I pulled my phone out to see that I had twenty-six missed calls and fifteen text messages.

"Oh my god." My stomach dropped. Why hadn't I brought both phones with me?

The first message was from Wynne. "Your dog is super sick and is having diarrhea. I have to take him downstairs. I texted your husband but haven't heard back. Hope it's okay."

The next text was from Iliya and came almost twenty minutes later. "Meg, pick up the PHONE. The fire department is at our apartment and the babysitter isn't answering."

The third text simply read: "MEGAN!"

I stopped reading the rest and called Iliya. He'd been trying to reach me since nine a.m. Which was three a.m. his time.

"Iliya!" I was relieved to hear his voice, but terrified of what he might tell me. He was seething. "Where the fuck were you?"

"I was… at a fashion show." As the words came out of my mouth I was flooded with guilt.

"That girl you hired." He was so furious that he could barely finish his sentences without stopping to catch his breath. "She isn't a nanny. She barely knows your friend. How could you be so insanely irresponsible!?"

"Stop, Iliya. Just tell me, are the kids okay?" My entire body was shaking.

"The kids are fine." He paused. "The apartment… isn't. The fire department had to break down the front door."

"What are you talking about?" I exclaimed.

"She was reheating pizza in the oven when she locked herself out."

"Why was she out of the apartment?"

"Red was having diarrhea all over the floor," he grunted. "She ran out with him and left her phone inside. The neighbors called Ken and he called me."

"Oh my god." I was crying.

"Roman was scared to death, Meg. I don't know what we are doing to that kid, but it isn't good."

"I'm so sorry." I was slobber-crying. "Can I talk to him?"

"Not right now." His voice was cold. "I just got him back to sleep. I'll see you tomorrow. You're still coming home, right?"

"Of course." I sniffled as I got off the phone.

"What the fuck is wrong with you?" Daphne seethed, bursting through the door.

"What the fuck is wrong with *me*?" I screamed. "Are you kidding? I thought you said that Wynne was trustworthy. She nearly killed my sons!"

"What kind of weird *Single White Female* game are you playing?" Daphne walked straight up to me, ripping a clip-in extension off my head. She was not concerned about the welfare of my family.

"You told me that Wynne was your nanny." Anger flooded my voice.

"I never said that," Daphne scoffed.

"Yes you did. You told me that she'd worked for you for ten years. That I could trust her with my children!" I shot back.

"Meg, you just hijacked my phone and went to the fucking Zoe show in my place! Is that what this has been all about? Do you think that you are me? Because you're not. And you never will be."

"Daphne, you were drunk and passed out in your own vomit. I went to save your ass!"

"Save me!? You wore the mustard silk culottes and that was the same look that Cardi B was in. That's all anybody is talking about!" She snatched her phone out of my hand. "I need some air." The door slammed behind her.

I sat there, paralyzed and scared of all that I was on the brink of losing, if I hadn't lost it already. Instead of giving in to my desire to start throwing furniture around the room like a member of Mötley Crüe, I washed off my war paint and ripped out the rest of my fake hair. I'd get on an earlier flight.

CHAPTER THIRTY-ONE

Twelve hours later, I slipped through the busted-up door to our apartment. It was nine p.m. New York time and Iliya was sitting in the living room waiting for me.

"Hey," I said cautiously. I couldn't read Iliya's expression. "Are the boys asleep?" I put down my things and walked over to Red. He was on his side. He let off the faintest of whimpers. "Maybe I should take him in tonight," I said, worried.

"Maybe," Iliya replied. "Or maybe you should just call Tom and Rita Hanks and see if they have any thoughts."

I was speechless.

"Tell me something." He got up to hand me a printed copy of my school statement. "Did you even read this thing through?"

"Apparently *you* did," I replied. "Is there a problem?"

"Do you even recall what you wrote? Because it's fucking insane!"

I glared at him. "You just don't like playing the game, but this is what everybody does."

"Claim to be Olympic athletes?"

"I was writing ad copy. And ads always overpromise!" I insisted.

Iliya shook his head in disbelief. "Do you hear yourself? Listen to how frantic you sound."

"I'm not frantic! I'm trying to keep our son from falling through the cracks!"

"How about you just work on keeping him safe in his own home! Do you understand what we could have been dealing with here? I thought the police were going to arrest me for child endangerment." Iliya's voice was getting froggy, the way it did when he was about to cry.

Before he could continue, we heard a thud from the kitchen. I turned to check on Red. The spot on the floor where he'd been resting was empty. I felt all the blood drain from my face.

It's weird when an animal drops dead. You just don't hear about it happening all too often, but that's what happens. Or happened to Red, anyway. One minute he was there, the next he'd toppled over and was gone. When I saw his sweet body on the kitchen floor, I let out a shriek. I threw myself on top of him, sobbing.

I'd had Red since he was a baby. Since I was baby. I was twenty-one years old when I got him. He'd known me longer than Iliya had. Our relationship changed when I moved in with Iliya and kept changing when I had Roman and then Felix, but he'd remained my faithful sidekick. I'd often pictured him dying, sometimes because of his age and other times because I didn't feel like walking him. But I always expected his passing to be more theoretical and gradual.

I would never get over what had just happened. I'd hardly petted him when I'd walked through the smashed-in door. I'd spent the last moments of his life screaming at my husband, and the last six months of his life staring at my phone. No wonder he'd collapsed. Who wouldn't have?

Iliya stayed home with the boys while I took Red's body to the 24-hour vet. The doctor explained that heart attacks in dogs were extremely rare and that any vet telling someone that their pet had a heart attack was in fact just lying out of sheer laziness. Maybe he had an aneurysm, maybe there had been internal bleeding. She couldn't really say without sending pieces of him to a lab. I wished that she would have just lied to me and said that it was a heart attack.

I left her office that night with nothing but a receipt and a small Ziploc bag filled with a mound of his hair for remembrance. When I returned, Iliya was sitting on the couch with Roman curled between his legs, fast asleep.

"I paid the extra hundred to have him cremated," I said. I walked toward Iliya and collapsed into his arms.

"Good." He enveloped me in a hug as I soaked his shirt with tears. Even if he was still angry, Iliya put that aside and was there for me in my moment of grief. Which only made me cry harder. I didn't deserve him. I kept crying as I mourned my former dog and my former self.

My sobbing eventually woke Roman. From the look on his face, I could tell that Iliya had already tried explaining what had happened. "Mommy, where is he? Where did you take him?"

"I…" As much as I wanted to shield my son from the harsh realities of human existence, I was not going to win a war against the world. "Red went to Kevin's, honey."

"Forever?" he asked.

"For now," I answered. I squeezed his body tightly, as if by applying pressure I could somehow stop his aching.

I waited until the next morning to text Daphne and tell her what had happened. I knew that I shouldn't reach out, but a part of me was still hoping she'd be the friend I thought she was.

"Oh, no. So sorry, babe!" she replied casually. "I'll tell Susan. I'm sure she can find another dog. They wanted to do it on New Year's Eve, which is just annoying. Who wants to spend their New Year's Eve working? It's for the best."

I was trembling. *What* was for the best… *My dog's death?* I wanted to shake her and make her see how hurtful she was being. But I didn't want to risk more rejection. So I let it go.

Two weeks after Red's passing, I found myself still reaching to fill his water bowl and searching for his torso in my bed. I was sleeping alone, since Iliya had co-opted the couch. He needed space and was still unable to speak with me about anything that didn't concern the kids. In other words, he was pissed. And he didn't even know the half of it.

In an effort to assuage Iliya's anger, I invited his family for Christmas Eve. Iliya seemed appreciative, though he could barely meet my eye. While the turkey cooked in our god-awful oven, Iliya caught up with his mother, sister, and her dentist date. I hid out in the bathroom.

From my perch on the toilet seat, I stared at a picture of Daphne and Kip in Saint Barts. Tanya and Howie were there, too, and Lauren and her husband appeared to be staying nearby, on someone's yacht. I assumed all the kids were in tow but hadn't yet seen them posted. All of the Insta stories were videos of sweaty women spraying each other with magnums of Champagne, claiming that they were "100 percent THAT BITCH."

I hadn't seen Daphne since Paris. It almost felt like it had all been a dream. In a picture that she captioned, "I've got 99 problems but a beach ain't one!" Daphne looked happy, without a care in the world. I missed her, but I also saw through her smile. She used to make my stomach do somersaults. Now she just made me nauseous.

I left her page but didn't get up. Instead, I posted a picture of myself sitting on the toilet and captioned it, "Somehow my mother-in-law managed to get herself re-invited to Christmas. If anybody needs me, I'll be in my office." I now had over 75,000 followers who were all waiting to hear what I'd done for the holidays. My bathroom selfie would likely disappoint them. But not posting anything would disappoint them more.

"Meg?" Iliya knocked on the door. "Everything okay?" He knew I hadn't so much as unbuttoned my pants. He knew I was sitting there staring at my screen, snorting up content.

"Yeah. One sec!" I said, deleting the picture and opening the door.

"This arrived." He held up an envelope. "Some weird dude."

Inside was a Christmas card along with the remainder of my NBD retainer fee. I looked at Iliya. "I looked at Ilya. Vigo?"

"Does he braid his bangs?" Iliya asked.

"No, that's Seth." I smiled softly. "That was cool of him."

I stepped into the living room feeling guilty for ever having doubted them. Seth and Vigo may have been nuts, but they were good nuts.

Roman burrowed into the pile of presents like a pig rooting around for truffles.

Dasha was grilling Irving, Marina's divorced dentist boyfriend. "So, what exactly is your intention with my Marina?"

Irving wasn't as old as I'd pictured. Whenever Marina had spoken about him or his kids, I'd envisioned him with an oxygen tank like that little man in the wheelchair who married Anna Nicole Smith. But Irving seemed youthful and sweet. He also clearly liked Marina a lot. I could tell he was the kind of guy who made plans and actually followed through. The kind of person who sent flowers and sat Shiva with you after you lost your dog. A memory of Red floated to mind, and I tried to push it back where it came from. Roman was simultaneously ripping into two presents. "Hey, kiddo!" I called out. "Save some for the morning."

Marina was telling her mother about her and Irving's plans for New Year's. "We're going to Boca!" Marina sounded giddy.

"I have a small condo there and a little time off," Irving said, modestly.

"Do you make a good living?" Dasha asked. "My Marina drives a Mercedes." I caught Iliya's eye, and we shook our heads at each other.

"He knows, Ma," Marina said.

Evidently mortified, Iliya announced he was taking Felix to bed.

"And you know she's studying to be a nurse." Dasha brought a game of Yahtzee and a small box over to Roman, then sat back down on her ever-present inflatable pillow on the couch.

"A nurse?" Irving shot Marina a look of confusion. "I didn't know that."

Marina hadn't been in nursing school in over a year, but still hadn't worked up the courage to tell her mother she'd dropped out.

"I'm a woman of many masks," she said.

I was pretty sure she meant "many talents" but Irving didn't seem to care. He placed a hand on her knee and smiled at her like a lovestruck teen.

"Open it," Dasha instructed Roman.

"Wow! A knife! Thank you!" Roman exclaimed.

"No knives!" I said, snatching the weapon out of Roman's clutches.

My objections were lost on Dasha, who was back to grilling Irving.

"How many kids do you have?" Dasha asked. "Where's the mother? She's probably feeling quite intimidated seeing my Marina on your arm."

"Well, I have two and they haven't met. I really don't want the kids knowing that I'm dating quite yet. This all happened so suddenly." Irving smiled.

"You don't want the kids knowing about her? Why not? She's perfect! She's a ten! No, she's a twelve!"

Iliya interrupted the interrogation as he returned to the room, presenting his mother with a gift.

Dasha opened the small box to find a pair of gold hoop earrings I'd picked out in the jewelry district and a larger box filled with a bunch of free face products that I'd been asked to post about.

"You shouldn't have!" she said, when I was pretty sure what she actually meant was, "You should have a long time ago!"

Marina explained some of the more cutting-edge creams to her mom while Irving pulled me aside. "How am I doing?"

"Good. I think she really likes you," I whispered. "Did you make her a night guard?"

"A great one."

"Cool. I know she's into that." I smiled, then looked over at Roman, who was chomping on a candy cane he'd pulled off the tree.

"Think he'll need braces?"

"Hard to tell." Irving shrugged. "Most kids do."

Our eyes met, and it took every ounce of restraint not to suggest that he and I do a "collab."

CHAPTER THIRTY-TWO

Our move was scheduled for January 2. Our bags were already packed, and there wasn't much to do but wait. Every time I looked on Instagram, I fell deeper into a depression. People's holiday vacations and adventures unfolded before me with up-to-the-moment footage from Grand Cayman, Whistler, Hawaii, Switzerland, Cabo, Aspen, and even the Maldives. Everyone but me was #livingtheirbestlife somewhere wildly romantic, sporting either Brazilian bikinis or brightly colored puffer jackets.

As luck would have it, NBD was shaping up to be one of the biggest earning products of the holiday season. Our campaign didn't just work — it *rocked*. Every time I logged into my account, a sponsored post popped up with Daphne's face. She was going to haunt me forever, and it was nobody's fault but my own.

Iliya had New Year's Eve off, but we had no real plans. Marina was in Boca with her darling dentist. Tanya and Lauren were still in the islands, and Daphne was now somewhere over New Jersey. I only knew because she posted a picture of her legs on a private jet heading into Teterboro.

We were free to pop by Chelsea House but going to a big party was the last thing Iliya was in the mood for. He went to pick up takeout from one of his favorite spots in Chinatown while I stayed back with the boys.

I was bathing Felix when my phone pinged. I couldn't resist checking to see if it was her. The notification was a message from Susan. "It could be you next time!" She'd attached a picture of Daphne standing next to none other than @JanesAddictions at the Doggy Detangler event. When I canceled, I didn't get into the details. I didn't want to relive the experience again or deal with any more condolence texts or flowers. I simply said that Red was unavail.

Daphne's caption talked about how a portion of the proceeds from each detangler would go to the ASPCA, and how she was honored to be involved with a company whose ethos and regard for pet welfare mirrored her own. I snarled at "ethos." Daphne didn't even know what that word meant. Not only did she not care that I was going through a personal tragedy, she was also selfish enough to take the twenty grand and do the detangling deal without me. I was trembling. People threw offers at Daphne all the time. She could have passed on this. She *should* have passed on this.

I scooped Felix out of the water, wrapping his body in a towel. After I wrangled him into his pjs, I caved and went to Daphne's feed to see what else she'd posted. I watched a clip of Cha Cha walking down a makeshift aisle toward Dagmar's dog, Helmut. He was wearing a tuxedo and looked like the canine version of Bernie from *Weekend at Bernie's*. "Red would have hated Cha Cha anyway," I told myself. She was too basic and purebred. It would have been over from the first butt sniff.

Feeling betrayed, I wrote a comment under the picture of the happy couple. "Cherish these moments," I typed. "They grow up so fast." I couldn't help myself. I had to say something just to let her know that she wasn't getting away with anything and that her dog would die someday too.

CHAPTER THIRTY-THREE

New York in January was all slush and drudgery, which was actually fine by me. There was comfort to be found in the joylessness permeating the entire city. I wasn't the only one having a rough go of it.

After dropping Roman off at school, I stopped in at a coffee shop to do some journaling before heading to work. I'd been trying to get my head back on straight and writing about it was cheaper than seeing a therapist. Seated at a table in the back corner, I wrote about my efforts to get acquainted with my new neighborhood via exploring every single corner market ("good deli cats, meh produce") and my search for a local gym ("nowhere where you have to learn a routine or sweat in the dark"). I wrote about how I still wondered if Iliya would ever stop hating me (he wouldn't), and I promised that I would not reach out to Daphne, nor would I comment on her posts "NO MATTER WHAT, pinky swear, dear diary." I made it to half a page of jottings before I gave in to the temptation to look at my phone. When I opened Instagram, I almost sprayed my espresso across the table as one of Daphne's posts appeared on my screen. She was holding a pregnancy test and frowning.

"It was a blighted ovum, which I guess is quite common, but this is my second miscarriage. And my hopes of having a third child are really starting to dwindle," Daphne wrote, followed by an announcement in all caps that she would be taking a hiatus from social media in order to give herself "TIME TO HEAL."

I clicked on her account, noting that her hiatus had lasted all of twenty-five minutes before she posted again with a video of her face trying not to move or blink, like she was one of those living statues you find in Washington Square Park. "I love you like Kanye loves Kanye," she wrote. The Visine that she'd clearly squirted into her eyes pooled in both tear ducts instead of falling down her cheeks, as I'm sure she would have preferred.

The blighted ovum story was a direct rip-off of Heidi Glick's share from the Mompire dinner. It was now clear that there was no boundary she wouldn't cross. No secret too sacred to share with the free world. Predictably, Daphne's follower count jumped by the hundreds each time I refreshed the page. Just then, a blocked number appeared on my phone. The only person I knew with a blocked number was Susan, who'd been angling to get me to sign with her ever since the doggy deal fell apart.

In a haze of disillusionment, I picked up. "Susan?"

"No, dear. It's Marilyn. I wanted to call because I was truly moved by your application and well, I just feel terrible that we aren't going to be able to accommodate your son Roman next year at Abington. Emails are going out today. I'm not sure if you've received yours yet."

I gulped. "I haven't." I tried to hear her out, but my mind had gone numb.

"We just had so many worthy candidates this season," she went on. "And the board can only offer so many scholarships."

I wanted to believe Marilyn, but I just couldn't. It didn't add up. Or rather, it did. I was paying the price for my misadventure. Daphne was still pissed and wanted to punish me.

"Is this because of Daphne?" I blurted out.

"I'm sorry?"

"Did Daphne Cole say something to you?" I asked, my head spinning. "Did she tell you not to accept my son?"

"I'm sorry, I still don't follow," Marilyn said. "Why would Daphne Cole weigh in when she doesn't even have children at this school?"

"What?" I could hardly see straight. I thought she was a school mom. Was there validity in anything I believed? Was Daphne even a real person? Was she even a *mom*?

I managed a meek "thank you" as I got off the phone with Marilyn and immediately started looking back through Daphne's page at the pictures of her pregnancy. She never showed her actual belly. She'd bounced back after a month. When I was at her place, there were no signs of children. It was all sinking in: The look of discomfort on her face when she'd held Felix, the fact that her alleged kids weren't with her at the goddamn cookie museum. My stomach was in knots.

Daphne didn't have kids. Of course she didn't. She didn't even have a real marriage. All of it was fabricated for financial gain. Being a mom not only opened new doors, it kept her relevant and relatable. OH. MY. GOD. This woman was nuts. She was a complete fucking sociopath and I'd let her commandeer my life.

Weeks went by before I finally heard from her.

"Hey," her text said. "We should talk…"

The message was short and direct. I wondered if she'd spoken with Marilyn.

"We should," I replied, trying to keep my emotions in check.

"I'll be near your place tomorrow, doing my Revolve shoot. Do you want to swing by?" I didn't bother to tell her that I'd moved to a far-off outer borough, to a basic two-bedroom apartment that was nowhere near swinging distance. I simply made the plan.

CHAPTER THIRTY-FOUR

It was bitingly cold when I took a cab to Daphne's Revolve shoot, the kind of weather that makes you wish you still lived in California.

A mighty gust pushed hard against my back as I thanked the driver and attempted to slam the car door behind me. The wind didn't want the door to close. It was a cosmic urging to simply get back in the vehicle and leave Daphne alone. But I couldn't leave her alone. She was like a pack of cigarettes in my glove compartment. I didn't trust that in a moment of weakness I wouldn't reach for her unless she was completely banished from my life.

The set was only three blocks from Ken's place and I could see my old apartment building from where I stood. A gaggle of crew members dressed in down jackets scurried up and down the sidewalk, trying to look busy. Daphne was huddled under a tent next to a heat lamp. She was scrolling on her phone and having her lipstick reapplied by a makeup artist.

"Meg!" she called out in a tone that was impossible to interpret. Was she happy? Was she sad? Was she even capable of any feeling at all?

Her eyes bore into mine as she walked toward me. Her coat was unbuttoned, and I noticed that she was wearing the exact same tie-dyed robe from the NBD shoot. She must have been freezing. She stopped just shy of hugging me, waiting for some kind of cue that it was okay. But I stood still.

"You finally found somewhere to wear the Etsy robe." I could see my breath in the air as I spoke.

"This is actually my design," Daphne said without flinching. It was as if she'd never told me about the art student online who'd originally designed it. "It's part of my capsule collection. I love the big pearl buttons," she said, not realizing — or not caring — that she said the exact same thing before.

"Right." I nodded. Daphne hadn't changed a bit. She started fidgeting from side to side, eager for me to follow her back under the heat lamp. But I didn't move.

"I thought you said you hated copycats." I couldn't hold back my irritation any longer.

Daphne laughed. "I don't know what you're talking about." She pulled her coat closed and folded her arms.

"I got a call from Marilyn at Abington," I told her. "She said your kids aren't even enrolled there." I looked at Daphne, waiting for an explanation. "Your *alleged* kids."

"You seem mad." Daphne spoke in a sickly sweet tone, the way I imagined people did to 1950s housewives who were being shipped off to mental asylums.

"Oh really? I seem mad?" I laughed. "Of course, I'm mad, Daphne! I trusted you. I..." Now tears started to well up in my eyes. "I cared about you. And I thought that you cared about me."

"I do care about you!" She reached out for my arm, and I pulled back. "But I care about a lot of people. And you were getting a little intense. I think you might be putting too much weight on what happened between us on the boat."

"This is not about the boat," I scoffed, trying to cover up my sense of hurt.

"I was just having a bit of fun," Daphne said casually. "Some girls just don't know how to separate that stuff. Why do you think I never took things further and fucked you? You would have been a total head case." Her words pierced my heart. "But babe, you are still my Galentine!" Daphne's tone suddenly turned cheery. She pulled a red box out of her coat pocket and handed it to me.

"I'm your what?" I looked at her in confusion.

"My *Gal*-entine," she said, lowering her voice to a whisper. "I know we're still a few weeks out, but Valentine's Day isn't just for lovers anymore. Open it." I took the lid off the box. It was filled to the brim with red-foil-wrapped chocolate lips.

"We got it!" a photographer called out from behind me, giving Daphne a thumbs up.

I could feel my knees buckling. "Is this..." I stared at Daphne in disbelief and loosened my grip on the box. The chocolate lips fell to the sidewalk. "Did you ask me here so you could use me for a paid post?"

"Oh come on, Meg, I also wanted to see you! And I was planning on sending them to you anyway. What's the difference?"

"You're absolutely insane."

Her lips curled. "*I'm* the one who's insane? I'm who I've always been, Meg. You're the one who has no idea who she is."

"Say you're sorry," I told her.

"For what? Those are Jacques Torres chocolates." She cast her eyes down on the sidewalk. "They *were*."

I shook my head, almost pleading with her to just fess up. "Maybe you can fool other people with your fake miscarriage, your fake gingerbread mansions, and your fake children, but you can't fool me. Not anymore."

"I was never fooling you," she said in a harsh whisper. "*You* were fooling yourself. You wanted a distraction from your boring life and an escape from your lonely marriage."

"I like my husband," I shot back. "I wanted a friend."

Daphne shook her head. Her eyes filled with pity. "You wanted a mommy. Someone to tell you what a pretty, talented girl you were."

I was burning with hurt. "You endangered my children's lives, Daphne. You let me leave them with someone that you BARELY KNEW!"

"That was a misunderstanding. And you might want to keep your voice down." I saw that members of the crew were starting to drift closer to us, clearly trying to eavesdrop. What did I care, though?

"You didn't give a shit when my dog died. All you cared about was that stupid doggy detangler deal. The deal that you went out of your way to do anyway."

"It's not like I —"

"It's almost like you wanted to hurt me. You could have sat this one out. Instead, you took the twenty thousand dollars when you specifically told me that Susan doesn't let you leave your house for under seventy-five. You can lie about who you are to other people, but don't do it to me."

"*You* were going to make twenty thousand. *I* made eighty-five," she said coolly.

Every cell in my body was vibrating with rage. "Good for you." I shook my head.

A PA interrupted, asking Daphne if he should call security. "I'm fine," she said, stepping away from me. "Good luck, Megan. I hope you get everything you want."

I watched as she tore off her coat and walked across the street, toward her mark on the corner of Canal and Mercer. Traffic whizzed by behind her as she glanced back at me with her saucer-like eyes and the chin dimple she always Facetuned out of photos. For a brief moment I was almost able to forget how crazy she was, how crazy *I* was, and just appreciate the beauty of the woman who had broken my heart.

"I'm sorry!" she called out to me. "For real." This was her last-ditch attempt to charm me into submission.

"Don't use that word, Daphne," I replied. "Nothing about you is real."

"I never claimed to be real." She looked at her crew and chuckled. "I'm selling fantasies out here."

"Maybe to other people," I said, playing the one card I knew she couldn't beat. "I unfollowed you."

Daphne reared back and stopped in the middle of the street, frozen. With the click of a button, I had erased her from my life. Not once in our six months together, not in any of the 4,892 photos of her that I had pored over online, had I ever seen her look so speechless. I was the one walking away. People didn't do that to Daphne. Passersby started to shout, but it was just noise. Neither of us saw what was coming next. An Uber rounded the corner and barreled straight into her. And with that, Daphne Cole was gone.

CHAPTER THIRTY-FIVE

Everybody wanted the gory details, even Iliya, who never wanted to talk about Daphne. The truth was, I hardly remembered a thing. Moments after the accident, I passed out, and when I came to, I was lying on the sidewalk, looking up at the wintry sky and the heads of people hovering over me. I heard offers of water. I heard sirens. There was a blur of movement in the background. It was paramedics carrying Daphne's body away, I realized later.

Daphne had once given an interview to *Hamptons* magazine in which she said that she wanted her ashes spread around the coast of Manhattan, starting at East Sixty-Fifth Street (where the city's biggest Chanel store was) and then all the way down and around the island, past the Statue of Liberty and up to Hudson Yards (where the second biggest Chanel store was). So that's what she got.

The farewell ceremony took place on a chartered motor yacht at sunset. Iliya offered to come, but I didn't want him to. I said I was sparing him the hell of being stuck on a boat yet again with some of the worst people he'd ever met. But I wasn't only operating out of kindness. I wanted a moment alone with Daphne. While I now understood that everything about her was fake, there was still something between us that had been real. At least on my end.

"Hey, baby." The words sent chills up my spine as I turned around to see Lauren standing behind me, wearing a full-length puffer coat and holding out a glass of Champagne. "Come have a drink with us?"

I followed her up to the top deck, passing familiar faces clustered around heat lamps. There was Christo, Daphne's personal shopper from Barney's; Javier, who had lightened my hair; superagent

Susan; Mia from Tramp Stamp; and a smattering of women who all looked eerily like me.

Near the bow I spied an older woman who was a dead ringer for Daphne. They had the exact same face, give or take twenty years. The woman looked monied and refined. She was wearing a navy wool coat and a dark pencil skirt.

"Not exactly how Daphne described her," I mumbled to nobody in particular.

Lauren turned to give me a quizzical look.

"That's the 'housekeeper mom from the Bronx'?" I asked.

"Connie, third-generation Sicilian from Summit, New Jersey. She works in real estate." Lauren rolled her eyes. "Daphne loved feeding people that bullshit story. Made her sound like the American Dream."

"I bought it," I said, shrugging.

"Didn't her accent ever tip you off? Like what was it even?" Lauren laughed.

I was too knotted up to speak. Daphne had told me that night in her closet that her entire life was a fabrication. She'd been clear. She hadn't hidden her red flags. I was just the fool who kept painting them white.

Lauren squeezed into a table next to Tanya and grimaced. Off in the corner, Kip was talking a little too cozily to Kiki. "And there goes the merry widower," Lauren said with a sigh. "The last thing Daphne's ashes need is another article in Page Six."

"Another article?" I didn't follow.

"They're running a piece about how he's been fucking Mia since the Tramp Stamp pop-up in East Hampton last year.

"That's old news." Tanya yawned. "The only person who didn't know that was Daphne."

"And you guys never bothered to tell her?" I looked at them.

"Hell no! It's not like she wasn't fucking around. Mia was the best trainer at Tramp Stamp. The real losers in that situation would have been our abs. You know she always had that rule, "Don't fuck where you sweat." She would have been furious!" Tanya turned to Lauren. "Speaking of workouts, did I tell you I found a new spot? Pump and Dump!"

"Oh, I've heard of them!" Lauren lit up. "Dance cardio, right?"

"It's more sculpty. You basically lift weights in a heated room for fifty minutes and then you get a colonic." Tanya smiled, then turned to me. "I'm really sorry about your dog."

"Thanks." I was genuinely shocked she'd remembered.

"Me too." Lauren feigned sympathy. "But you seem to be holding up. Your numbers must be jumping because of all this drama! How many followers do you have now?"

"I— I actually haven't looked in a few days," I lied. My count was now well past 90,000.

"Even Howie is getting work out of all of this," Tanya admitted. "Three women scheduled nose jobs this morning! Oh, and Daphne's numbers are through the roof!"

"Yeah, I'm thinking we'll make it into a tribute page for a bit. Gonna post a bunch of her best stuff, the greatest hits if you will, then maybe move into funny outtakes before I merge it with my own," Lauren added.

"You're taking over Daphne's account?" I looked at her.

"More like carrying the torch," she told me. "Can you watch my things for a second? I need to go say hi to Susan."

I sat there, soaking it all in. The likelihood of Lauren being able to pull off what Daphne had achieved was slim to none. But even Daphne's fiction was quietly falling apart, according to her "friends." Daphne's body had barely cooled before Kip was being asked to move out of the apartment. Half their rent was paid in trade and contingent upon Daphne talking on her feed about how the building was the best place to live.

Kip now stood at the center of the deck, calling out for everyone's attention. "Hi, everyone. Thank you so much for coming. It means so much to our family."

What family? I wondered.

"Before we do this," he went on, "I thought it would be great to get one last epic selfie with the queen of selfies herself." Kip held up a brass urn and my stomach recoiled as he gave it an Eskimo kiss with his Keebler elf nose. "Everybody, let's all squeeze in. And if you don't mind, tag the picture #WomanCrushWednesday. We'd also love it if you could kindly tag Triton Yachts, Krunktown Gin, and Ashes2Ashes, who did the most beautiful cremation I've ever seen."

I stood back and watched as Daphne's mother poured her daughter's remains into the river, each dusty particle delicately sinking into the abyss. Some onlookers cried, but most of the people on the boat just gossiped and chatted with friends as if they were on a sunset booze cruise.

Not in the mood for talking, I disappeared into a corner and stared out at the Manhattan skyline. I wondered if I'd made the right decision in coming here. In LA everybody was trying to find themselves, while in New York everybody was trying to become someone else. Where did I belong? Tears ran down my cheeks and I didn't even know who I was crying for.

I was done with trying to sell myself to strangers as somebody who they should aspire to be. I was done exploiting my children's childhood for bullshit chickpea puffs and organic sunscreen. Here I was, quite literally, lost at sea.

"Cigarette?" I looked up to see Tabitha Rose taking off her shearling-lined gloves and opening up her pack of American Spirits.

"Thanks," I said. "I don't smoke." The breeze sprayed cold water against my cheeks.

"Me neither." She smiled coyly. Tabitha lit two cigarettes, handing one to me. "Such a shame, isn't it? An Uber X whose driver only had like a three-star rating. Thank god Daphne will never know what pancaked her."

It was my turn to feign amusement, but I felt heavy inside. I held my unsmoked cigarette over the ledge and watched as it disintegrated to ash, meeting Daphne in the brackish water below. "I'll miss her," I finally said.

"Will you?" She paused, lost in thought. "I'll just miss her clothes." Tabitha tossed her butt over the railing and walked off as if our conversation had never happened.

A moment later, Susan came around the corner holding a plateful of crab cakes and a glass of Champagne. "Meg! It's just so sad."

Her eyes were red, and her nose was puffy. I could tell that she was genuinely upset, which made me like her more than I ever had. "I don't know how I'm going to spin this," she said, biting into a crab cake. "Can you describe the driver to me? I'm so glad it was a man. If it had been a woman, this would be *so* much less relatable."

"It's all sort of a blur," I told her.

Susan drew a deep breath. "I'm already over this year."

"Only, what, eleven months to go?" I said.

Susan inched closer to me and raised her eyebrows. "I sort of have a small ask. *The Today Show* wants to do a piece about Daphne's death and influencers and has this all gone too far, yada, yada. Not to be morbid or anything, but you watched it happen. Would you be interested in talking to Jenna and Hoda?"

I gave a slow shake of the head. "I don't think so."

"Come on! It's national television. You'd for sure get a few thousand more followers."

"I'm really not in the market for any more followers."

I saw that Susan was distracted, pulling a dark curly hair out of her crab cake. She shuddered.

"Nice," I deadpanned. "Comes with its own floss."

She snorted. "Daphne was right. You *are* funny! Look, I just need you to say a few things. Keep people believing in the art of influencing." Desperation filled her eyes. "A lot of people's livelihoods depend on this, Meg. If Lauren goes on the air, we're in trouble." I was unable to argue with her point. Susan looked at me imploringly. "Daphne would have wanted it to be you."

CHAPTER THIRTY-SIX

Two days later, I sat in a makeup chair in *The Today Show* green-room as a disinterested makeup artist slapped concealer under my eyes.

"I can't thank you enough for doing this," Susan said. She was standing beside me wearing a bright pink sweater and eating a stale bagel.

"We're going to move you guys up to set at the next break," a production assistant whispered to Susan.

I heard a familiar voice coming from behind and looked into the dressing room. There sat Marilyn from Abington, drinking a Dunkin Donuts coffee and talking on the phone. A young woman was at her side.

"Next!" the makeup artist called out.

"Ready for me?" Marilyn popped her head out. Her glasses sat crooked on her nose. She pushed them up, then did a double take when she saw me. "Megan!" she cried, then introduced me to her companion. Her name was Justine, and she was a reporter from the *New York Times*.

"So tragic what happened," Justine said. "I'd love to speak with you at some point. Maybe I can get your number before you go?"

I was too confused to give her an answer. "Are you also going on air?" I asked Marilyn. "I thought Daphne *wasn't* an Abington mom."

"Lauren and a few of the other parents are setting up a scholar-ship in her honor," Marilyn informed me. "She wasn't a part of the school per se, but she was a big part of the community." Marilyn looked down. "A new scholarship will mean a new opportunity. I know we weren't able to accommodate Roman initially, but that was before these unforeseen events… I can't imagine anyone who Daphne would have wanted to help more."

Before I could respond, the production assistant flew over to move us along. "Sorry, guys. We gotta scoot you up to set. We have Tom Hanks coming in to promote his new movie and he has an entourage of about ten people."

My stomach bottomed out. "Tom Hanks? He's here right now?"

The assistant went back to a conversation that was happening on his walkie-talkie. He then turned to me and nodded silently.

"I'd love to meet him if you'd feel comfortable introducing me, Meg," Marilyn said with an eager smile. "*Green Mile* is my favorite movie of all time."

Susan's ears perked up. "You know Tom Hanks?"

Blood rushed to my temples. My stupid application essay. "Like they say on Facebook: It's complicated." I smiled meekly.

Once I was on set, the sound guy clipped on my microphone, then handed me over to the AD. I was then led out onto the stage, where I took my seat next to Jenna and Hoda. They were just like I'd expected, only tinier.

"Now, don't look directly into the camera, and remember we are live. No cursing," the AD instructed before disappearing into a sea of light.

I smiled quickly and mouthed an awkward "hi" to Jenna before a red light indicated that we were rolling. Hoda turned to the camera, introducing our segment. "The Age of Influence," she said in an ominous *Dateline*-esque tone. "Has it gone too far?"

I tried not to look like I was on the verge of a panic attack as she caught the audience up to speed on what had happened. "Today we have one of Daphne's close friends, Megan Chernoff, here to share some insights," she started. "So, Meg, first of all I want to say I'm so sorry for your loss." I mumbled a thank you and shifted uncomfortably in my seat. Luckily for me, she didn't want to dwell on the condolences. "A hundred thousand followers, two kids, a husband, and a full-time career. I don't get it. It seems so exhausting. How do women like you and Daphne do it all?

"Well…" I started. The bright lights made me feel like I was under interrogation. I could feel my head throbbing and my knees shaking as I looked over at Marilyn, who stood next to Susan. My old friend Tom Hanks was across the studio, getting his mic checked. It was all too much.

"But seriously, what's the secret to keeping it so real?" Jenna chimed in.

My secret… I thought about Iliya, who I'd been keeping so much from, then I thought about my kids, who deserved better than what I was giving them. I owed it to all of them to tell the truth. And the truth was that I wasn't showing up in the way that I should have been. I was ignoring my real life in favor of a fucking app. I was no better than Daphne.

"I've been thinking about what I was going to tell you guys all morning," I started. "I don't keep it so real." I let off an awkward laugh. "The truth, Jenna and Hoda, is that nothing that's documented is real when you think about it. Once the cameras are on, it's all subjective. I'm lying all the time. We all are. And Daphne was no exception. She wasn't some superhero. She was a curator. She created a fantasy for women, for moms like you and me who desperately want to believe that motherhood can be summed up in a hashtag, that you can have it all if only you just own the right lunchbox or use the right face roller."

My hosts were nodding fervently.

"Stop!" Hoda said to me with a jokey smile. "I *love* my filters. I'm not sure I want to see the real me, or anyone else to see it, for that matter."

"But Daphne was in a league of her own," Jenna said, getting us back on track.

"She was," I agreed. "She knew how to take what people wanted and feed it back to them. She was a master marketer, but she certainly wasn't mom goals." I took a deep inhale. "In fact, she wasn't even a mom."

I saw Susan's eyes go wide.

Jenna gasped.

Hoda stared at me in disbelief.

Before either of them could formulate a question, I continued. "But I'm not here to tear down someone who can't defend herself. I'm here to clean up my own mess. My platform made me feel like the master of my own universe. I got to choose what people saw and what they didn't see. But that ability to play God started to permeate my real life. I've spent the last six months lying to everyone I know... I tried to get my son into private school by claiming that he was some sort of genius and that I was close friends with Tom Hanks." I peered into the studio and saw America's favorite actor look up at the sound of his name. "Hi, Tom Hanks, I'm Meg Chernoff. We've never met. I loved you in *Forrest Gump*. *The 'Burbs* was probably my favorite. *Splash* was great too!"

Tom gave one of his humble Tom Hanks waves. There was a kindness to the gesture that encouraged me to keep going. I turned back to Hoda and Jenna, trying to block out Marilyn, who was twitching with rage in the opposite corner. "Sure," I went on, "the outfits and captions were fun. But it was all a show. And it erased anything that actually mattered. I was so busy trying to prove what a good parent I was that I stopped being a good parent."

"Then why do it?" Jenna probed.

"I was addicted to the praise. To the external validation. To the free stuff," I admitted.

"But like my husband says, nothing is ever free. And it's never enough. It was never enough for Daphne either. 'More is more.' That's what she used to say. And I guess the biggest thing I've learned since her passing is that more is just more. It's not better. It doesn't fill the hole. It is the hole."

The studio was silent, and I could hear the buzzing from the lights overhead. Finally, Jenna came to her senses and called for a commercial break. "I'm sorry if that wasn't what you were expecting," I told her when I stood to leave.

She shook her head and embraced me. "Thank you for your honesty. It's refreshing."

I walked past Marilyn, who refused to make eye contact. She was really bummed that I didn't know Tom Hanks. Susan didn't seem too happy either.

"You realize you just brought down half my clientele, so I should hate your guts. But that whole bit about mom guilt? Genius," Susan said when we were alone. "You've probably blown it with most mainstream brands; they like their influencers a bit less Machiavellian. But what you're doing is different. It's fresh. If you ever want to talk about representation… my offer stands."

"Thanks, but I was serious up there, Susan. It wasn't a bit."

We walked out an exit where a row of black SUVs waited next to a cluster of autograph hunters holding Tom Hanks headshots.

My phone was blowing up with messages, some from Iliya and others from friends I hadn't spoken to in years. I turned to go, then stopped. "Hey, Susan? Out of

curiosity, were there others? I mean, more than a couple?"

Susan shot me a look that said nothing and everything all at once.

"You were one of her most favorites."

CHAPTER THIRTY-SEVEN

After watching *The Today Show*, Marina agreed to postpone her date with Irving and stay to watch the boys. At Iliya's behest, I met him after work for a much-needed chat.

We went to Veselka, the Ukrainian diner on Second Avenue that Iliya had managed in his youth and still talked about in rhapsodic tones. We were seated in a booth up front. A knot of Russian men congregated at the counter, along with a smattering of aging East Village punks. The hipster foodies one booth over were asking the grumpy waitress which menu items were on the Infatuation's current top-ten list.

"I haven't been back here in ages," Iliya said, biting into a piping hot pierogi. "You have to have one of these." He gave me a fork, but I was still too sick to my stomach to eat.

I chugged some ice water and took a deep breath. "I owe you an apology."

"Maybe," he said. His eyes twinkled in a way that gave me a modicum of hope.

"I fucked up." He nodded and motioned for me to keep going. "And I don't know if you'll ever forgive me, but I really want you to because I love you and I need you and I'm never going to be that person again. I let this whole thing control me. I let it take priority over everything — you, the kids, us. I don't know if you can hear this and believe it, but I want you to know that I'm sorry and I'm going to work every day to show you that you and the boys are all that matter."

"Thank you." He got started on another pierogi.

"I can't have you thinking that I'm a bad mom. That I'd ever intentionally—" I was on the verge of weeping.

He stopped chewing and looked at me. "I don't think that you are a bad mom. If I did, we wouldn't be sitting here." He put down his fork and paused. "And I should have supported you more."

I sat up straighter. "What do you mean?"

"I should have seen that you were struggling. I was just trying to push through. When what you needed, or at least what I think you needed, was just someone to listen."

Tears spilled down my face. I was overwhelmed with gratitude and remorse.

"Did you love her?" Iliya looked down, his voice cracking ever so slightly.

"Not like I love you…" I shook my head. "Nothing like I love you," I said, more certain than ever.

"Glad to hear it. So, what do we do now?" He resumed eating. "I stop with the influencing." I was digging my fingernails into my thighs under the table. We go back to normal?

"No more toot puffs?" He rubbed his eyelids and gave me a smile.

I shook my head and laughed. "No more," I told him. "No more private school applications, no more silly trampoline classes, no more cardboard boxes blocking our front door."

Iliya pursed his lips and let off a slow exhale. "That sounds like a good place to start."

I felt an unclenching within. "I want to be with you, Iliya. I want to make this work."

"Me too." A smile came to his face. We were going to be okay. "Let's start with you trying a pierogi before I eat 'em all."

CHAPTER THIRTY-EIGHT

It had been an unseasonably warm winter, according to lifelong New Yorkers. We were only halfway through March and cherry blossoms were already starting to bloom.

I was almost hot in my parka when I arrived at the playground. It was 4:40 p.m. Felix's first birthday party was due to start in twenty minutes. I'd taken the day off work to run party errands. The subway from Long Island City had been slower than I'd hoped, and I had a ton of setting up to do. The party was downtown to make it easier for Iliya to join us after work.

Marina and the kids had gone directly to the park after school pickup. She waved to me from on top of the slide, where Felix was straining to touch his big brother, who was hanging from the monkey bars. I dropped my copious belongings on a long wooden bench and started preparing the picnic table. I was only halfway done separating the towers of party hats when my phone rang. It was Vigo, calling to ask if he and Seth could bring anything.

"No! Just come."

"Tell her that we didn't know what he was into," Seth said in the background.

"Tell Seth he's turning *one*," I reminded Vigo. "He's not into anything."

"Turn left!" Vigo said, presumably to the driver. "No, left. LEFT!"

"I'll see you guys soon." I smiled and hung up. Then I looked at my messages and saw that Bubby had texted to say that she was en route but stopping at Magnolia for the cupcakes. I took a short inhale when I saw there was only fifteen minutes to go.

Dasha's sciatica was acting up, so she wasn't going to make it, but Irving was coming with both his kids. This would be the first time they were meeting Marina, and we were all instructed to be on our best behavior.

Ken was back in New York and planning to stop by. He was coming solo. His girlfriend was working on a zombie movie in Budapest and was rumored to be hooking up with Wesley Snipes. Ken was a wreck, and Iliya made me promise not to bring up anything to do with zombies when Ken arrived. "That's going to be hard," I'd told him. "What else does anyone talk about at a one-year-old's birthday party where the theme is *Bubble Guppies*?"

Sari fumbled with the large iron gate at the entrance as Waverly effortlessly slipped through the bars and ran to join Roman on the swings. I went to help Sari unload goody bags from her car.

She lit up when she saw me. "Congrats, Meg! Is the deal officially closed?" Sari inquired, digging into her trunk for the candies to fill our piñata. I nodded, still unable to believe that it was real.

After the *Times* piece had come out, things changed rather quickly. I took two weeks off from launching Seth's shower gels to cobble together a book proposal based on my experience with Daphne and the world of influencing. It was pitched as a fairytale meets cautionary tale, and my agent had only been out with it for two days when three editors bid on the book. All that journaling had come in handy.

"I'm really proud of you," Sari said as we walked back into the park. "You've made me reevaluate how much weight I give this cursed thing." She waved her cellphone in the air. "I'm thinking I might go on one of those retreats where there's no Wi-Fi or Chardonnay."

As we put the finishing touches on the table, guests started to trickle in. There was Eszti, a mom friend I'd recently made in Queens, and her two boys. Then came Sylvia, one of Roman's favorite teachers, followed by Joanne, my new editor, with her wife, Laura.

Everyone was giddy over the signs of spring. Good weather was something we all took for granted in Los Angeles. But the changes in seasons seemed to bond New Yorkers, and I kind of liked it. It wasn't just a way to mark the passage of time, but a shared experience that we were all enduring, a common thread.

Our crew colonized the entire front corner of the park. Iliya was on the scene, entertaining a gaggle of guests with his boyhood tales of Coney Island mischief.

Sari nudged me. "Did you read that Daphne is being sued posthumously for that tie-dye robe she knocked off?"

"I missed that," I said, still figuring out how to hang a piñata from the leaning limb of a tree.

"Girl, there's a whole paper trail of her promising to post in exchange for free merch and then never following through. She was sending the stuff off to China and having it reproduced under her label for that Revolve collab. I can't believe you haven't heard. It's even on Diet Prada." Sari raised her eyebrows at me. "Do you not check your gram *at all* these days?"

"I have ten days under my belt," I said proudly.

"Well, when you have a moment of weakness, you really should peek, because they mentioned NBD."

"What did they say?" Apprehensive, I pulled my phone out of my back pocket. My finger hovered over the app's rainbow-colored icon.

"Mom! Mommy! Look how high I'm swinging!" I heard Roman screaming from the swings. "Mommy! Mommy! Look at me!" he called out again.

I looked up at my son, who was swinging his heart out. The

sunlight was refracting into thick segments and the sky was the truest blue I'd ever seen. It was so beautiful. Prettier than any filter. I asked Sari if she could finish rigging up the piñata and stuffed my phone back into my pocket.

"Roman!" I called out as I headed over to him. "I see you!"

ACKNOWLEDGEMENTS

Thank you to Lauren Mechling, who saw my vision from day one and elevated my work to levels I never dreamed possible.

And Haley Heidemann who championed this book through a literal pandemic and never stopped believing in its worthiness.

Thank you to my PR dream team Jami Kandel and Megan Beattie, who followed me fearlessly through the darkest of hours.

Thanks to Richard Pine, for convincing me to try fiction.

Thank you to Julia Bodner, Hilary Zaits Michael, Alicia Everett, Lauren Rogoff, at WME and my lawyer, Julian Zajfen.

Thank you to Ben Denzer and Aaron Bernstein for letting me micromanage the fuck out of this cover.

Thank you to Lauren Moffat, Lauren Stein, Christopher King and Jessica Casey at Sony and the incomparable Jamie Tarses, who I wish could have seen this one come to fruition.

Thank you to Brian Volk-Weiss, Rich Mayerik, and the entire Nacelle team.

And thank you to my friends, family and allies who have always helped propel me forward, Mom, Dad, Samantha, Mema, Poppi, and Chiara… Diablo Cody, Joe Veltre, Adrienne

Miller, Joanne Spataro, Charlotte Groeneveld, Stephanie Danler, Katie Sturino, Chelsea Handler, Stacey Bendet, Melody Young, Margret Riley King, Sophie Flack, Michael Kravit, Liz Vaccariello, Grant Ginder, Jessica Hartshorn, Jenny Hutt, Jill Kargman, Jess Glick, Curtis Rich, Victoria Gray, Breanna Schultz, Brent Neale, Shandiz Zandi, Beth Becker, Lauren Gershell, Emily Henry, Caitlin Mehner, Bethany D'Meza, Oren Tepper, Justin Bartha, Rebecca Serle, Jennifer Lancaster, Jennifer Eatz, Julia Chebotar, Olga Grinberg, Wynne Hamerman, Reid Rolls, Amber Mazzola, Miriam Tarver, Ashley Bellman, Ashlee Glazer, Dan Powers, Katie Taylor, Zibby Owens, Lauren Bochner, Jamie Rosenblit, Juan the lifeguard, Edsel the doorman, Lou, Max, Scottie, Nugget, Miguel, Rudy, Eszti, Jehan, Juju, Sylvia, Gina, Chad Gervich, and ALWAYS the ghost of MuthafuckingTeets.

Also to my sons, Sid and Lazlo who told me to quit writing and go back to being an out of work actor because then I could always pick them up from school.

And of course to my husband Jason… Jason, Jason, Jason. Only you know what writing this cost me, cost us emotionally. Thank you for being my cheerleader, my copyeditor and my confidant. You, are the only reason people think I know how to use a comma. I couldn't have done it without you. Or maybe I could have. It just wouldn't have been legible. I love you.

ABOUT THE AUTHOR

JENNY MOLLEN is a writer, actor, Instagram personality and *New York Times* bestselling author of the essay collections *I Like You Just the Way I Am* and *Live Fast Die Hot*. Her digital series, "I Like You Just the Way I Am," which she wrote and in which she stars, currently streams on ABC Digital. Heralded by *The Huffington Post* as one of the funniest women on both Twitter and Instagram and named one of "Five to Follow" by *T Magazine*, Jenny wrote a standing column for *Parents* magazine and has contributed to *Cosmopolitan, Glamour, New York*, Elle.com, Grub Hub, and Wake Up Call with Katie Couric.

Jacket Design: Ben Denzer
Jacket Photograph: Aaron Bernstein
Author Photograph: Reid Rolls